A Dragon's Promise

Paranormal Council - Legacy

Book Two

A Dragon's Promise

Paranormal Council - Legacy

Book Two

Written by Sheri Eleese

Table of Contents

Note From the Author

Hello to all my readers,

To enhance your reading experience, I thought it would be helpful to provide a little background for some minor characters who make an appearance in this book, who were first introduced in the **Reforming the Paranormal Council** series.

First, we have Ruth, the remaining Elder from the original ruling body of all paranormals (which has since been replaced by the Paranormal Council). In their quest for power, the Council of Elders, led by Ruth, schemed to bring a demon to the earthly dimension with the intent of using its power to rule the world.
To the surprise of no one, except Ruth, the demon crossed over and immediately took control of her mind, turning her into its servant. Irony at its finest.

At present, Ruth is imprisoned in the dungeons beneath the Council building.

Next, we have Leon, a vampire from the now defunct Rossi coven. Chafing under the leadership of Carlos Rossi,

Leon spearheaded a revolt, killing all vampires loyal to Carlos, before he and his fellow rebels joined with Elder Ruth to act as her private army. Even when informed of Ruth's intention to destroy all vampires, Leon was convinced he was integral to her success and would be spared the annihilation of the vampire community.

No one ever accused Leon of being intelligent.

And last, but not least, we have Officer Sanders, a disgruntled member of the NOPD who despises all paranormals, but has a focused and bitter hatred for Carlos Rossi. Sanders habitually arrests any paranormal unfortunate to cross his path, fabricating charges, if necessary, to put them in jail. When his actions came to light, he temporarily lost his badge and was forced to attend paranormal sensitivity training. The lessons failed spectacularly as the only thing they did was reinforce his belief that paranormals are abominations and the cause of everything wrong in his life. However, not completely clueless, Sanders hid his true feelings and bided his time until his gun and badge were returned. Which they were. Yeesh.

Seriously, who thought it was a good idea to give this guy a weapon? Twice.

Happy reading,
Sheri

To Dara

Who loves dragons as much as I do.
One day we'll both have one.
Love you, Auntie.

Prologue

Demon Realm, Queen's throne room...

Aldrich, the Father of Dragons, also known as the Great One, gasped as more of his power was ripped from him. He clenched his teeth to bite back a cry of pain, determined not to show vulnerability to the demon queen as she siphoned off another tendril, but it was a losing battle. And the queen knew it. Her eyes glowed, reveling in the knowledge he was at her complete mercy...something the dreaded monarch didn't have. When she pulled harder on his magic, Aldrich staggered back a step before catching himself, then locked his knees, refusing to allow any further weakness. He glared through slitted eyes, silently promising retribution.

The queen laughed and twisted her hands, yanking more magic from a well almost gone dry. Black spots clouded his vision.

And still, she fed on.

Aldrich was swaying in place, no longer able to see, when the demon queen finally cut their connection, releasing him from her hold. He collapsed, falling against the bars of his cage, then slid to the ground before slowly toppling to his side.

The demon queen, blazing bright with his stolen magic, slammed her tail against his cage before turning and making her ponderous way to her throne, shrieking orders at her assembled lieutenants as she did, and killing the ones who didn't move quickly enough. By the time the queen reached her throne, a quarter of her servants were dead, and the reeking smell of fear filled the room, the surviving demons quailing before her might.

Aldrich watched it all from where he lay curled in a ball at the bottom of his cage, an interdimensional prison designed specifically to contain his dragon powers. It was an insidious trap, one that kept him alive by shielding him from the lethal environment of the demon realm that would have long since killed him, and also prevented him from using his magic to escape.

Or so the demon queen thought.

Perhaps not realizing the risk, the queen had unwisely forced a hole through the barrier surrounding his cage, a small opening she used to feed off his energy. But the hole had created a weakness, giving him a way through the wards of his prison, a backdoor he exploited to send his spirit to the earthly realm to keep watch over his children, and position them to where they most needed to be.

So, although it looked like Aldrich was trapped and completely helpless, he was far from it. From the moment the queen had captured him, he'd paid close attention to everything that had happened in her throne room. From her daily orders to her lieutenants, to her many attempts to break through the dimensional walls to invade other realms, he'd been witness. And for everything she'd attempted, he'd devised ways to stop her.

And now, the demon queen in her arrogance of thinking Aldrich broken and cowed, had no hesitation in speaking freely in front of him about her plans to breach the divide and bring the full might of her demon forces to bear against the earthly dimension, never once suspecting the greatest threat to the success of her plans was him.

It was a critical error on the queen's part that would lead to her undoing.

With only a couple of pieces still needing to be put into play, Aldrich's sacrifice was almost done. He needed only to hold on, to stay alive until it was time. Then, if everything fell into place, if he was strong enough, if his savior was brave enough, Aldrich would join with his children and end the queen's threat to all of the realms, once and for all.

And then he would finally claim the one destined to be his.

A hidden grotto in the Bayou…

"I know it's down here somewhere."

"Leon, why do you care so much about a stupid rock?"

"Because that stupid rock is the demon stone that gave Ruth her power, and I want it."

"It also made her batshit crazy."

"She was always crazy," Leon said, sliding along the moss-covered wall. "I earned that stone. I'm not leaving here until I have it."

"Whatever. Just hurry the fuck up. This place gives me the creeps."

Leon clenched his teeth, pricking his lip with his fangs. Why was it always the idiots who survived? He'd rather have Aaron at his side. Or Benny. Anyone other than Lukas. But since none of them had escaped Ruth's betrayal, he was stuck with this fucking coward.

Glaring over his shoulder, Leon sneered, "If you're afraid of the dark, you can just fucking leave."

"You'd like that, wouldn't you?'

Yes, he certainly would. Lukas' constant whining was becoming tiresome. Lethally so. For him.

"Stay. Go. I don't fucking care. Just shut the fuck up so I can find my stone."

"Fuck you, Leon. It's our stone, not just yours."

Leon spun around and grabbed Lukas by the throat, slamming him against the cave wall. "What did you just say?"

"I said it's our stone, not yours. I have as much right to it as you do."

Leon sank his claws into Luka's neck. "You have no rights except the ones I give you. Be thankful I let you live."

"Fuck you!" Lukas grabbed his wrist and tore Leon's hand off of him, ignoring the blood spurting from the deep gouges in his neck. He grabbed Leon as he spun and shoved him face first into the wall. "You owe me, fucker. You couldn't have overthrown Carlos without my help. Or escaped from Ruth when she tried to kill us."

"That doesn't mean I still need you."

Luka bared his fangs. "You're not strong enough to take me out."

No, he wasn't. Not yet. But once he had the stone, Lukas would be the first to die. Leon jerked his head back, slamming it into Lukas' face.

"Fuck." Lukas backed up a step and grabbed hold of his nose, snapping it back in place.

Before he could close in again, Leon drove his fists into Lukas' chest, sending him flying back down the tunnel, then turned and stormed down the path, no longer concerned with stealth.

Leon slowed when the tunnel opened up into a small, dank grotto. He scanned the area, his eyes moving from the bloodstained altar to a desiccated body lying off to the side. He raced over to it, hissing when he recognized Zachary. He'd wondered what had happened to him. Then Leon saw the knife sticking from his back and laughed at the irony, thinking it was a fitting end to the backstabbing bastard.

He pulled the knife free and slid it down the inside of his boot, peering at Lukas from the corner of his eye as he walked down the tunnel toward him. Leon knew exactly how he was going to christen his new blade.

Kicking the Elder's body out of his way, Leon began searching the surrounding ground. Zachary being here meant he was on the right track to finding the stone. And when he did, he'd finally have the power he'd been promised and could go after everyone who'd fucked him over. Starting with that bastard, Carlos. Leon shivered in excitement thinking about his nemesis' blood spilling over his hands when he had his long overdue revenge on the ex-coven leader.

Not finding the stone where Zachary's body had lain, Leon moved to the altar and began kicking at the clumps of vegetation piled against the side of it. An angry hiss was his only warning before a snake reared up at him. Leon jumped back, the snake's fangs missing him by inches. He laughed as he snatched it out of the air and whipped it across the cavern to smack against the far wall. That'd teach the stupid, fucking snake for trying to bite him.

He walked to the other side of the altar, shoving the rotted vegetation aside with his foot. Seeing nothing, he gave the cavern another once over, then smirked when he saw a glint of red.

"Leon!"

He turned and saw the snake slithering toward him. Then he hissed in disgust when he realized Lukas was backing away from it, letting it herd him closer to Leon. "Could you stop being such a fucking coward for once? It's only a fucking snake."

"There's something wrong with it."

"Yeah. It's too fucking stupid to have learned its lesson the first time."

"I'm serious," Lukas said, sidling up to Leon. The snake hissed, its head moving back and forth as it slithered closer.

Leon rolled his eyes. "For fuck's sake. Just kill the fucking thing."

"You do it." Lukas ducked behind him and ran to the other side of the altar.

The movement startled the snake, who hissed and reared up. Leon flashed his fangs and hissed back, then darted toward it, drawing back his foot to kick it.

Its eyes flashed red before the snake sprang into the air, its powerful jaws clamping down on Leon's face.

"Fuck!" Leon tore the snake free and flung it across the cave, then clamped a hand to his face when the burn of the snake's venom raced through his veins like liquid fire. "Mother fucker! What the fuck kind of fucking snake is that?"

He turned to lean on the altar when red clouded his vision. His face went numb, his eyelid drooping and blinding him on that side. Leon staggered, falling to his knees when his legs stopped working.

Then he heard another hiss. Squinting through his good eye, he saw the snake coming at him again.

"Fucking fuck." Leon scrabbled at the side of the altar, using it to pull himself up, but the snake was on him before he could get to his feet. Its fangs drove deep into

Leon's thigh. Screaming as fire burned through him, Leon grabbed hold of the snake behind its head and ripped the fangs from his leg, before tearing the head from its body, flinging both parts after Lukas, who was running away like the cowardly fuck he was. Leon was going to tear his fucking head off next.

Lurching to his feet, he stumbled, falling to the ground in a crumpled heap when his legs wouldn't support him. He moaned at the burn of the snake's venom as it moved through him, changing him. It felt as if an alien presence had entered him and was trying to take control of his body. What the fuck?

Red light flickered in the corner, catching his attention. Leon's head jerked toward it. Fuck. Was that another snake? Then the red flashed again, burning its image into his eye.

Leon cackled, saliva dripping from his swollen and numb lips. He knew what that was. It was the stone he'd been looking for. Groaning as he fought to make his uncooperative body obey his commands, Leon slowly rolled to his stomach, then dug his fingers deep into the damp soil to pull himself forward. He had to get to the stone before his body failed him. It would give him the power he needed to heal himself. And drive out the presence he could feel twisting inside of him.

The stone flashed again, spurring him on when he faltered. Leon dragged himself closer, using every last bit of energy he had in a desperate bid to reach the stone before the numbness completely overtook his body.

His arms finally giving out, Leon dropped to the ground. Breathing heavily into the musty soil, he craned his neck and stretched his hand toward the stone, cursing when he saw it was still out of reach. Fuck, no. He was so close. He dug into the ground with his toes and shoved himself forward a few inches more. Straining with everything he had, his trembling fingers finally grazed its surface.

The stone flashed again, flaring a thousand times brighter than before, burning his eyes as the cave was lit with crimson fire. His long draw out scream filled the cavern as his skin boiled, before abruptly cutting off.

The stone pulsed one final time, then went dark.

The Council dungeons…

Ruth slowly became aware of the presence outside her cell, but couldn't raise enough interest to see who'd come to bother her today. All they ever wanted was to talk about her plans to destroy the paranormal communities. Plans that no longer mattered. Not that she could fully remember them. Or cared. Whoever was waiting could leave. She had nothing to say.

Surprise flickered when the door to her cell flew open. That was new. Ruth raised her head, squinting at the strange man standing on the other side of the bars. When her eyes met his, he smiled. The menace in them caused a ripple of worry to flare before it quickly faded, even that not enough to break through her apathy.

Until the stranger stepped through the open door and walked toward her.

Ruth rose to her feet and stood with her back pressed against the wall, watching as the stranger came closer.

"W-who are you?" The shredded roughness of her voice was barely audible in the heavy stillness of her cell.

"Your savior."

Ruth blinked, trying to pull the tattered fragments of her thoughts together to make sense of what he said. "W-what?"

"I came to free you."

Free her? "I-I…don't under—"

"It's time for you to go," the man said, coming even closer.

Sensing danger, Ruth shuffled sideways, a kernel of fear finally breaking through the numbness surrounding her mind. She stopped when the man cut off her retreat.

"Who are you?" she asked again.

The man's smile grew teeth as he reached for her. "I am…you."

Some buried reflex of self-preservation warned of danger. Ruth held her hands up to fend him off and shifted to the side, trying to slide away from him.

"S-stop. L-leave."

"Not until I get what I came for." The man grabbed hold of her head.

Ruth's mind splintered when a presence drove into her skull. She clawed weakly at the hand holding her, harsh cries tearing from her throat as everything she had been, and all she was now, was ripped away, leaving only an empty husk.

Ruth's eyes rolled back in her head as her body jerked in the man's hold before dropping lifelessly to the ground.

The man closed his eyes and inhaled, breathing deep. His image wavered, flashing through several visages before finally settling into Ruth's ancient features. Breathing out, she opened her eyes and smiled, then ran her hands down the front of her dusty robes, smoothing out the wrinkles. A small onyx gem fell from its folds, glittering in the dim light as it bounced across the hard-packed ground before rolling under a seam in the wall.

Ruth gazed dispassionately at the shriveled body on the ground. Stepping over it, she exited through the open door of the cell—power sparking against her skin when she passed the threshold—then headed down the pathway to search for her next victim.

Only the rats, frozen in terror, were witnesses to the sound of her footsteps as they faded in the distance.

Chapter One

Noah

The Galway mansion, where we left off…

A mate? How could he have a mate? And not just any mate, but a wolf shifter mate. A young, incredibly bold, gorgeous, amazing smelling wolf shifter mate. And he'd been matched with Noah, who was definitely not bold, or young—no matter what anyone thought—and while some might consider him good looking, it was all for show. Noah took great effort to present a highly polished exterior to hide how flawed and insecure he really was. And for the most part, it worked. But a mate would see right through his pretense and realize he'd gotten the short end of the deal.

Which wasn't how it was supposed to go.

A mate was meant to be your perfect match, the other half of your soul, the yin to your yang, not an anchor around your neck that would drag you down. Who in their right mind thought putting him and the wolf together was a good idea? Noah glared at the ceiling, knowing exactly who was to blame. He caught himself before he could shake his fist and express his opinion verbally, some part of him retaining enough sense to realize he was about to cross a line. He really didn't want to call down the Goddess' anger on himself by disrespecting Her, no matter how annoyed he was at being a pawn in whatever game She was playing.

Blowing out a frustrated breath, Noah jammed his hand in his hair, then froze, carefully extracting it before he mussed the gelled masterpiece it had taken almost an hour to perfect. Just because he was dealing with some crazy existential mating crisis was no reason for him not to look his best. It was, after all, what everyone expected of him.

He dropped heavily to the mattress. A mate. Shit. Now what was he supposed to do? He'd only come to the Galway mansion at the request of his brother because Reid needed his help—something that rarely happened—not so he could become the Goddess' next victim.

The skin over his heart started burning.

His eyes slowly rolled toward the ceiling.

Noah cleared his throat. "So, I, uhm, would really appreciate it if you didn't light me on fire. Just so we're clear, I'm happy I found my mate. Mostly." The patch of skin on his chest grew hotter. "Really, I am. It's just...the timing is wrong."

The heat intensified, spreading across his chest. Noah held up his hands. "Sorry, sorry. Forgive me. I didn't mean to imply you made a mistake...except, well, you kind of did."

He jumped when the lamp on the bedside table popped, then rushed to the other side of the room and put his back to the wall when it started sparking.

Eying it nervously, he said, "You have to know I'm not in a position to take a mate right now. I have to make some changes in my life, big ones, before I can safely claim him." Holding his breath, Noah waited, then slowly let it out when the lamp didn't explode. He felt a slight tension in the air before there was a gentle brush against his cheek that felt like understanding. Or that he was being an idiot. It was hard to tell. Either way, his chest stopped burning.

Collapsing against the wall in relief, Noah whispered, "I'm very grateful you brought him to me and I promise, I will claim him. I just have to fix everything first. But when the time is right, I'll accept him with my whole heart."

And he truly meant it. Noah had dreamed of the day he'd meet his fated mate, that special someone selected just for him. That moment, when Noah had first seen him and realized who he was, burned bright in his mind. The confident way the wolf stalked him and boldly staked his claim. Even when Noah tried to deny him, his mate had refused to back down, calling him out on his lie. He closed his eyes, shuddering as he remembered how his mate had leaned in and sniffed his neck before licking him. His skin still tingled from the wolf's touch.

But now was not the time. Not even for someone as spectacular as his wolf.

Unfortunately, his dragon hadn't gotten the message and was roaring inside him in excitement and joy, wanting to come out so he could be with their mate. Noah shoved him back, struggling to keep control when his dragon pushed even harder, growling and lashing his tail as he tried to convince—force—Noah to go back and find their mate, to claim him and take what was theirs.

His dragon was so persuasive, Noah turned to the door. Should he? Was it possible everything could work out? Before he could decide, images flashed into his mind, visions of him presenting the wolf to the Dragon Court, to the cruel, overcritical, and antagonistic ruling families. His mate, young, sweet, and bold, standing proudly in his torn and faded jeans, with hair as wild and as untamed as he was. Noah grimaced, all too easily imagining their scornful words and the scathing insults they'd fling at him. Cuts, honed over centuries of practice, that would strike true and deep, drawing blood with the precision of an assassin's blade. Wounds that would hurt to the deepest level and strip the smile from his mate's face and the joy from his eyes.

Just the thought of his mate being subjected to the derision of the dragon Court had Noah seeing red and made him want to shove their spiteful and judgmental words down their stupid lizard throats until they choked on them. But they'd laugh if he tried.

It was a cruel joke that he was the only one standing between his mate and the terrors of the ruling families, because he was no one's savior. Hell, he couldn't even save himself from their judgment and cruelty.

Only a small minority of the Court respected him or thought him anything more than a screw up. To the rest, he was hopeless, a dragon with a lifetime of poor choices and badly thought-out decisions behind him. He'd proven time after time he'd always do the worst thing possible in any situation. He was an embarrassment to his family and if everyone wasn't so afraid of his brother, his shortcomings would be a weapon that could be wielded against them.

Noah crossed the room and sat back on the bed. Shit, but he wished he'd done better, made wiser choices, done something good in his life. Then he'd be able to claim his mate, his beautiful, wild wolf, who smelled really, really good.

Ugh. Noah threw the pillow across the room. He shouldn't be thinking about that. What he should be doing was finding a way to put off this mating, even though he suspected it was already too late. His mating instinct had stirred the moment he'd seen the young shifter. And rose to fullness when the wolf licked him.

He shivered again just thinking about it, then groaned and threw himself backward, grabbing the other pillow and covering his face, for once not thinking about what he was doing to his hair.

He had to stop this line of thinking. His only way forward, the best way to protect his mate, was to keep his distance to prevent the bond from getting any stronger. Once he'd earned everyone's respect, proven he was a powerful dragon, ready and able to defend his mate, then, and only then, would it be safe to claim him.

And though the decision hurt his heart, Noah knew it was the right thing to do. It would kill him if his mate came to harm because of his weakness. It would shred him if the happiness he'd seen on the wolf's face was dampened, if the spark in his eyes dimmed. Or if bleakness and uncertainty took the place of his mate's passion for life and fierce confidence.

So yes, until Noah could protect his mate from the worst of dragon society, it was better to stay far away from him. Fortunately, it wouldn't be for long, as he knew exactly how he could prove himself. But he needed time to execute his plan.

Except…his time may have just run out.

Noah jumped up from the bed when he heard scratching at the door. Ignoring the way his skin tingled in response to his mate's presence, he looked frantically around the room, searching for a way out.

The magic of a shift washed over his skin.

The doorknob rattled. "Let me in, pretty dragon."

Noah flushed at the nickname, instinctively taking a step toward the door before he could stop himself. How could the wolf have this much of an effect on him already?

"I know you're in there. Let me in before I huff, and puff, and blow the door down."

Noah snorted, then frowned at the wooden panel, determined to stay strong. But when he found himself taking another step forward, Noah knew he was in trouble. Young though he might be, it was apparent the wolf was the more dominant shifter between them.

Which meant Noah needed to get away immediately before the pull got any worse and ruined everything he was trying to accomplish.

"Last chance, pretty dragon." There was a deep laugh. "Unless you really want to see how much of a big, bad wolf I can be." The doorknob rattled again before something slammed into the wood, rattling the door in its frame.

Noah froze. There was another crash against the door. He nervously watched as it vibrated, but it held firm. He waited, but when no further sound was forthcoming, Noah slowly let out his breath. The sensation of his mate faded.

Good. The wolf must have realized he couldn't get in and left. Great. That's just what Noah wanted. Really.

He pressed his hand against the ache in his chest.

Casting a last glance at the door, Noah resumed his pacing as he worked out his plan to recreate himself. The first thing he needed to do was return home to New York. Next, he'd have to reassign his workload. Then, he'd...

Noah's steps slowed when he felt his mate's presence getting stronger, coming closer. What was the wolf up to now? There was a scrape of metal on metal. Turning to the door, his eye went wide when the tumblers in the lock moved. Shit. His mate hadn't left. He'd just gone to get the key.

Noah's heart bumped when the doorknob slowly turned.

He was out of time.

Jory

Jory smiled as he pushed open the door. "Hey pretty dragon. why'd you leave so qui—" He stopped when he got a look at his mate, who was halfway out the window.

Eyes full of regret stared back at him.

Jory reached for him. "Wait. Don't go."

"I'm sorry. I have no choice."

Then his mate jumped out the window.

Jory sped across the room and leaped through the window after him, landing on the soft grass in a diving tuck and roll, before coming to his feet and chasing him to an open space a few yards from the house. Before he could reach him, his mate sprang into the air and shifted into a blue dragon. Jory stumbled to a halt, unable to tear his eyes away from his magnificence.

It took his mate flying away to bring him to his senses.

Jory chased after him. "Stop. Come back."

His mate circled around and hovered just out of Jory's reach before letting out a mournful cry. Then he flapped his wings, rising higher in the sky before turning and flying away, ignoring the silent pleading of Jory's hands reaching out to him.

He folded over, the pain of his mate running from him crushing. Goddess, but he was tired of the most important people in his life leaving him. First his mother and now his mate. And he didn't even know why. Was it because he was a wolf? The thought made him angry.

Jory glared after the dragon until he disappeared from sight. He had no idea how long he stared at the empty sky before the hurt returned, overshadowing his anger. What made him so unlovable that nobody wanted to stay with him?

When his mother had abandoned him, he'd understood. Actually, that was a lie. He would never understand why she'd left him. Especially because she'd done it so easily. How could someone who loved him as much as his mother had just walk away? Even though she'd warned him she was going to take off when he came of age, Jory hadn't believed her, thinking there was no way, not his mother. Until he'd come home and found her gone, leaving him with only a picture and a note telling him to search for his brother.

But his mate was a different story. He'd been chosen especially for Jory and Jory for him. So how could his dragon have run from him and everything they were meant to be to each other?

It took him far too long to notice the scent of his mate's worry and fear that lingered in the air, as well as his regret and shame. And strangely enough, determination. Whatever had caused the tangled mess of emotions in his dragon stemmed from much more than just finding out Jory was his mate.

The hurt that had been squeezing Jory's chest eased, but now his heart ached for his pretty dragon, wanting to know who or what had hurt him so badly he'd been driven to run.

When he found out, he would make them pay, because his mate was Jory's to protect, his to cherish, and eventually, his to love. From now on, Jory would stand between his mate and his enemies so no one could hurt him again.

But he had to find him first.

Giving a last glance at the empty sky, Jory jumped back through the window and headed toward the office. Someone there should be able to tell him where his mate had gone.

And then the hunt would be on.

Chapter Two

Jory

Jory grabbed his pants from the clothes piled on the chair and turned to his brother as he finished explaining what had gone on with his mate.

"By the time I got into the room, he was halfway out the window. Then he just flew away." He was pretty sure he'd kept any lingering hurt from showing on his face, but his brother picked up on it anyway.

"I'm so sorry, Jory," Lysander said, putting his hand on his shoulder. "I have no idea why Noah took off like that."

"I do," Carlos said. "It's because he's a pretentious asshole who doesn't want a lowly shifter for a mate."

"Hey." Jory stopped in the middle of pulling on his pants to scowl at him. "My mate is not an asshole. His running had nothing to do with me being a wolf." Of that, he was sure. The scent of his mate's fear was something Jory wasn't going to forget anytime soon.

"Sorry, pup, but you're wrong." Carlos' look of sympathy seemed sincere, cooling Jory's anger...until his next words. "I've known Noah a lot longer than you and appearances are all that matter to him."

But Jory knew that wasn't true. How, he couldn't say. He just knew it in his heart. Something else was driving Noah. And he was going to find out what it was. Jory zipped up his pants. "Does anyone have any idea where he might have gone?"

"He probably flew back home," Lysander said.

"That's my thought as well."

Jory turned to the dragon who'd spoken. "Who are you again?"

"Reid. Noah's brother." He smiled at the small magic-user sitting next to him. "And this is my mate, Fionn."

Jory nodded. "It's nice to meet you both." He reached for his shirt and looked at Reid. "Where is home, exactly?"

"New York."

Shit. How was he supposed to get there? Jory pulled his shirt over his head and turned to Roman as he shoved his arms through his sleeves. "Any chance you'd be willing to lend me your plane?"

Roman's lips twitched. If Jory didn't know any better, he'd think his brother's stoic mate was amused by him. Why, he had no idea. But given Roman was reaching for his phone, he could laugh at Jory all he wanted if it got him to his mate quicker. "I will have the pilot get it ready for you."

"Thanks, Roman."

"That won't be necessary," a musical voice said. "It would be my pleasure to take you, Jory."

Jory turned to see who had spoken. His breath caught when he saw the woman sitting next to Fionn. How had he missed noticing her? She was absolutely glorious and so powerful the air around her sparkled. He returned her smile with an awkward bow while the room exploded around them.

"Mother, no," Gideon said, standing. "I can't let you do that."

"Sophia, are you sure that's wise?" Lysander asked.

"Fly Jory?" Bryan's eyes darted from Sophia to Jory and back. "B-but, you're the queen."

The queen? Holy shit. That explained why she looked like a princess…or he guessed, a queen. And she'd offered to give him a ride? Jory was going to refuse her offer…until she turned to him, her eyes filled with glee, and winked. All right then. Choking back a laugh, he pulled on his socks and left her to it.

"Listen to Bryan, Mother. You can't carry Jory on your back."

"I don't see why not."

"Because it's just not done. Royals do not transport passengers."

"Funny. I don't recall seeing that rule."

"It's not a rule. It's a matter of propriety."

Sophia lifted her eyebrow. "Since when did you become concerned about propriety?"

"Since I…well…I don't…damn it." Gideon looked at her helplessly.

Carlos laughed. "She's got you there."

"I know," Gideon said, shaking his head. "I can't think of a single reason why Mother shouldn't fly Jory that doesn't make me sound like an asshole."

"Then let her be, dragon," Carlos said. "If Sophia is willing to carry him, who are we to tell her she can't?"

Sophia ginned. "Thank you, Carlos. I knew there was a reason you're my favorite."

"Mother!"

Her tinkling laughter filled the air. "Well, you're being ridiculous, Gideon. This is not that big of a deal."

Gideon huffed. "I'm not being ridiculous, Mother. And it is a big deal. Ferrying someone is not something you would normally do."

"You're right. I wouldn't," Sophia said, smiling gently at him. "But Jory needs to get to his mate. And since I'm leaving shortly to tell Edmond what's transpired here, it only makes sense for me to take him with me."

Finished tying his shoes, Jory crossed his arms and leaned against the wall, waiting while they sorted out his life for him. Personally, he didn't care how he got to New York. It only mattered that he did.

"Sophia, it might be best to let Roman send Jory in his plane," Lysander said. "I'm not sure dragonkind would approve of you doing this."

"Excellent point, beloved." Roman got to his feet and nodded to Sophia. "It will take but a moment to arrange for my pilot to have the plane prepared."

"I appreciate the offer, Roman, but please don't trouble yourself. I'm more than happy to get Jory there myself."

Lysander's eyes narrowed. "Wait a minute." He pointed a finger at Sophia. "What happened to our agreement to not get involved with Jory's mating? This looks a lot like involvement to me."

"That was for you, dear. I made no such promise."

Lysander blinked, then snorted, shaking his head. "I'm pretty sure you said Jory needed to pursue his mating on his own so he could prove himself to Noah? Or did I mishear?"

"No, you're correct. I did say that."

"Exactly! So what is this?" Lysander asked, pointing between her and Jory.

"This is about getting Jory to the same part of the world as Noah. Once he's there, he'll have plenty of opportunities to prove himself."

"True, but you—"

All amusement dropped from Sophia's face. "I suspect this is another situation where there's a limited amount of time to get things accomplished. We might not have the luxury of waiting for him to get to New York by his own means." She glanced up. "Or Roman's plane."

Lysander stilled. He studied Jory, then turned back to Sophia and nodded. "You might have a point."

Jory's eyes narrowed. "Is there something I should know?"

"Nothing I can say for sure," Lysander said. "It's just a feeling."

"Is it about my mate? Is he in danger?"

Lysander paused, then shook his head. "Not as far as I can tell. But you know how quickly things can change."

"Yeah." Wasn't that the truth? Jory turned to Sophia. "I appreciate you agreeing to take me. Do you think we could go soon? I'd really like to get to my mate."

"We'll leave right now." Sophia looked at Gideon and Reid. "Are you boys coming with us or will you be staying here?"

"Carlos and I will be flying with you," Gideon said.

"Damn right," Carlos said, jumping up to stand next to Gideon. "There's no way we'll let you go by yourself."

"We'll be going as well," Reid said as he helped Fionn to his feet.

"Very good." Sophia turned to Roman and Lysander. "I'm sorry to cut our visit short, but it's time to take Jory to his mate."

"Oh course," Roman said. "I hope all of you have a pleasant flight."

Lysander came over and gave her a hug. "It was good to see you again. Hopefully next time you'll be able to stay longer."

"That depends. Will you be able to stay out of trouble?"

"Probably not. But I'll try my best."

"You always do, dear."

Lysander laughed and gave her another hug before walking over to Jory. "Be careful. If you need anything, you call me. I don't care what time of day or night it is."

Jory nodded. "I will. Thanks."

Lysander gave his shoulder a squeeze, then returned to Roman.

Sophia said a final goodbye to Roman and Lysander, then left the office through the French doors leading off to the garden.

Jory pushed off the wall and followed her without looking back, so didn't see the worry in his brother's eyes.

Arriving at the Dragon Court, New York...

The wind whistling past his ears slowed, then stopped when Sophia dropped to the ground. Cracking his jaw to pop his ears, Jory took his first full breath since they'd taken off, then immediately clenched his jaw so he didn't vomit on the queen. Breathing heavily through his nose, he gave it a moment, then cracked open an eyelid, slamming it shut when his stomach lurched. Maybe he'd just wait until everything stopped spinning before he climbed down...if he could get his fingers to unlock their death grip.

Whatever thoughts he'd previously had about riding a dragon, which, to be honest, had been none, Jory now knew for sure wolves didn't belong in the sky. The next time he had to travel a great distance, he'd use whatever mode of transportation he could get his hands on. Hell, he'd even run, no matter how long it took, if it meant he'd never have to fly on a dragon's back again.

"Are you coming down or not, Jory?" Carlos yelled up at him.

"Take your time, dear. Flying by dragonback can be a bit overwhelming at first."

His eyes snapped open to see who'd climbed on Sophia's back, the voice so close it almost sounded like it was in his head, but there was no one with him. "Who said that?"

"It was me, Sophia."

"Sophia?" Knowing the queen was speaking directly into his head startled Jory so much one of his hands jerked free. "W-what? How'd you do that?"

"C'mon, pup. We haven't got all day. Let go of the queen so she can shift and greet her mate," Carlos said, crossing his arms. "Unless you're too scared."

Jory used his free hand to flip him off.

Quiet laughter from the other side of Sophia floated up to him. He cautiously leaned over enough to see past his leg and saw Fionn smiling up at him.

"Don't let him get to you," Fionn whispered up to Jory, his eyes full of understanding. "The first ride by dragonback is a lot."

"So, I've heard."

Sophia giggled in his mind.

Jory leaned a bit further, holding on tightly to the ridge of scales on Sophia's upper back and whispered to Fionn, "Were you scared too?"

"Not exactly." Fionn's face twisted in apology. "I wish I could tell you I was, but no. My first flight with

Reid was amazing. It was the most wonderful thing I'd ever experienced."

"Oh."

Fionn shrugged. "But that might have been because Reid's my mate so I knew I could trust him." He patted Jory's lower leg. "I'm sure it will be a much different experience when you fly with Noah."

Jory didn't know if flying on his mate's back would be any better. But maybe Fionn was right. Not that he was in a hurry to find out.

Sophia's large head swung back to him. "How are you doing, dear?" Her clawed hand gestured to the side of the field. "Edmund is waiting whenever you're ready to get down."

Fionn gasped. "I didn't know you could speak in dragon form?" He turned to Reid. "Why didn't you tell me you could talk when you were shifted?"

"Because I can't."

"What?" Fionn turned back to Sophia. "But...you just spoke, didn't you?"

"I did. All members of my line can speak while shifted."

"You can speak in dragon form?" Carlos asked, bumping Gideon. "How come I didn't know that?" He squinted. "Are you keeping secrets?"

"Sorry, treasure. Once we established our mind link, I never thought to mention it."

"Uh, huh. What else have you forgotten to tell me?"

"Nothing of importance."

"I'll be the judge of that," Carlos muttered.

Gideon laughed and wrapped an arm around his neck, pulling him close to kiss his forehead. "I promise. You know everything that matters."

Tuning them out, Jory looked over Sophia's side and measured the distance to the ground as he tried to work out the best way to get down. If he slid off her side, he wasn't sure his legs would hold when he landed. And since he'd already embarrassed himself enough in front of everyone, the last thing he wanted was to do a face plant on the grass. He could try lowering himself by his arms, but it looked like it was still too far of a drop for him to have a clean dismount. Jory twisted and looked behind himself. Huh. If he slid further down Sophia's back towards her tail and didn't topple over getting into position, he'd be a lot closer to the ground, so shouldn't make a fool of himself when he landed.

He nodded, his decision made. Now if only he could convince his fingers to let go.

Jory let out a very manly yelp when Sophia shifted and lowered her body some more, then wrapped her tail around her side.

"Step on my tail, dear. I'll help lower you down."

He looked down and calculated again. With the ledge she'd given him, it was only a short hop to the ground, relatively speaking. Surely he could manage that.

In the end, it took knowing he couldn't start searching for his mate unless he got down, to get him moving.

His face feeling hot, knowing everyone's eyes were on him, Jory pulled his leg over Sophia's back, then holding tight to her scale-ridge, lowered himself to her tail. Once his legs stopped trembling, he let go with his hands and jumped to the ground, locking his knees when he landed. Fionn was there to grab him when he wobbled taking his first step. Fortunately, his next was steadier.

Then Sophia was before him. Taking hold of his hands, she smiled, then leaned forward to whisper in his ear. "Well done, dear. We'll make a rider of you yet."

Yeah. He didn't think so. But he wasn't about to tell the queen that. Not after what she'd done for him. Nodding and giving her a half smile, he followed her as she skipped across the lush grass into the waiting arms of her mate, King Edmund.

After Edmund finished greeting her, he smiled warmly at Jory and held out his hand. "Welcome, Jory. Sophia's told me all about you."

She had? When? When Edmund gave him a wink, he realized it was more secret dragon mind stuff.

Edmund tapped his temple, confirming Jory's thoughts, then said, "We're pleased to have you stay with us."

"Thank you for inviting me," Jory said, including both the King and Queen. Then, taking his cues from Fionn, he dropped into a slightly less awkward bow than he'd given Sophia before.

"That was lovely, dear," Sophia said, nodding approvingly. She glanced over at Edmund, then whispered to him conspiratorially, "But there's no need for such formality unless we're at Court. It gets somewhat tedious."

Edmund sighed.

Giggling, the queen winked at Jory. "Come with us and I'll have someone show you to your room," Sophia said, before linking her arm with Edmund's and walking down the mosaic tiled path to the castle entrance.

Following the royal couple inside, they were immediately surrounded by guards and castle staff. Before Jory had a chance to ask about Noah, he was whisked away to a suite of rooms he was told were his to use for the duration of his stay.

The moment he was alone in his room, Jory flung himself on his bed, glad to be away from everyone. He needed a few minutes of peace and quiet to process everything that had happened since he'd first walked into Roman's office and seen his mate.

He had no idea how much time had passed when there was a knock on his door. Propping himself up on his elbows, he called out for them to come in, not surprised when it was Reid and Fionn.

Rolling off the bed, he met them at the door.

"Are you settling in okay?" Reid asked.

Jory shrugged. There wasn't much to settle since he hadn't brought anything other than the clothes on his back and his phone. "I guess. Are you here to take me to Noah?"

Reid shook his head. "Fionn and I are going to visit with Mother. But before we go, I wanted to give you Noah's contact information." Reid handed Jory a sheet of paper.

He glanced over the information Reid had given him, which included Noah's home address, business address, work and personal phone numbers, and email addresses. He noted Reid had also included his and Fionn's phone numbers. Jory pulled out his phone and began inputting the information, then tilted his head to look at Reid from the corner of his eye. "If you're not going to take me to Noah, how do you suggest I find him?"

"If I were you, I'd wait until tomorrow morning. You should be able to catch him in the office."

"Tomorrow?" So not what Jory wanted to hear. His wolf wanted them to go after their runaway mate immediately.

Obviously knowing the direction of his thoughts, Reid held up his hand. "I know you want to start looking right away, but it'll be better if you give Noah time to process. He'll be more open to accepting the bond once he's had a chance to think through everything."

Jory grunted, not sure he agreed.

"Trust me, Jory. I know my brother. Giving him some time will only work in your favor."

"Fine." Entering the last digit into his phone, he folded the paper into a small square and shoved it in the back pocket of his jeans,

"And Jory"

He raised his eyes to Reid.

"Don't give up on him, no matter how difficult he might make things. Noah has issues about the way people see him." He winced. "Something I haven't helped with. It won't be easy getting him to accept you as his mate, but once you do, you'll find there's no one more loyal than my brother."

"Is he running because I'm a wolf?" Jory was pretty sure that wasn't it, but it didn't hurt to ask.

Reid hesitated, then shook his head. "That may be part of it, but no, I don't think that's what the problem is."

Which was a relief, but still didn't tell him what he needed to know. "So, what do you think it is?"

Reid shrugged. "I'm not sure."

"You can't even guess?"

"I could, but I'm not going to. Noah's issues are his own. You'll have to find out his reasons for yourself."

"Big help you are."

Reid laughed. "I know. But you're going to have to earn Noah's trust if you want to learn what's in his heart."

Which was fair. In fact, it was probably better if Jory found out for himself rather than letting someone else's opinion influence him. Didn't mean Reid wasn't still an asshole for not telling him, it just meant he was a smart asshole. "I get what you're saying. I need to show Noah his secrets are safe with me, because without that trust, we'll have nothing but the bond keeping us together."

"Exactly."

And though it went against every instinct he had to not begin searching for his mate immediately, Jory found himself saying, "So then, tomorrow?"

"Yes."

"When's the best time to find him at the office?"

Reid frowned. "Why don't you come after ten. That'll give me a chance to talk to him. Get an idea of where his head is at." He clapped Jory on the shoulder. "I'll make sure he's there when you show up."

"Thanks."

Fionn gave him two thumbs up.

Jory snorted, then walked them to the door. Closing it behind them, he threw himself back on the bed, then pulled out his phone to scroll through the contact information Reid had given him. He checked the time, sighing when he saw how many hours he still had to wait before he'd see his mate again.

Telling his wolf it wasn't going to kill him to wait a bit longer, Jory ignored his whimpering and began planning his strategy for the next day.

Chapter Three

Noah

Noah put another file on the stack to his left, groaning when he saw the mountain of paperwork still waiting to be sorted. He'd known he'd fallen behind when Reid had been out of the country, but this was ridiculous. It was going to take him hours to redistribute his workload. But since his plan to recreate his image was dependent on finding the thief who was stealing from their hoards, it had to be done if he was going to free up his time. And he couldn't stick his brother with all of his work. Not after Reid said he trusted Noah to take care of the thief, which had to have been a huge sacrifice for his control-freak brother. Noah wasn't going to let him down. And not only because this was his big chance to prove himself, to show Reid he could be counted on, but because he wanted to make his brother proud.

Picking up the next folder in the pile, he glanced through its contents and dropped it on the stack he was handing over to his assistant, then grabbed another. He flipped open the cover, but instead of seeing the page in front of him, his mind was filled with images of his mate, from first seeing him across the room and realizing what he was, to when the wolf stood proudly in front of Noah asserting his claim, to the look on his face when Noah jumped out of the bedroom window. His stomach twisted as he recalled his mate's stunned surprise—and hurt—when he flew away. Something he was now regretting.

It was possible, just maybe, that he might have overreacted. With a night's sleep and a few states' distance between him and his mate, Noah could see things a bit clearer. At least enough to realize he could have handled the situation better. But in the heat of the moment, fleeing had seemed like the only thing he could do. Time would tell how much of a mistake it had been. Or if his mate would forgive him for running.

Sighing, he dropped the folder on a random pile and picked up the next one.

Noah looked up at a sharp rap on his door, smiling when he saw his brother standing outside of his office. He motioned him in. "What are you doing here so early?"

"Just thought I'd check up on you." Reid strolled over to Noah, a huge grin on his face. "You left in quite a hurry yesterday. You didn't even take time to say goodbye to anyone."

Noah groaned inwardly. He should have known Reid wouldn't let that pass. "I know."

"Care to explain why you took off like the hounds of hell were chasing you, or should I take a guess?" Reid asked with a laugh.

"I had my reasons."

"I'm sure you did. Question is, are they good ones?"

"I thought so."

"Huh. I wonder what your mate would think?"

Noah was trying really hard not to think about that. Instead of responding, he picked up another folder, feeling the weight of Reid's stare as he thumbed through it. Asshole.

After a moment, Reid sighed. "Alright. I'll let it go for now." He rested a hip against Noah's desk and picked up a folder, glanced inside then tossed it back. "What's this all about?" he asked, waving his hand over the stacks.

"I'm trying to reassign my workload so I can be out of the office for a few days." He put the folder he was holding on Reid's pile.

"Good." Reid smiled at him. "I'm glad you're taking time for your mate."

Noah glanced up. "That's not why I'm doing it."

Reid blinked. "It's not?"

"No."

"Then what do you need time for?"

"I'm working on something."

"Which tells me exactly nothing."

At the exasperation in his brother's voice, Noah snickered. "I need the time so I can look for the person who's been stealing from our hoards."

His answer seemed to surprise his brother. "Oh. You don't need to worry about that. I'll look after it so you can spend time with your mate."

Noah shook his head. "You said you trusted me to take care of it, so that's what I'm going to do."

"But it's not necessary. I can—"

"It is necessary. I need to prove you didn't make a mistake leaving it with me."

"You don't have to prove anything to me."

"Don't I?"

Reid hesitated a second too long before answering. "No."

"Uh, huh." Noah raised his eyebrow.

"I'm serious."

"Sure, you are. You think I'm nothing but a screw up."

"You may have made a few mistakes in the past, but—"

"But nothing. This is my chance to show you I'm not a total failure."

"I never said you were a failure."

"It was implied."

Reid's mouth opened and closed before he pressed his lips tightly together.

Noah snorted. "You can't even deny it."

Reid's sigh sounded pained. "I may have thought something like that in the past, but not now."

"Why not? Nothing's changed to make you think any differently." Except for one thing. He narrowed his eyes. "Does this have something to do with Fionn?"

"He might have made me see I was judging you unfairly."

"Or maybe you weren't. But it doesn't matter. This is my chance to prove I can be counted on."

"True," Reid said slowly. "It also gives you an excuse to avoid your mate."

Noah flinched before he could catch himself. It was unfortunate Reid noticed.

"Please tell me that's not what you're doing."

"Of course not."

"Noah." Was that disappointment in his voice?

"Look. You know how important it is to recover our money."

"Yes, but—"

"So I'm going to find the person who took it and get it back." Noah picked up another folder and stared blankly at its pages.

"You didn't let me finish," Reid said, taking the folder from him. "I was going to say I used to think money was important. Then I met Fionn and realized he's more valuable than any amount of money could ever be."

"Yes, well, Fionn's special."

"And so is Jory."

Noah startled at hearing his mate's name for the first time. He couldn't believe he hadn't thought to ask before now. What kind of mate did that? Goddess but he needed to start doing better by his wolf. And he would. As soon as he took care of this one task.

"You can't avoid him forever."

Noah looked at him. "I don't want to avoid him forever. Just until I find the thief."

"You shouldn't put off your mating," Reid said quietly. "You never know what could happen if you do."

Seeing the haunted look in his eyes, Noah knew his brother was reliving what had happened to Fionn. He reached out and squeezed his arm. "I know what you're saying, and I don't want any harm to come to Jory, but I…I can't have a mate right now. I need to…I have to—" He stopped, not sure how to finish. He didn't want to tell Reid he didn't think he could keep Jory safe.

"Noah, you know you don't have to prove anything to Jory. He'll want you just the way you are."

"I'm not worried about that."

"Then what? Why are you avoiding him and putting off your mating?"

"Because maybe I need to prove something to myself first."

Reid stilled, then his eyes narrowed. "It's not just yourself though, is it? You want to prove something to everyone."

Noah nodded, wishing he could deny it.

"You shouldn't care what anyone else thinks."

"That's easy for you to say. Nobody thinks you're a screw up."

"I know, but—"

"This is something I need to do. To prove I've changed. To show everyone they're wrong about me."

"To hell with everyone else, Noah. Your mate's what's important."

"I know. He's the reason I'm doing this. I need to prove I'm more than the mistakes of my past. I need to earn everyone's respect so I can stand between him and them. I need them to believe I'm worthy, even if I'm not." Noah found it hard to hold his brother's gaze when he admitted that, but he did. Barely.

"Noah." Reid's voice was strangled. "You are worthy of a mate. Please tell me you believe that."

"Sure."

After studying him for a moment, Reid gave a resigned sigh. "You don't. I hope you realize how wrong you are before you harm your relationship with your mate."

Noah hoped so to.

"And I get it why you think you need to protect Jory from the Court, but you're making a mistake. And not giving yourself or your mate enough credit."

"Maybe I'm not. But I'm still going to look for the thief." He stared Reid down when it looked like he wanted to argue some more. "It should only take a few days. I'm sure Jory will be fine waiting until then."

Reid barked out a laugh, the haunted look fading from his eyes. "You're kidding yourself if you think that."

Noah frowned. "What do you mean?"

"Do you honestly expect your mate to patiently wait until you decide you're ready for him? After the way he claimed you in front of everyone?"

"Well, no, but since he doesn't know where I am…"

"I wouldn't be too sure about that."

Noah dropped the file he'd just picked up and pointed a finger at him. "What did you do?"

Reid blinked, his wide, innocent eyes fooling no one. "What makes you think I did anything?"

"Because I know you too well. Now spill."

Reid snorted and shook his head. "Sorry. Can't do that."

Noah crossed his arms and glared. "Please tell me you didn't tell him where I am."

"Okay. I won't."

"Damn it, Reid."

His brother laughed, rapped his knuckles on the desk, then walked out of the office. A few seconds later, he stuck his head back in. "Hey. There's a delivery out here for you. You need to sign for it."

Noah looked at the mess on his desk. "I'm a little busy. Can you take care of it for me?"

Reid turned to talk to someone, their voices too quiet for him to make out, then he was back, shaking his head. "Sorry, Noah. You're going to have to unbusy yourself. They say you're the only one who can accept it."

Noah's eyes narrowed. His brother's voice sounded strange, like he was trying not to laugh. "What's going on?"

Reid looked at his watch. "Oh, would you look at the time? I'm late for an appointment. Gotta run." He winked, then ducked out of sight.

Why was his brother acting— No. He wouldn't have.

"Reid, my mate better not be—"

Jory appeared in the doorway.

He totally was. "You're an asshole, Reid."

His brother's laughter floated back to him. Oh, he was going to make his brother pay for this.

Noah shook his head when Jory went to step in. "Sorry, I'm not seeing anyone today." He snapped his fingers. The office door slammed shut and locked.

Ignoring the knocking, Noah looked at the folders he'd been sorting through, then scooped everything into one big pile in the center of his desk. Screw it. Reid could look after all of it. It served him right.

With that taken care of, there was nothing else keeping him there…other than his mate on the other side of the door. But once Jory realized Noah wasn't going to let him in, he'd have no choice but to leave. Then Noah could get out of here and begin his search.

He slipped on his jacket, then pulled out his phone and began scrolling through his social media accounts as he waited out his mate. After a few minutes, the knocking stopped. Smirking, Noah finished posting an update, then put his phone in his pocket.

His head snapped toward the door when he heard a soft snick as it opened. What the hell? Jory strolled in with a huge grin on his face.

Oh, he was going to kill his brother.

"You ass. Why'd you unlock the door?"

Jory stopped. "Are you talking to me?"

"No. I'm talking to my stupid brother."

"Reid? He's not here."

"Yes, he is."

"No, he's not. He left a couple of minutes ago."

Noah rolled his eyes. "You don't need to lie for him. I know he unlocked the door for you."

Jory turned and looked behind him, then back to Noah. "Uhm, the door wasn't locked."

"Yes, it was."

Jory shook his head. "No, it wasn't."

"I know it was because I locked it myself."

"Okaaay. I don't want to argue about it. But you might want to have someone take a look at it because it wasn't locked."

"Listen—"

Jory whistled, cutting him off as he looked around the room. "Nice office."

"Thanks," Noah muttered. It was just an office. One he needed to get his mate out of.

Jory smiled at him. "I guess we have some things we need to talk about."

"No, we don't." They really did.

"Sure, we do. Let's start with why you—"

Noah looked at his watch. "This isn't a good time for me."

"Okay, then. When is?"

"How about next week?"

Jory laughed. "I was hoping for something a little sooner."

"Well, I'm all booked up. It's going to have to wait until then."

Jory looked taken aback, then he crossed his arms, a spark of annoyance flaring in his eyes. "Yeah, I don't think so. I'm not leaving until you talk to me."

Noah shook his head. "That's not going to work for me."

"Too bad." When Jory started walking toward him, Noah flicked his fingers and put up a shield between them, smirking when his mate bumped into it. Smugness turned to confusion, then quickly to shock when Jory pushed his way through like it wasn't even there.

"What did you just do?"

"Uhm, nothing."

Noah just stared at him.

Jory gave him a confused look, then twisted and looked behind him. "Or perhaps I did. What's going on?"

"You walked through my shield."

"Is that what that was? I thought I felt something, but it vanished so quickly, I figured I was mistaken."

"You weren't. It was my shield and it should have stopped you."

Jory blinked, then smiled. "But it didn't. Isn't that interesting?"

"No, it's not interesting. It's a huge freaking problem."

"Maybe for you." Jory waved his hand back and forth through the space he'd just walked through. "The air feels tingly here. Is this where your shield is?"

"Yes." Not that it was doing any good.

Jory turned back. "I guess your magic recognizes me as your mate."

"That shouldn't make any difference." Noah put up another shield. A thicker, stronger one that would definitely stop his mate.

Jory stepped forward, passing through it without any resistance. "Whoa." He held up his arm where his hair was standing on end. "That one was pretty powerful, huh?"

"How do you keep doing that?"

Jory shrugged as he brushed his hand down his arm. "I think your magic likes me."

Noah growled, annoyed his magic wasn't working properly? Or perhaps it was. He squinted at the ceiling, starting to suspect someone was interfering.

He looked back when Jory came closer and held out his hands to stop him. "You need to stay back."

"Why?"

"Because I said so."

"But we're mates. I want to be near you. Don't you want to be near me too?"

Not able to lie to his mate, a strangled yes escaped his lips before he could stop it.

Jory moved fast, closing in until they were chest to chest. He buried his face in Noah's neck and took a deep breath, then sighed. "I missed you, pretty dragon."

Noah shivered, barely holding back a groan. He dropped his head forward, unable to resist breathing in his mate. His arms started to come up. Then he realized what he was doing. Shit. He needed to be stronger than this. Noah shoved Jory back, then slid sideways behind his desk.

Expecting his mate to be angry—or Goddess forgive him, hurt—Noah was surprised when Jory grinned at him.

"You do realize the harder you try to escape, the more determined I am to catch you?" Jory's eyes flashed yellow as he rounded the desk.

Noah backed up and looked around, starting to understand what being hunted felt like. "I can't do this right now."

Obviously sensing something in his voice, Jory pulled up, the smile dropping off his face. "What can't you do?"

"I can't be your mate."

"But you are my mate."

"I know that. But I can't bond with you right now."

"Why not?"

Was that hurt in his voice? "Because I just...I can't."

Jory studied him, his glowing eyes seeing right through Noah, rooting out all his secrets. His voice was soft when he said, "You don't need to be afraid of me. I promise I won't hurt you."

Pheromones wafted off of him, coating Noah's skin.

Noah bit back a moan when the wild, forest scent of his mate curled around him. It called to him, speaking of companionship, loyalty, and joy. It promised forever, if only he was brave enough to accept. Noah floundered, feeling himself sinking beneath the lure of his mate. It took all of his strength and his determination to keep to his plan, to force himself to back away when every part of him wanted to get closer.

Then what Jory said registered. Noah shook his head to clear it, and gasped out, "I'm not afraid of you."

Jory's nostrils flared. "But I can smell your fear. If you're not afraid of me, then who?" His head tilted. "Is it…are you afraid of yourself?"

Before Noah could respond, Jory shook his head. "No. That's not right either. What are you afraid of, pretty dragon?"

"Nothing."

At his mate's doubtful look, Noah shook his head. Jory didn't need to know how messed up he was inside. He couldn't even begin to explain the emotions choking him. The regret, the shame, his feelings of inadequacy, and the guilt. Yes, let's not forget the guilt for what he was doing to his mate. But he had a plan and needed to see it through to the end. It was the only way he could think of to prove himself worthy.

When the doubt on Jory's face changed to concern and he moved a little closer, Noah knew he needed to get away before he gave in. He looked toward his door, measuring the distance between himself, his mate, and his exit point. If he timed it right, created a distraction, he should be able to get around his desk and get to it first.

As if realizing what he was planning, or perhaps it was just an unlucky coincidence, Jory moved to the side and cut off his escape route.

With no option left, Noah sent his magic to the window next to him, shattering the glass. He was up on the ledge before Jory could react. Noah jumped just as his mate lunged for him, Jory's fingers slipping off the hem of his jacket as Noah sailed through the opening.

Noah shifted as he fell, then rose and turned back, his wings faltering when he saw his mate dangling from the window ledge by one hand.

Shit. Noah quickly angled to get under him. By the time he was in place to catch his mate, Jory had managed to grab hold of the ledge with his other hand and pull himself up. Noah waited until he was safely back in the office, then moved back from the building, hovering just out of reach.

"You don't have to run, pretty dragon," Jory said, stepping back from the window. "I'll give you some space."

Noah let out a high-pitched whine that tapered off at the end, hoping Jory could hear his apology. Then he fled.

Jory rushed back toward the opening and shouted after him, but his words were lost in the wind created by Noah's wings as he flew away from his mate and everything they could be to each other.

The pull on his heart told him he was making a mistake, but Noah didn't turn back. What was one more bad decision in a lifetime filled with them?

Chapter Four

Jory

Most of Jory's weight was supported by the ledge as he leaned forward, pulled by the invisible cord connecting his soul to Noah's. His heart yearned to follow his mate, so he kept watching after him as he grew smaller and smaller until Noah was nothing more than a speck on the distant horizon. And still Jory kept his eyes locked on him, hoping against hope he would turn around, that their fragile bond would be strong enough to overcome his mate's fears and bring him back.

But Noah kept going.

Jory finally gave up and turned away from the window when his mate disappeared from sight. He sighed, resting his hands against the ledge as he leaned back and stared at the ceiling. What was driving his mate to run? Jory could feel the connection between them. He knew Noah was drawn to him. He could feel how much the dragon wanted to be close to his wolf. Jory had also smelled his mate's arousal, felt his excitement, and for a brief moment, his joy. Then he'd run.

The sting of rejection tried to rise, but he pushed it back. His bruised feelings were insignificant compared to the complex mix of emotions that had swirled around his mate. Ones that worried Jory, stirring every protective instinct he had. Emotions that made him determined to find his mate so he could shield him from whatever was causing him pain.

After he tracked him down. Again.

He pushed off the ledge when the person who'd be able to help him with that ran through the door.

"I heard a crash. What happened?" Reid's eyebrows shot up when he saw the broken window. "Where's Noah?"

Jory jabbed his thumb over his shoulder. "He jumped through the window."

"He did what?" Reid raced over and leaned out, then spun around and glared accusingly at Jory. "I was gone for less than five minutes. What the hell happened?"

Jory shrugged, not sure where to even start."

"For fuck's sake, Jory. He went through unbreakable glass. What did you say to him?"

"It didn't look that unbreakable to me," Jory muttered.

"Well, it is." Reid glanced over his shoulder and frowned. "Or was. We outfitted the entire building with top-of-the-line glass specially designed to withstand paranormal strength. Then had additional layers of strength and protection spelled into it."

"You might want to look into whoever magicked the glass. It didn't even slow Noah down."

"And why is that, Jory? What did you do that made my brother so desperate to escape he jumped through the window?"

Jory wasn't going to tell Reid about Noah being scared. That was between him and his mate. So, he picked the next best thing. "I think he freaked out because I walked through his shields."

Reid gave him a look, then shook his head. "That couldn't have been it. Nobody can break through dragon magic."

Jory held up his hand. "I did."

"If you got through Noah's shields, it's because he let you."

"Nope." Jory shook his head. "He definitely didn't let me through. He almost lost his mind when he realized he couldn't block me."

Reid's eyes widened. "You're serious?"

Jory nodded.

"But…how?"

"I have no idea. There was a little bit of resistance the first time, but then the magic let me through. All the next shield did was make my skin super tingly."

"Holy shit." Reid fell back against Noah's desk. "No wonder he freaked."

"So what? His magic must like me. It's not that big of a deal."

"It's a very big deal. You shouldn't have been able to go through Noah's shields."

Jory bit his lip as he thought about it, then remembered Noah saying the same thing. "Do you think it has anything to do with me being his mate?"

Reid shook his head. "That wouldn't make any difference. Fionn can't break through my magic, and he's a lot more powerful than you are."

"Huh. Then I don't know how to explain it."

"Me either." Reid studied him. Long enough for Jory to get jittery. "There is something different about you, Jory. I just can't put my finger on what."

"I'm just me. What you see is what you get."

"Yeah, I don't think so." Reid shook his head and snorted. "My brother's definitely going to have his hands full with you. And that's not a bad thing. Not a bad thing at all."

Jory was glad he thought so, because he was going to need his help. "Do you have any idea where he might have gone this time?"

Reid rubbed his chin, thinking. "He'll stay in the city. At least for a couple of days."

"Are you sure? He's gotta know I'll be looking for him."

"I'm positive. Noah has some personal business to take care of."

"Oh? Anything I should know about?"

Reid hesitated, then nodded. He crossed his arms and leaned back on the desk. "I'm only telling you this because you're his mate. You can't let this information get out, understand?"

Jory nodded.

"Someone's been stealing money from mine and Noah's hoards."

"Holy crap." Jory was stunned, not having expected that. "How would someone even do that? I thought dragons were super secretive about where their hoards are hidden."

"We are. And our physical hoards weren't touched. At least, not as far as I know." He frowned. "I probably should check to make sure." His face brightened. "I bet Fionn would love to see my hoard."

Jory chuckled. "I'm sure he would. And I bet your dragon would love to see him covered in jewels."

Reid gave him a goofy grin. "He would."

But what Reid had said wasn't making sense. "If your hoards weren't touched, why do you think someone's been stealing from them?"

"I said our physical hoards are fine. But a significant portion of our wealth is in the bank, locked behind some of the greatest security on the planet. There are so many layers of protection and security approvals required, nobody should be able to get to our money. Yet they did."

"That's crazy."

"That's one way of putting it. What it is; however, is a big problem. One that needs to be dealt with. So, Noah's looking after it."

"By himself? Shouldn't you be helping him?"

"I offered, but Noah is determined to catch the thief on his own."

"Why?"

"He needs to prove something."

"My mate doesn't have to prove anything," Jory said through clenched teeth, instantly angry on his mate's behalf. How dare Reid say that about him? He raised his fists, ready to throw down.

Reid held up his hands. "Peace, Jory. I'm not the one saying he needs to prove something. Noah's the one who thinks that."

"Why should he have to prove anything? He's a dragon. strong, intelligent, powerful. Why would he even think—" Jory stopped. This might be a part of what he'd sensed from his mate earlier. His anger drained away. "Why does Noah feel like he has to prove himself?" he asked more calmly.

Reid pinched his nose and sighed. "Mostly because he has a habit of making poor choices and making a mess of things. It's come to the point where everyone expects it of him. Including himself. I think that's a big part of why he's running. I'm not sure he feels he deserves a mate. At least, not until he proves himself worthy."

"That's crap."

"I agree. But that doesn't change how he feels, or how everyone's made him feel."

Aaand, his anger was back. Jory was incensed at the thought of anyone looking down at his mate. But what Reid said helped explain the twisted mix of emotions of fear, worry, and shame he'd picked up from Noah. But underlying all the rest, had been a fierce determination. Which, now that he knew what Noah intended to do, told Jory everything he needed to know about his mate's character.

Reid bumped his arm as he handed him a piece of paper, breaking him out of his thoughts. "Here's the contact information for the bank that handles our accounts and our brokerage firm. If it were me, that's where I'd start my search."

Jory nodded. "Noah will probably do the same." He scanned the page and pointed to the last line. "Who's this number for?"

"Our mother."

His head shot up. "Why are you giving me your mother's number?"

Reid's lips twitched. "Because she'll be very interested in meeting Noah's mate. Even more so if you show up without him. But if I were you, I'd save her for a last resort if you can't find him anywhere else. Once mother gets her hands on you, she's not likely to let you leave. At least, not anytime soon."

Jory folded the paper and shoved it in his pocket with the other note from Reid, thinking that wouldn't be an issue. The last thing he wanted to do was meet Noah's mother while looking for him. He could only imagine how that conversation would go.

Reid laughed as if he knew what he was thinking. Then he turned serious. "Just promise me one thing, Jory. No matter how much trouble he gives you, please don't give up on my brother."

"Don't worry. No matter how far he runs, I'm not going to let him get away."

"Good. My brother needs someone like you in his life." Giving him a hard slap on the shoulder, Reid walked out of the office.

Jory stared after him, pleased by his words and the acceptance in them. A small part of him had been worried Noah's family would have trouble accepting him because he was a wolf. It was good to know Reid didn't have a problem with that.

Now, to find his dragon.

He left Noah's office, closing the door behind him, and pulled out his phone. As he headed for the stairs, Jory typed out a message to his mate. A little heads up to let Noah know he was coming. But really, he just wanted him to know Jory wasn't giving up on him. He wanted to show Noah he was worth fighting for. That Jory was willing to chase him to the ends of the earth if necessary.

A grin spread across Jory's face when he hit send. He wished he could be there to see his mate's reaction when he read it.

Chapter Five

By the time Noah landed on the roof of the building where his bank was located, his common sense had reasserted itself. Along with no small amount of embarrassment at the way he'd panicked and fled from his mate. And not just any old panic. No, he had to go and break the window in his office and fly through the opening. What, did he think no one was going to notice a dragon diving from the sixteenth floor? For someone who was supposed to be reinventing himself, he wasn't off to a very good start.

His brother was going to laugh himself silly when he found out.

Noah sighed. The mocking coming his way was no less than he deserved for running from his mate. Again. Which, this time, was more than just a mistake, but something that must have hurt his mate. Even worse, since his magic didn't seem to work against Jory, obviously recognizing and accepting him—something he'd never heard of happening to another dragon—it meant his mate was special. Noah freaking out might have jeopardized their bond. It wouldn't surprise him if Jory, who was only acting on his instincts to claim him, regretted being stuck with Noah as his mate by now.

Noah walked across the roof toward the exit, trying to ignore the voice inside his head—one that sounded a lot like his dragon—telling him to stop being a stubborn fool and claim their mate. And he would. Eventually. But since he'd already set himself on this path, willfully burning his bridges behind him, he might as well keep going until he'd successfully completed his mission.

Opening the door for the rooftop staircase, Noah pulled out his phone and saw he'd missed some texts while he was airborne. Unlocking his phone, he pulled them up, then stumbled to a halt.

"Did you think jumping out of the window would discourage me?"

Noah snorted. That would be a no. Considering Jory followed him from New Orleans, a little jump from an office tower wasn't going to slow him down for long. The best Noah was hoping for was to keep in front of him long enough to find the thief.

He moved to the next text.

"Did you know wolves love to hunt?"

"And the longer the chase, the sweeter the victory when we capture our prey."

Noah rolled his eyes. A dragon was no one's prey. Not even his mate's. Noah swiped his screen and slid his phone into his pocket. He was exiting the stairwell door that led into the lobby of the building when more texts came in.

"So, run, pretty dragon. Run as fast as you can."

"Note to self. I guess that should be, note to you. A wolf always gets his man. At least, this one does."

"Can you feel me closing in?"

His pulse leaped. Even knowing his mate had no idea where he was, Noah couldn't stop himself from looking through the main glass doors, half expecting to see a wolf on the sidewalk. Then he shook his head. He was worrying over nothing. Jory had no way of knowing where he was. And on the off chance Reid had guessed and told him, Noah had too much of a lead for his mate to catch up.

Noah grinned as he pictured Jory's wolf chasing his dragon through the streets of New York, dodging pedestrians, food carts, and traffic, while Noah sailed high above it all. He was chuckling as he entered the bank and headed for the offices lining one side.

His phone chirped again. And again. And then a few more times in quick succession. Looking at the screen, he couldn't help but laugh.

"Slight delay. Had to stop and help a lady get her purse back."

"Can't get the taste of thief out of my mouth. Do you think lemonade will help?"

"In case you were wondering, it didn't."

"On my way again. I'll be there as fast as I can."

"I promise. I won't let you get away."

He was putting his phone away when another text came in.

"I'm almost there. See you soon."

His skin suddenly tingling, Noah looked over his shoulder through the glass doors, but saw nothing more than the usual heavy flow of pedestrian traffic typical for this time of day. He laughed at himself for jumping at shadows and started walking again. He made it another few steps before he slowed, then stopped, unable to shake the sensation that his mate was close by. Noah turned and scanned the activity on the streets outside, almost positive Jory would appear out of the crowds if he watched long enough.

"Mr. Davenport?"

Jumping slightly, Noah spun around, then dropped his phone in his pocket and held out his hand to the bank's manager, who was looking at him expectantly.

"Gerard," Noah said, clasping his hand and shaking it. "I appreciate you making time to see me on such short notice."

"Of course. It sounded urgent." Gerard gave him an indulgent smile. "It's the least I could do for one of the bank's larger clients."

Noah's eyes narrowed. Gerard was downplaying the value of their portfolio. He and Reid weren't just one of anything. They were the largest and most important clients the bank had. And Gerard knew it. Perhaps he needed to be reminded of how integral the Davenport holdings were to the bank's continued prosperity.

"This way please, Mr. Davenport," Gerard said, holding out his arm, "I've cleared my calendar for the next couple of hours."

Squaring his shoulders, Noah took a deep breath, feeling like he was going into battle. And in a way, he was. This was the first step in his fight to prove himself worthy. He couldn't afford to screw this up. There was too much at stake. As he followed Gerard, he reasoned his best chance for success would be to emulate his brother.

By the time Noah stepped through the doorway of Gerard's office, he'd wrapped a mantle of the confidence and strength that Reid so effortlessly wielded around himself.

Let the battle begin.

Noah's phone beeped as he slipped the buttons from his coat. Taking a quick glance at the screen, his lips curled when he read the latest text, then he silenced his phone and slid it into his pocket. He couldn't afford to be distracted by his mate. Not when he needed all of his attention focused on what was sure to be an unpleasant conversation with Gerard.

Taking the seat across from him, Gerard leaned back in his chair and clasped his hands with a supercilious air. Noah raised an eyebrow at him not bothering to offer coffee, tea, or water as he would have done with Reid. Oblivious, or uncaring, of the insult he'd given, Gerard gave him another fake smile.

"So, what can I help you with today, Mr. Davenport? If you require some investment advice, I can arrange to have one of our financial planners made available for you."

"That won't be necessary."

"I see." Gerard's head tilted as he studied Noah, who stared back, not giving anything away. He was curious to see what the manager would do next. Hopefully, he'd be smart enough to give Noah the same level of respect he gave Reid. Unfortunately for Gerard, that didn't prove to be the case.

Gerard leaned forward, his tone nothing less than patronizing, as he asked, "Has some bauble or trinket caught your fancy, Mr. Davenport? Or did you perhaps wish to acquire a new car or yacht and have found yourself short of funds?"

Noah's eyebrow went up. "Gerard—"

Ignoring the warning in his voice, Gerard blithely continued. "No need to worry, Mr. Davenport. Whatever your latest indulgence is, I'd be more than happy to arrange for funds to be transferred into your personal account to finance it."

Noah's back, already stiff, went ramrod straight at his words. Where the hell did Gerard get off speaking to Noah this way? Whatever Gerard thought he knew about him, he was wrong. So very, very wrong. As he would soon find out.

Not that he seemed to realize it. The condescendingly indulgent smile on Gerard's face made his true feelings for the youngest Davenport brother quite clear. He was about to learn Noah had as much clout as Reid, and wasn't afraid to use it.

Gerard dug his grave even deeper when he smirked as he picked up his phone. "I'll have one of my staff arrange the transfer of funds for you immediately. How much were you looking to spend?"

Noah eyed him coldly. "I think you've given away quite enough of my money, wouldn't you say, Gerard?"

Gerard's eyes widened. "I beg your pardon."

Noah motioned for him to hang up the phone. When he hesitated a moment too long, Noah allowed his dragon to rise.

Gerard gasped and hurriedly set the handset back in the cradle, his hand trembling as he finally realized his danger.

Keeping Gerard's eyes captive, Noah said, "I didn't come here for financial advice. Mine and my brother's expertise in financial matters far exceeds that of anyone you can provide."

"T-then I don't understand. W-why did you wish to see me today?"

"I'd like an explanation for why you've been transferring money from our accounts." He waited a beat. "Transfers that were not authorized by either my brother or myself."

"W-what?"

"Someone's been stealing from us, Gerard, and you've helped them."

Gerard's eyes widened in shock, but he recovered quickly. "I've done no such thing."

"You most certainly have. I strongly recommend you locate our money and return it to our accounts immediately." He let a bit of growl enter his voice. "Before I'm forced to take steps."

The blood draining from Gerard's face was gratifying. As was his dawning respect, which had been absent up to this point. The fear oozing from him was just the icing on Noah's cake.

"Th-there must be some mistake," Gerald sputtered.

"There's no mistake." Noah relaxed back in his chair, with his legs crossed and hands folded in his lap. "Substantial amounts were transferred from both our personal and business accounts, bypassing the protocols put in place to protect our finances, without proper authorization for any of the transactions."

Gerald stiffened at the accusation. "I can assure you, no transfers would have been made without full and proper authorizations."

"And yet, that is exactly what happened."

"That's impossible," Gerard said as he turned to his computer and began quickly tapping on his keyboard. "Give me one moment and I will prove to you the transactions in question followed all security protocols and procedures."

This should prove interesting. Noah brushed his hand over the pocket holding his phone as he watched Gerard pound away at his keyboard. He wondered if he had enough time to check the last text from his mate.

Paper began spitting from the printer. Guess not then. Noah sat back in his chair, sighing when the stack of pages accumulating in the printer's tray began spilling onto the floor.

Noah scanned the documents spread across the desk, then looked at the image Gerard had pulled up on his computer screen, frowning when he noted the date and time stamp from the week before. Leaning back, he tapped the papers in front of him.

"According to these, you transferred funds from our accounts at the behest of our Director of Finance, William Smith."

"Yes, that is correct," Gerard said smugly.

"Interesting. I don't remember getting a call."

"A call?"

"Yes. The call I should have received to get my approval for the transactions. Did you misdial my number?"

Gerard blinked. "Uh, no. But—"

"But nothing. How dare you release our funds without bothering to check with Reid or myself first?"

"I-uh…what?"

Noah jabbed at the computer screen. "Check your system. There is a clearly detailed process for how our finances are to be managed. I want to know, firstly, why you didn't challenge Smith when he presented you with a request to transfer funds from our accounts, and secondly, how you could, without a moment's thought, approve his transfer request without calling us to confirm it first?"

"He provided an original document signed by Mr. Reid Davenport."

"Which Reid couldn't have signed since he wasn't in the country at the time."

"B-but everything checked out. There was no reason to suspect anything was wrong with the paperwork."

"No?" Noah stood and planted his hands on the desk. "Did it not occur to you that in our long history of dealing with this institution, there has never, not once, been a withdrawal made on either of the personal accounts since they were first established over two hundred years ago?"

"T-there hasn't?" Gerard asked weakly.

"No. The fact someone, who is not an owner of either of those accounts, showed up with a request to transfer funds from accounts which had never seen a withdrawal over their lifetime, should have sent up every red flag you had. That it didn't, makes me seriously question your capabilities of heading this branch."

Gerard's face paled further, something Noah hadn't thought possible. Not that it deterred him from hammering his point home.

"The level of incompetence and carelessness displayed by you is something your predecessors would never have allowed. Your gross negligence in this matter has proven you cannot be trusted to look after our assets; therefore, you leave me with no choice but to pull all of our business from your institution."

Gerard swayed in his chair before lurching to his feet. "Mr. Davenport, sir. You can't do that. You'll ruin me."

"You should have thought of that before you gave our money away."

"But Noah, you—"

"It's Mr. Davenport. I haven't given you leave to call me by my name."

"My apologies, Mr. Davenport." A drop of sweat rolled down the side of Gerard's face. "Please, you must reconsider. My daughter's university bills. My wife's lakeside cottage. I can't...you can't...please, you must give me a chance to fix this."

Noah crossed his arms and scowled at the trembling bank manager. If Reid were here, Noah was sure he'd have already cut their losses and kicked Gerard out the door. At least, the old Reid would have. Mating with Fionn had mellowed his brother, making him somewhat more forgiving. The present-day Reid would probably be inclined to give Gerard a chance to make everything right. But only one.

Which is exactly what Noah was going to do, since he didn't want to disappoint his new brother-in-law. Gerard had no idea how fortunate he was that Fionn was now part of the Davenport family.

"I'll give you one chance to make this right."

Gerard swayed in his seat. "Oh, thank you, sir. Tell me what you want me to do."

Speaking so low Gerard had to strain to hear every word, Noah said, "Find out where our money is and have it put back into our accounts. You have three days to get it done."

Gerard gulped. "And if I can't"

"Then we'll close all of our accounts and recommend to the rest of the Dragon Court they do the same, which will include any holdings for the King and Queen."

"Y-you can't do that."

"Oh, I very much can, and I will. Make this right Gerard, or you'll lose everything you hold dear."

Noah figured he'd made his point when Gerard's eyes rolled back in his head and he slithered from his chair to the floor under his desk.

———

Noah was a block away from his brokerage firm, the next stop in his investigations, when he recalled the text that he'd silenced earlier.

"I'm almost there, pretty dragon."

Before he could put his phone back in his pocket, it vibrated again. Noah smirked as he shook his head. Did Jory seriously not have anything better to do than send him texts all day long? He tried to ignore the warmth of his skin and the pounding of his heart, uncontrollable side effects of his pleasure at being the focus of his mate's attention, but it was a lost cause.

"What did you do to that poor man at the bank? I could smell his fear a block away."

Noah's eyebrow shot up. How had Jory tracked him to the bank so quickly? Especially since he'd flown and left no trail for the wolf to follow.

The next text that made him think his mate had a direct line to his brain.

"No matter how far you go or how fast you fly, I'll always be able to find you."

Noah grunted. Was that so? Challenge accepted.

Noah picked up his pace, almost running by the time he reached his broker's office. He crashed through the front doors and charged up the stairs to his account manager's office on the seventeenth floor. By the time he pounded past the landing on the fifth floor, he was in a full-on sprint and grinning from ear to ear.

If his mate wanted to catch him, he was going to have to work for it.

Thirty minutes later, Noah was fuming as he exited the stairwell after leaving his broker's office. Another large portion of their assets had been liquidated, with William Smith once again providing paperwork with their signatures authorizing the transaction. What in the hell was going on?

He was almost to the main doors when he spotted Jory on the sidewalk outside. Stepping back until he was out of sight of the doors, Noah spun around and sprinted for the stairs. He'd just leave from the roof.

Noah hurtled through the steel door that opened onto the roof and skidded to a stop. Glancing around, he hurried across the graveled surface to the far side and prepared to shift. Another text arrived to join the other that came through while he was running up the stairs.

"Which floor are you on?"

"Not going to answer? No worries. I'll keep looking."

Noah couldn't stop his mouth from twitching. His mate's relentless pursuit was rather flattering. Distracting, slightly worrisome, but mostly flattering. And he was getting closer, so it was time to go.

Noah's phone beeped again.

"The nice man on seventeen said I just missed you. Where'd you go next?"

Yes. He was definitely out of time. Noah dropped his phone in his pocket, but before he could shift, it started ringing with Reid's ringtone. Shit. He couldn't leave without telling his brother what he'd discovered.

Keeping an eye on the door to watch for his mate, he answered the call.

"Hey, Reid. What's up?"

"How's it going, little brother?"

Noah eyed his phone. Reid sounded a little too gleeful to be trusted. "It's been interesting. I found out—"

"You do realize your window is broken? Were you in too much of a hurry to use the door?

He rolled his eyes at the laughter in his brother's voice. "Something like that."

"I'm going to deduct the cost of replacing it from your paycheck."

"You do what you have to."

"You can't keep avoiding him forever."

Noah grunted. He could try.

"I'm telling you, Noah, if you keep running, it's going to bite you in the ass. At probably the worst possible time."

"I know. And I'll worry about it later. Right now, you need to listen to what I found out."

"Okay. Hit me."

"Gerard's the one who approved transfers of our money."

"The hell? Why did he do that?"

"Because Smith gave him a transfer request, authorized by the both of us, to move our funds out."

"What? I didn't sign any transfer request."

"Me either." Noah patted the packet of papers in his breast pocket. "I got Gerard to give me copies. The signatures look legit."

"That's bullshit. You and I both know they're fake."

"Which is what I told Gerard. We need to talk to Smith. Can you set something up?"

"Sure. Hang on a minute."

"Wait. I'll call you back." But his brother was already gone. Noah sighed and leaned against the ledge as he waited for Reid.

His neck began to itch as he got another text.

"You tried to throw me off by backtracking. Sneaky, sneaky, pretty dragon."

Keeping an eye on the stairwell door, Noah was about to hang up when Reid came back on the line.

"I checked with the Finance department. Nobody's seen Smith in about a week. Apparently, there was some kind of family emergency."

"Pretty weak cover for a guy who's embezzling our money."

"Unless he didn't think we'd catch on, which is stupid on his part."

"No more stupid that stealing from us in the first place."

"True. I think you should pay him a visit."

"I think you're right. Send me his address."

"Already on its way."

Noah's phone beeped. He checked, seeing an address for the Upper East Side. "Got it. I'll let you know what I find."

"While you're doing that, I'll look around his office. We can compare notes when you get back."

"Sounds good. Talk to you soon." Disconnecting the call, he glanced at the screen when his phone chimed in his hand.

"I've got you now, pretty dragon."

Noah shoved his phone in his pocket and jumped onto the low surrounding wall before leaping off the edge of the roof. Shifting as he fell, he snapped his wings out, rising above the building in time to see Jory crash through the rooftop door and race to where he'd been standing.

He hovered above the roof, playfully shooting flames over his mate's head. Jory crossed his arms and crooked one finger, daring him to come closer. Noah flicked his tail and released another blast of fire, circled once, then began heading north. As he flew away, he wondered how long it would take his mate to find him this time?

Knowing Jory would filled Noah's heart with joy, whether he was ready to acknowledge it or not.

———

Noah poked his head around the tree and looked over the top of the tall hedge encircling the yard two houses down from the brownstone he was spying on. He held his breath as the kid he'd hired rang the doorbell, then bounced from foot to foot. When no one answered after he rang again, he looked over to where Noah was hiding. Stepping away from the tree, Noah signaled that he could go. Grinning, the kid waved back, then jumped off the front step and raced down the sidewalk to where his friends were waiting on the corner. There was some pushing and shoving, fist bumps, even a few shouts of "thanks mister" before the group of teens jumped on their skateboards and took off, presumably to spend the money Noah had given them.

Noah tapped his fingers against the tree trunk as he contemplated his next move. There'd been no answer when he'd tried calling Smith earlier, and now that he hadn't come to the door, he had no idea where to look for him. But since Noah was here—and Smith wasn't—it might be worthwhile to have a look around his house. He might get lucky and find some clues as to what Smith had done with their money.

Noah's attention was so focused on the brownstone he didn't realize someone was sneaking up on him until a voice whispered in his ear.

"What are you doing?"

Noah shrieked—a sound no dragon should make…ever—then spun around and shoved Jory away from him.

"What the hell? You almost gave me a heart attack."

"Sorry," Jory said, his eyes filled with humor. "I called your name, but I guess you didn't hear me."

"I guess not."

"You must have been too busy with whatever you were doing." Jory came up beside him and looked over the hedge. "What are you looking at?"

"Nothing."

"You're concentrating pretty hard on nothing, then."

"So what if I am?"

"Maybe I can help."

"Thanks, but I've got this."

"I'd really like to help," Jory said, taking his hand. "Who are you watching?"

"None of your business." Noah shook his hand loose, ignoring the tingles that ran down his arm. "Could you please go before someone wonders what we're doing and calls the police."

Noah turned back to the brownstone, hoping he hadn't missed anything. It would be just his luck if Smith came home while he'd been distracted by his mate.

Jory's warmth surrounded him as he molded himself to Noah's back, his breath ruffling Noah's hair as he rested his chin on his shoulder. "Come on, pretty dragon. Tell me what we're doing."

"There is no we." Noah elbowed him in the stomach. "Now please go before you ruin everything."

Jory grunted when his elbow landed, then wrapped his arms around Noah, pinning his arms to his sides.

"Do you mind?" Noah growled. Which might have been more effective if he wasn't so damned breathless. "I'm kind of busy here. I don't have time to deal with you right now."

"Don't be so cranky, pretty dragon. Let me help," Jory crooned, then licked at his ear.

Noah's insides turned to mush. Which only annoyed him further. "Stop that." He turned his head and glared. "And stop calling me pretty."

"But you are."

"I don't care. Just…don't do it."

"But I want to." Jory pressed his face in Noah's neck, raising goosebumps all over his body. Then the damn wolf licked him again.

He shuddered, swallowing back a moan. Jory really needed to let go of him before he forgot why he was there.

"Tell me, mate," Jory husked, the vibrations of his voice strumming along Noah's nerves. Pheromones wrapped around him, drowning him in a sea of desire. "What's so interesting about that house?"

House? What house?

Jory snickered and squeezed him around the waist.

Noah blinked, then shook his head, trying to clear the fog covering his mind. His mate had asked a question. At least, he thought so, even if he couldn't recall the words. "What'd you say?"

Jory cradled Noah's chin between his thumb and forefinger and pointed it toward the brownstone. "Why are you watching that house?"

"Uh, no reason." At least none that concerned his mate.

"Okay. Then you won't mind if I check it out."

Wait. What?

Jory took off before Noah could stop him.

"Get back here," he hissed, then groaned and banged his head against the tree when Jory zipped past the first house, then winked at him before he hurdled Smith's fence and ran up to the front door.

Damn it. Noah was going to kick his ass if he somehow scared Smith away.

Giving up on stealth, he chased after his mate. When he caught up to Jory, he was sniffing around the door, a frown on his face.

"What is it?"

"Check out the smell."

Noah did as he asked, then coughed. He rubbed his nose to wipe away the acrid odor of wrongness that stung his nostrils. Whatever was inside smelled of rot and decay, mixed with tainted magic.

"Things just got serious," Jory whispered. "It's time for you to tell me why you were watching this place."

Noah hesitated at telling Jory he'd allowed someone to steal from him. The theft of a hoard was a dragon's greatest shame. But this was his mate. Surely, he wouldn't judge.

Hoping Jory would understand the sensitivity of what he was telling him, Noah whispered, "This is where our Director of Finance, William Smith, lives. I found out he's been stealing from my hoard."

Jory nodded. "And you want to talk to him."

Noah frowned. "You don't sound surprised."

"Reid might have mentioned what you were doing."

"He did? Why would he…never mind." Noah shook his head. He should have guessed Reid would tell Jory everything. "But you're right. I want to talk to Smith. Find out what's going on."

Jory grimaced. "Judging by the smell, you might be too late."

Noah sighed. "I know."

"We should probably check anyway." Jory reached for the doorknob, which turned easily in his hand. "It's open," he said, his eyes flying to Noah's.

Noah tensed, and reached out with his senses. A menacing darkness lingered in the air.

Jory nudged the door open.

"Wait," Noah hissed, reaching for him.

Jory shrugged his hand off and slipped inside.

"Shit."

Noah glanced over both shoulders, checking to see if anyone was watching, then slid sideways past the door, closing it quietly behind him.

He had a feeling they were making a big mistake. If they were lucky, they'd only get arrested for breaking and entering. Taking a look at the broken furniture in the living room, he added vandalism to their possible charges.

As he made his way down the hallway and saw the butcher knife sticking out from the wall with streaks of red running from it, Noah revised the list to include murder.

Sheri Eleese

Chapter Six

Jory

Jory made it two steps into the brownstone, then gagged. He buried his nose in the crook of his elbow to block the overpowering stench of wrongness and scanned the interior. Taking note of the toppled and broken furniture, he eased through the front room to avoid touching anything, then cautiously made his way down the hallway. His steps slowed when he saw a knife jammed into the wall, trails of dried blood running from it. Giving it a wide berth, he continued to the back of the house, where the smell seemed to originate.

He was standing in front of a closed door near the end of the hallway when Noah caught up to him, his jacket pulled over the lower half of his face. He grabbed Jory's arm before he could turn the knob and whispered, "Be careful. I don't know what happened here, but it feels wrong."

"Okay," Jory said, his voice muffled behind his arm. Covering his hand with the bottom of his sleeve, he slowly turned the knob, gasping as fetid air, thick with rot and an overpowering sense of evil, rolled out into the hallway. He jerked the door closed, then bent over and retched.

Noah made a strangled sound as he choked on the thick air, his body hitting the wall as he fell into a fit of coughing.

Tears streaming from his eyes, Jory flapped his hand in front of his face, and trying not to breathe, gasped, "Can you do something about the smell?"

Noah nodded and flicked his fingers. The air glinted with magic as a breeze blew down the hallway, taking the offensive odor with it.

Jory breathed deep, filling his lungs with fresh air, then scrubbed his nose where the foul smell of rot still lingered. "Thanks."

"Sorry I didn't think of it sooner."

"No problem." He reached for the doorknob, stopping when Noah touched his wrist.

"I still have to clean the room, so you might want to hold your breath before going in."

"Gotcha." Taking a deep breath, Jory steeled himself, then opened the door and went in. Even holding his breath, the concentrated smell in the small space hit him like a punch in the face. Behind him, he could hear Noah gag, then fresh, crisp air swirled around him.

It took a few more minutes to cleanse the room than it did the hallway, but once he could breathe without wanting to hurl, Jory wiped his streaming eyes and took another step into the room. When he saw the darkened, shriveled body on the ground, he jerked back, stumbling into Noah, who caught hold of him.

Noah leaned around him. "What is…is that a body?"

Jory swallowed. "Yep."

"Why does it look like that?"

"I don't know." Jory turned his head to the side. "We'll have to get closer to see."

Noah grimaced. "I, uh, I'd rather not."

"Me either, but we should try to figure out what happened." Jory stepped closer to the figure on the floor, then realized Noah hadn't moved. Noting the pallor of his face, he said, "I take it you don't see a lot of dead bodies."

Noah swallowed and shook his head. "Not generally, no. I'm more used to the bloodless skirmishes at the Dragon Court, where words are the weapons used to cut your opponent. I don't deal well with blood." He glanced at the body and shuddered. "I try to avoid things like this."

Taking in his mate's pristine suit, overly styled hair, and face that was looking a little green around the edges, Jory realized how out of his comfort zone Noah was. That he hadn't run screaming from the room or fainted told Jory a lot. The more he learned about his mate, the greater his respect for Noah grew.

Since both of them weren't needed to inspect the body, Jory said, "How about I examine the body while you stay back there?"

"Are you sure?"

"Yeah, I've got this."

Noah's eyes flicked to the body, then back to Jory. "Okay, thanks."

Jory gave him a half smile, then crept up to the figure curled on the carpet at the end of the bed. The body's skin was brownish-gray, shriveled and weathered, as if baked under a hot desert sun for a hundred years. The flesh on its skull was dark and tight, with sunken sockets where the eyes should have been and its lips were pulled back, its face frozen in a rictus of terror.

Jory looked back at Noah. "Do you think this could be your Mr. Smith?"

Noah took a couple of steps further into the room and squinted at the body. After a minute, he nodded, then he shook his head, then tilted his head to the side. "I'm not sure. It could be. But…" He came a few feet closer and studied the body, before giving Jory a helpless shrug. "I'm sorry. There's not enough left there to tell."

"What do you mean?"

"I mean, there's nothing there. Even in death, there are always traces of a person's essence, something, left behind. But this," he gestured to the body, "it's like everything that made him who he was has been drained out of him."

"Except for the smell."

"Which I think has less to do with the body and more about how he was killed. Or rather, whatever killed him."

"Which is what?" Jory asked, prodding the desiccated corpse with his toe. "What could have done this to him?"

"I, uh, I don't know."

"Could it be something from another dimension? Like a demon or something like that?"

Noah shook his head. "No. We would have known if something crossed over."

"We?"

Noah tore his eyes off the body to look at him. "I mean dragons."

"Dragons can tell when something from another dimension comes here?" Jory asked, surprised to hear that. He'd had no idea. He wondered if his brother did.

Noah nodded. "Dragons are more in tune with the forces that make up the universe than anything else. If something crossed over to the earthly dimension that didn't belong, we would have felt it."

"Then how do you explain whatever killed him?"

"I can't. But Sophia or Edmund might know. I'll have to check with them later." He pulled out his phone and took a couple of pictures.

Jory stepped back from the body and glanced over the room. "Assuming this is Smith, we should take a look around to see if we can find any clues as to what happened to your missing money."

He went to the dresser and pulled out the top drawer, then rifled through it. Finding nothing, he moved onto the next, then glanced over his shoulder. "It'll go faster if you help."

"Right. Sorry." Avoiding the body, Noah went to the nightstand on the far side of the bed and opened the bottom drawer.

Working together, they made quick work of inspecting the room, including some boxes stacked on the shelf in the closet, but came up with nothing.

Jory leaned against the dresser with his arms crossed. "I have a feeling we'd be wasting our time going through the rest of the house. Let's see if Smith has an office and concentrate our efforts there. If nothing else, there should at least be a computer we can take for your IT guys to have a look through."

"Good idea," Noah said. Giving the body on the floor a last look, he walked out the door, turning left down the hallway.

Jory pushed off the dresser to follow him when something on the floor caught his attention. Crouching, he saw a small black crystal half buried in the nap of the carpet. Picking it up, he held it to the light, then rolled it between his fingers, before clenching it tight in his fist. Standing, Jory dropped the stone in his pocket, not exactly sure why he took it, but he had a strong feeling it was important that he did.

———

Carrying Smith's laptop under his arm, Jory followed Noah into his office and set it on the desk. Two minutes later, Reid walked in, smirking when he saw them together. Until he saw their grim expressions.

"What happened?" Reid asked.

Noah dropped into his chair. "Smith's dead."

"Our Smith?"

Noah nodded. "Yes. At least, I think it was him. It was hard to tell."

"What do you mean?"

"The body we found was too desiccated to know for sure."

"Vampire?"

Noah shook his head. "No. It was something else."

"Then it couldn't have been Smith. He's only been out of the office for a week. If he died sometime in the last few days, his body wouldn't have deteriorated that much."

"I'd agree with you, except there was something off about how he died."

"Off how?"

"Whatever killed him sucked him completely dry, stripping away every bit of his essence. There was nothing left behind."

Reid frowned. "That can't be right. There's always something."

"Not this time."

"You must have missed something. Nothing can do that to a body."

"I know that," Noah groaned, leaning back in his chair as he scrubbed his face. "But I'm telling you, there was nothing there. I have no idea what happened to him."

"I don't know if it'll help, but I found this." Jory pulled out the stone and set it on Noah's desk.

Noah squinted at it. "Where'd you find that?"

"Next to the body. I noticed it when I was leaving the bedroom."

Reid picked up the gem and held it up to the light. "Interesting. What made you decide to take it?" He looked at Jory questioningly.

"I'm not really sure. It seemed out of place." Jory frowned, trying to recall what had prompted him to take it. "I just had the feeling it was important. That we needed it."

Reid's eyebrow shot up. "A feeling?" He glanced over at Noah. "That can't be good."

Noah groaned again. "Probably not. But I've come to expect that lately." He gestured toward the stone. "Do you sense anything from it?"

"Not much." Reid set it back on the desk. "It has a strange echo about it, like an impression. But it's very faint."

"Of what? Smith?"

"Possibly. Or it could be from whatever drained him."

Jory picked up the black gem to see if he could feel this echo Reid was talking about—which he couldn't— then handed it to Noah when he held out his hand. "Do you think it's safe for me to carry it around?"

Noah pushed it around on his palm as he examined it. "I don't sense any danger in it, but since I don't know what it is, I can't say for sure."

"I think I'll have to risk it. I have a feeling we're going to need it." He held out his hand to Noah, who started to hand it to him, then hesitated. A whisper of magic flowed over his skin, then Noah dropped the gem into his hand.

Jory held it up, noting the way the light wavered around it. "What did you do?"

"I put a shield around it. I don't like the idea of you carrying around something that could possibly harm you."

Jory smiled as he put it in his pocket. "I didn't realize you cared."

Reid snorted.

Noah rolled his eyes at Jory, at the same time flipping off his brother. "Of course, I care. You're my mate."

"Does that mean you're going to stop running?"

"Probably not."

"That's okay," Jory said with a grin. "I enjoy hunting you down."

Reid choked on a breath before he started laughing.

Noah shook his head, his lips twitching as he tried to hold back a smile. "You're both idiots."

"You should know," Reid said, chuckling as he sat in one of the chairs in front of Noah's desk. "So what's your next move now that Smith's a dead end?" He winced. "Shit. I didn't mean for it to sound like that."

Shaking his head, Noah said, "We know what you meant. But to answer your question, it's time to follow the money. I already have Gerard looking into it."

"We took Smith's computer," Jory said, sliding the laptop over to Reid. "It might have something helpful in it."

Reid took it. "I'll drop it off with the IT team. Knowing how careful Smith was, it probably has great security on it. Which should be fun for them. They do love a challenge."

"Why? Are they hackers?" Jory asked, snickering.

"We prefer to say information gatherers."

Jory almost swallowed his tongue. "Seriously? You employ criminals?" He looked at Noah, who shrugged.

"It's better to hire them than have them try to hack our systems."

"Besides," Reid said, shrugging like it was no big deal they had criminals working for them. "Talent like that is hard to come by. We much prefer them working for us than our competitors."

Before Jory could respond, his mate's phone rang.

Noah pulled it from his pocket, his eyebrow going up when he glanced at the screen. "It's Gerard."

"Hey, maybe he's already tracked down your money," Jory said.

"We can only hope." Noah set the phone on his desk and answered it. "Hello Gerard."

"Mr. Davenport. I'm so glad I reached you."

"Do you have good news for me?"

"Unfortunately, no. I'm sorry to have to inform you the money has already been removed from the account it was transferred to. I have no way to get it back."

"That's a problem, Gerard."

"I understand, sir. And that's not the only one."

Reid leaned forward in his chair. "What's going on, Gerard?"

"Mr. Davenport. I didn't realize you were there as well."

"I am. So is my brother's mate, Jory. Please tell us what you found?"

Having a bad feeling about what Gerard was going to say, Jory moved around the desk so he could be near his mate if he needed him. Noah watched carefully, but didn't shift away when Jory put his hand on his shoulder. He was going to take that as a win.

"Right." There was a pause, then the sound of typing on a keyboard, then Gerard came back. *"I wish I had better news. After my conversation earlier today with the other Mr.*

Davenport, I took it upon myself to lock down all of your accounts to prevent further debit transactions from being made against them."

"A wise precaution."

"I wish that were the case. A few minutes ago, I received a notification from our sister branch in NOLA that some rather large sums of money were transferred from those accounts."

"What?" Reid growled. "How did that happen if you put a lock on them?"

"It appears the manager of the NOLA branch overrode it."

"He did what?" Reid yelled.

"Under whose authority?" Noah asked, waving his brother to silence.

"Yours and the other Mr. Davenport. Mr. Smith had a transfer request signed by both of you. It appears when the notification message on the accounts popped up, Smith provided a document overriding the hold."

"When did this happen?" Reid snarled.

"Two hours ago, sir."

"That's impossible," Noah said. "Smith is dead."

"I'm afraid he can't be, sir."

"Why do you say that?"

"I had the manager send the security footage to me in case you had questions. I just finished watching it and I can confirm it's the same person who arranged for the transfers at my branch. The individual you identified earlier as your Financial Director, William Smith."

"What the hell?"

Jory squeezed Noah's shoulders when they tensed up.

"I tried to get the transaction reversed, but the manager I spoke with was quite uncooperative."

"I'll take care of it," Noah growled. When smoke started wafting from his nose, Jory stroked his thumb up and down on the back of his neck, hoping his touch would calm him.

"*Sir?*"

"Gerard," Reid said, "we're going to have to call you back."

"*Very well, sir.*"

Reid ended the call, then jumped up and began to pace. "What the hell is going on?"

"I have no idea." Noah rubbed his forehead. "I thought the body we found was Smith's, but it couldn't have been if he's in New Orleans."

"What if it's someone pretending to be him?" Jory offered.

Reid and Noah both shook their heads.

He frowned at their quick response. "Why not?"

Jory stepped back when Noah turned his chair to face him. "Financial institutions have special protections to prevent anyone from disguising their identity. You can't hide who you are or pretend to be anyone else."

"But—"

Noah held up his hand, cutting him off. "These protections are created with dragon magic. No glamor or spell can fool them or get past them."

"Except it did, since Smith is dead."

"If that was actually Smith's body we found. It's possible it could have been someone else."

Reid stopped pacing. "I'll have some of our people clear the scene. One way or another, we'll find out who that was."

"While you do that, I'll fly to NOLA and have a chat with the bank manager," Noah said.

Jory cleared his throat. "I think what you meant to say is we'll fly to NOLA."

"No, I didn't." Noah stood and pointed his finger at Jory. "You can stay here and help Reid."

Jory snorted. "I don't think so."

"Well, I do."

"Too bad. If you leave without me, I'll ask Sophia to fly me back."

Noah frowned. "Why would you ask our queen?"

"Because she's the one who gave me a ride here."

"She did what?" Noah turned to Reid. "You let our queen carry him on her back?"

Reid barked out a laugh. "There was no let. Sophia insisted."

"I can't believe she'd carry a complete stranger on her back."

"Uhm, standing right here," Jory said.

Noah squinted at him. "What did you say to make her?"

Jory choked back a laugh at how annoyed his mate was. "I didn't have to say anything. She volunteered."

"She wouldn't have without a good reason. You must have done something."

"I didn't do anything," Jory growled, getting annoyed himself. He jabbed a finger in Noah's chest. "You did."

"Me?"

"Yes, you." When Noah began edging away, Jory stayed with him. "Sophia giving me a ride was all your fault."

"My fault?"

"Yes. She wouldn't have had to give me a ride if you hadn't run off scared."

"I wasn't scared—"

"You were," Jory said, bumping his chest into Noah, who quickly took another step back. Tempering his tone, he continued softly. "I know you had reasons for running.

I could smell them. And if this was any other situation, I'd let you leave me behind. But things have changed now."

"Let me?" Noah squeaked.

"Yes, let you. And I would have kept chasing you." Crowding him up against the wall, Jory cupped Noah's face, brushing his thumb over his cheekbone. "Because we were both enjoying it." Jory held back a smile when he felt him tremble. "But this isn't a normal situation, and I refuse to allow my mate to leave me behind while he walks into danger. If you don't want the queen flying me back to NOLA, then you'd better take me yourself because you're not going alone."

"Allow me?" Noah sputtered. "You can't...I won't...who the hell do you think you are telling me what to do?"

"I'm your mate," Jory said, pressing up against him. "And it's my job to keep you safe. You're not going anywhere without me, pretty dragon. Not this time."

Noah's mouth dropped open in shock, an opening Jory couldn't resist.

He slammed their mouths together.

Noah froze, his hands coming up as if to push Jory away, then he sighed and all but melted into him.

Groaning at his mate's submission, Jory pushed his tongue past Noah's lips. The smoky spice of his mate exploded in his mouth as he licked deep, searching out every bit of flavor. Blood pounded in Jory's ears as sparks of magic flickered around them, making his skin tingle and sending shocks of energy zinging through his veins.

Noah rose to his toes, his tongue eagerly pushing against Jory's as he tried to take over the kiss. Jory growled in warning. Noah jerked, then moaned, the scent of his arousal filling Jory's nostrils. When Noah backed down, he rumbled his approval and attacked his mate's mouth, taking everything Noah had to give.

When the need to breathe became too great, Jory slowed the kiss, nipping gently at Noah's lips, then running his tongue over them to soothe the sting. When he pulled away, Noah clutched at his shirt, his eyes slowly opening, the dazed expression on his face making Jory smile. He brushed Noah's bangs out of his eyes, then gave a startled laugh when his mate yanked him back into the kiss and bit his lip. Hard.

Jory growled at the taste of blood and bit him back. He slid his hands around Noah's neck, cupping his jaw as he held him right where he wanted, then took his mouth again, biting at his lips and sucking on his tongue as he fed his hunger for his mate, driving both of their passions higher.

The need pouring off of Noah appeased Jory's wolf—and healed the small wound on his heart—as much as the hands clutching at his back as if they never wanted to let him go.

Chapter Seven

Noah

Heat. His body was consumed by heat. And need. A need so fierce he was drowning in it. The tight grip he had on his mate was all that was keeping Noah afloat. His hands clenched the fabric of Jory's shirt as he pulled him closer—if that was even possible—and tried to take control of the kiss. The warning growl vibrating in Jory's chest sent tingles of excitement through his body and made him want to submit.

So he did.

The rumble of approval warmed his heart.

Wanting to hear that sound again, he bit at Jory's lip. In his excitement, he bit harder than he intended, breaking the skin. The small drops of his mate's blood on his tongue were like gasoline on the fire of his need.

And ignited the wolf's dominance. Noah gave way to his mate's greater power as he held him in place, accepting the stinging bites to his lips that drove his need higher, succumbed to the tongue that lashed and soothed in a dizzying mix of sensations. The ground shifted beneath his feet as the hot and hungry kisses swept him away.

Stirred by his passions, Noah's dragon rose, urging him to bond with his mate. Telling him to wait no longer. When Noah hesitated, his mind was flooded with images of him tackling Jory to the ground and uniting them in flames, blood, and magic.

Groaning, caught between the hunger of his mate and the needs of his dragon, Noah's fingers tightened on Jory's shirt as he tried to climb his body without losing connection with his mouth.

Then his brother laughed, jolting him back to an awareness of where they were. And the fact they weren't alone. The flames of his passion cooled as if plunged into a glacier cold lake.

Tearing his mouth free, Noah rested his head on Jory's shoulder, panting as he tried to catch his breath, then he pushed him back. Wiping his mouth, Noah ran his hands down the front of his shirt, then straightened his tie and jacket, hoping the other two didn't notice the way his fingers trembled. The heat in Jory's eyes and the curl of his lip as he watched him let Noah know his sharp eyes hadn't missed his reaction. And that he was pleased by the effect he'd had on him.

Noah growled and glared at him, not sure he pulled it off with puffy lips and flushed skin, but he gave it his best shot. Ignoring Jory's snort of laughter, he brushed past his mate and walked unsteadily back to his desk.

He stiffened when Jory crowded against his back and took hold of his hips. The kiss to the back of his neck almost melted his resolve but he was determined to resist his mate. Then he sighed, and relaxed, giving his weight to Jory. It was ridiculous of him to keep fighting a battle he'd already spectacularly lost. His heart bumped when Jory's arms slipped around his waist and pulled him closer.

"Thank you, pretty dragon," Jory breathed in his ear, for only him to hear. "I won't betray the trust you've given me."

Noah tried, but couldn't hold back the heat that crawled up his face. Especially not with his stupid dragon cooing and prancing around, thrilled at pleasing their mate. Jory's low rumble of approval that sounded almost like purring wasn't helping much either.

"It's good to see you two have everything worked out," Reid said, his eyes dancing.

Noah tried to scowl but failed dismally, too content from being held by his mate.

"I told you Jory was perfect for you."

Noah squinted at his brother. "No, you didn't."

"I didn't?" Reid asked, feigning confusion. "Are you sure?"

"Trust me, you didn't."

"Well, I was thinking it, so close enough." He waived his hand airily. "And as usual, your big brother was right."

Jory snorted behind him.

Noah rolled his eyes. "Nobody likes a know-it-all, Reid. Please try to control yourself."

"Fionn does," Reid said, a smile spreading across his face.

"Yes, well, he really doesn't have a choice but to tell you that. But take it from me, nobody else does."

Reid started laughing. "You might have a point. It still doesn't change the fact I was right about you being perfect for each other. Maybe next time you should listen to me and save everyone a lot of hassle. If nothing else, it'll keep us from having to replace any more office windows."

Noah flipped him off. "Asshole."

Jory buried his face in his hair, his body shaking with laughter.

———

Landing in New Orleans the following day…

Noah flared out his wings to slow his descent, then touched down lightly on the plush green grass. He folded his wings to his sides, then twisted his neck back, and gently bumped Jory's leg with his head.

After they'd left New York, Noah had been so excited about taking his first flight with his mate it had taken far too long to realize something was wrong with Jory. He'd gotten his first inkling when Jory's body had stiffened when he flew through the clouds. But it wasn't until he'd dropped and leveled out that Noah had felt the panic and fear flowing through their barely established bond. He'd been crushed when he realized the thing that brought him his greatest joy and that he'd looked forward to sharing with his mate, terrified him.

Noah had kept the rest of the flight as smooth as possible, carefully adjusting for the changing air pressures so his mate wouldn't get bounced around by varying shifts in altitude. As he'd gotten closer to their destination, his mind reeled, unable to believe his mate was afraid of flying. But now, seeing Jory's white face and rigid body, Noah knew it to be true. The fact Jory hadn't hesitated even the slightest to climb on his back before they left New York only proved how strong and brave he really was.

Unfortunately, Jory's fear was going to be a problem. A dragon's mate was expected to fly with their dragon. And as much as he wished he could to tell Jory he didn't have to, he really couldn't, because it was a weakness others could exploit. Their only choice was to find a way to get Jory over his fear…and as quickly as possible before the wrong people found out.

But first, he had to get his mate off his back because they couldn't stay in the park forever.

Noah flattened himself, going as low as he could, then adjusted his wings so Jory could slide down them to the ground. When Jory didn't make a move to dismount, Noah nudged his leg again, then rubbed his leathery cheek against it as his throat vibrated with a low-pitched croon.

Jory blinked. His weight shifted. Then he froze.

Noah quickly sent waves of encouragement and support through their connection, hoping it would be enough to get his mate to let go.

Jory's eyes flicked to the side, locking onto his. Then he turned away, his fingers tightening further on Noah's scale ridge.

Noah ran his cheek up and down his mate's leg, then nudged his shoulder…but bumped him a bit too hard.

Jory shouted when he was knocked sideways, his hands scrabbling frantically as he tried to find a handhold, but his fingers slid over the smooth surface of Noah's tightly interlocked scales, unable to get a grip. Jory yelled as he rolled down Noah's wing, landing on the grass in a graceless sprawl.

Noah immediately shifted and dropped to his knees, pulling his mate's trembling body into his arms. "I'm so sorry. I didn't mean to knock you off."

Jory stayed still in his arms. But only for a moment, then his pride must have kicked in. He pushed at Noah, struggling to get away. "Let go. I'm fine."

But Noah could feel through their bond he really wasn't, so held him tighter.

Jory slid his arms between them and pushed against his chest, but when Noah refused to let go, he growled. "I'm not some weakling you have to coddle."

"I know you're not. You're amazing, and so brave. The furthest thing from weak, but—"

"Then let me go."

"I can't. My dragon knows your wolf is scared. We need to care for him. Please let me hold you until we know your wolf's okay."

Jory tentatively pushed against him again, then sighed and tucked his face into Noah's neck. "Fine. But only for a bit."

"Thank you."

After a few minutes, Jory's trembling finally stopped. "I'm okay. You can let go now."

Noah let his arms drop, then kissed his lips before climbing to his feet and stepping back. He turned away and pulled out his phone, under the guise of checking the time, to give Jory some privacy to pull himself together. When he heard Jory walking around behind him, Noah turned back.

Holding up his phone, he said, "We still have a few hours before the bank closes." He took in his mate's still pale face. "Unless you want to wait until tomorrow."

Jory shook his head. "No. Let's go now and get it done. That way we'll be one step closer to finding the person who's hurting you."

Noah held back a grin. There was his fierce wolf. Then what Jory said registered. "Umm, they're not actually hurting me."

"Aren't they?" Jory asked, his eyes locking onto Noah's. "They're stealing from your hoard. Isn't that the most important thing to a dragon?"

"It is." Then Noah paused and shook his head. "Actually, that's not completely true. A hoard is the most important thing to a dragon…unless they find their fated mate. Mates trump hoard every time."

"Are you saying I'm more important than your hoard?"

"Maybe," Noah said teasingly.

A grin spread across Jory's face. He leaned in and kissed Noah on the cheek. "That's good to know, pretty dragon. Thanks for telling me."

Clearing his throat, Noah stepped back. "So, shall we go see what the bank manager has to say now?"

"Yes. I can't wait to talk to the asshole who helped someone steal from you."

Noah's heart skipped a beat at hearing the angry growl in his voice. It was a heady feeling knowing he had someone at his side who completely supported him. And always would.

———

"As you can see, Mr. Davenport, the transfer documents have clearly been signed by you and the other Mr. Davenport, so you're mistaken in thinking one of my people made an error," the snooty bank manager said.

Noah stared at him a moment. What the hell? Was there some special school for bank managers that taught them to be condescending bastards? Did none of them know anything about client services or were they all just a bunch of pretentious assholes?

Shaking his head in disgust—but knowing Boudreaux would soon learn the error of being so dismissive of him—Noah took the pages from his hands and flipped through them. Rolling them into a tube, he tapped them idly against the edge of the desk. "I was under the impression Gerard from the New York branch explained that the signatures on the documents provided to you were forged, which would make the transfers your bank processed using them illegal. I'm also aware you willfully bypassed the holds Gerard put on the accounts, thus making you solely responsible for the illegal transactions. Further to that, you were also advised by Gerard that said transactions were to be reversed." Noah cocked an eyebrow. "Or am I mistaken in that as well, Mr. Boudreaux?"

"He might have mentioned something to that effect," Boudreaux muttered.

"Then we should have no problem," Noah said, knowing from the resentful expression on Boudreaux's face they in fact had a very big problem. "When can I expect the money to be returned?"

"But…we didn't do anything wrong."

"I would have to disagree."

"Mr. Davenport, I can assure you, the transactions were handled with the same care as every other transaction we've done on your behalf."

"And that is another problem," Noah said as he leaned back in his chair and crossed his arms. "There should not have been any other transactions. In fact, there has never been a withdrawal transaction authorized by my brother or myself for these accounts. Ever."

"That can't be."

"I suggest you check your records."

Boudreaux turned to his computer and pressed a few keys. "According to this, Mr. Davenport," Boudreaux said, his hands trembling slightly, "there were a number of transactions processed over the last week."

"And before that?"

Boudreaux typed on his keyboard. Then some more. He looked at Noah from the corner of his eye and hit the keys again, his fingers flying so fast they were a blur.

Noah tapped his fingers and gave it a minute. When he saw sweat pop out on Boudreaux's brow, he murmured, "Find anything yet?"

Boudreaux slammed his hands down on the keyboard then pushed it to the side. "No. Nothing other than the transactions from last week."

"And I can assure you, not a single one of them was authorized by myself or my brother." Noah pointed to his computer. "And as history shows, withdrawals are not made against those accounts."

"I don't understand," Boudreaux said, working his finger in the front of his collar to loosen his tie. "We have a stellar reputation. Our customers know they can trust us to handle their financial needs with discretion and professionalism. We would not make a mistake of this magnitude. There must be some other explanation."

"There is no explanation other than that you and your branch made a critical mistake. One that will cost you dearly."

Boudreaux's lips tightened. Before he could spit out the angry words that had to be burning his tongue, he was interrupted by Jory.

"It's a wonder you managed to achieve such a stellar reputation when not only do you disrespect your clients when they seek your help, but you also carelessly give away their money," Jory said, his voice carrying a rumble worthy of any dragon. "How many of your major clients do you think will stay once word gets out that you're not capable of protecting their investments?"

Boudreaux drew himself up, fire sparking in his eyes as he glared at Jory. "Are you threatening me, young man?"

"No, he's not," Noah said, tapping the desk to bring Boudreaux's attention back to him. "I am. I'll tell you the same thing I told Gerard. Find a way to return the money taken from our accounts or I'll ruin you."

"You can't do that. We did nothing wrong."

Noah set the documents on the desk and pushed them toward Boudreaux. "Since these are not our signatures, you are complicit in the theft of our money."

Boudreaux froze, then his eyes narrowed, a smug expression crossing his face. "I can prove it was your man who brought the transfer documents. Look." He pounded a few keys on his keyboard, then turned his monitor toward them. "That's your Mr. Smith, correct?"

Noah studied the image frozen on the screen. It certainly looked like Smith. Glancing at the timestamp, he noted it was for earlier that day, just as Gerard reported. Which meant it couldn't be Smith, not if the body they'd found had been his.

When Boudreaux started the video, Noah kept his eyes glued to the screen watching as Smith handed some documents to one of the bank tellers. The teller did something on her computer, then placed a call— presumably to Boudreaux to bypass the account freeze— then handed Smith a sheet of paper, which he signed and returned to her. He then leaned against the counter, his eyes moving back and forth over the other customers while she processed his transaction, then took the packet of pages she handed him and put it in his inner jacket pocket. After tipping his hat at the teller, he looked directly into the camera for a few seconds, then turned and walked away.

The playback paused.

Noah leaned back in his chair, frowning as he tapped his finger against his lip. There was something wrong with that scene. But what? "Play it again."

Boudreaux frowned, but restarted the video.

Noah watched closely, trying to figure out what had caught his attention. Smith signed the slip the teller presented to him, waited, took the papers, tipped his hat, looked at the camera, and left.

"Again," he said to Boudreaux.

It was the third time watching it when it hit him.

Glancing up at Boudreaux, Noah asked, "When was the last time you had the bank's protections tested?"

"Excuse me?"

"Your security magic isn't working properly. When was the last time you had them checked?

"I can assure you they're working just fine."

"I'm telling you they're not. Our Mr. Smith is left-handed. If you watch," Noah said, pointing at the screen, "you'll notice the man who requested the transfer is right-handed. Which means he's an imposter. Which also means your security protections are not working."

Boudreaux rewound the security feed and watched. Then blanched. He rewound it again.

Noah bit back a smile as Boudreaux banged on the keyboard as he kept rewinding the video, his forehead dripping with sweat as he finally realized how much trouble he was in. Though it was possible he was reacting to the continuous stream of growls coming from Jory as he stared Boudreaux down, his wolf flashing in his eyes.

Noah should probably tell Jory to stop. And he would. Eventually. Maybe after he'd had time to forget what a condescending ass Boudreaux had been from the moment they'd been shown into his office.

Eventually, Boudreaux shoved the keyboard away. "Bah. This proves nothing. I have only your word that Mr. Smith is left-handed."

Noah's eyebrow shot up. "Are you calling me a liar?"

Boudreaux shook his head, holding out his hands in a calming motion, which had the complete opposite effect on Noah. "Not at all. I'm merely suggesting you may have made a mistake."

"The only mistake being made here is yours in not taking my grievance seriously. Unless you have a plan for how you're going to fix this that you haven't shared."

Boudreaux looked between him and Jory, then, as though the last thirty minutes hadn't happened, donned the haughty, self-important expression he'd had when they first arrived. "I'm not sure what you expect me to do."

Noah's eyes narrowed. "I thought I made it clear I expect you to return the money to our accounts."

Boudreaux folded his hands and leaned back in his chair. "Unfortunately, Mr. Davenport, that's out of my hands. As we have original documentation signed by yourself and the other Mr. Davenport, there is nothing further I can do."

Noah fumed. Had this fool listened to nothing he'd said? "Is that your final answer?"

"It is."

Noah nodded, then stood and adjusted his jacket. "You should call your lawyer."

"I beg your pardon?"

"As a crime has been perpetrated against me, I have no choice but to report it to the police. I will also be in touch with my lawyers who will undoubtedly recommend additional charges be laid against you."

Boudreaux's chair shot up. "The police. There's no need to resort to threats—"

Noah slashed his hand, cutting him off. "I'll also strongly suggest to any dragons who have accounts with you, that they should immediately request a full audit of their finances. The fact you allowed an imposter to steal from us, yet refuse to do anything about it, means that not only are you an idiot who overruled an account hold resulting in a theft, your business practices borderline illegal, and your client care policies reprehensible, but your faulty protections and willful blindness may have also allowed the same mismanagement of funds to happen to the rest of your clients."

Boudreaux slammed his hands on his desk as he stood. "You can't prove any of that. It's only your word against mine. I'll sue you for slander. You'll—"

"Do nothing. You can't be trusted, Boudreaux. And I'll make sure everyone is aware of it. Starting with the King and Queen."

"You can't do that. It will ruin this branch. Ruin me."

"Then you should have listened and tried to resolve my concern instead of washing your hands of it," Noah said, allowing his dragon to rise. Boudreaux fell back in his chair. "In future, it would behoove you to remember the customer is always right, not you and your over-inflated ego. Instead of trying to prove me wrong, you should have been looking for ways to help me. It is your responsibility to assist the clients who put their trust in you, not ridicule them or call them liars. This is something you have obviously forgotten, blinded as you are by your own self-importance. A few years in jail should help you remember that."

"B-but, I didn't...I'm not...you can't..."

"You did, you are, and I most certainly can. But don't worry, Boudreaux. If you manage to stay out of jail, rest assured your importance or lack thereof won't be an issue for you in any managerial capacity. The best you can hope to achieve in the future is to service customers by flipping burgers and cleaning up their garbage." Noah fixed him in place by the force of his glare. "I'll make certain of it."

Noah led Jory out of Boudreaux's office, thinking that was as fitting an exit line as any.

Chapter Eight

Jory

The plastic bottle crackled in Jory's hand as he took another sip of water, hoping it would cool him off. A hot coal of anger still burned in his chest at the dismissive way that dickhead Boudreaux had spoken to his mate.

Listening with one ear as Noah updated his brother on what they'd found out, Jory was seriously contemplating going back to the bank to kick Boudreaux's ass. Not that he really needed to after the way Noah had eviscerated the man, but it might make him feel better.

Thinking of how Noah had taken charge at the bank had him swallowing another mouthful of water, needing its cooling properties for an entirely different reason. The calm, controlled way his mate had torn Boudreaux to shreds had really done it for Jory. He held his bottle up to his face and wondered if it wouldn't be better to just pour it over his head. His mate in action had been hot. So incredibly scorching hot Jory wanted to drag Noah into the nearest alley to show him how much he'd appreciated the show.

Obviously feeling the heat of his stare, Noah looked over at him, then winked, before going back to his call.

Smirking, Jory tipped his bottle at him and paid closer attention to what Noah and Reid were saying.

"Have IT tap into all the security feeds in the area. I want to know where this fake Smith went after he left the bank."

"I'll have Gilbert start working on it right away. What are you and Jory going to do next?"

"We're going to check around the neighborhood. See if we can find anyone who recognizes Smith."

"All right. I'll call you back when we have something."

"Thanks."

Noah ended his call, then shook his head at Jory. "Whatever you're thinking will have to wait. Right now, we need to search for this Smith imposter."

"Gotcha. Business before pleasure," Jory said with a grin.

"Exactly." Noah gave him another wink, then strode off, a man on a mission.

Jory took a moment to watch him walk down the sidewalk, unable to hide his pleasure at seeing his mate bursting with confidence and exuding power. It was such a change from when Noah had first seen, then run from him. Jory couldn't be any prouder of him. Or want him more.

It was a damn good thing they had a mission. After listening to Noah's take-charge voice as he ordered his brother to break the law—who knew he could be such a badass—Jory knew it wouldn't take much more to push him over the edge. Smirking as he imagined Noah's reaction if he tackled his dignified mate to the ground and mussed him up, Jory poured the last of his water over his head, which did nothing to dampen the fire in his blood.

Tossing his empty bottle in the recycle bin, he followed his mate looking forward to seeing what he'd do next.

———

Oh where, oh where, has Mr. Smith gone…

They lost the trail.

Jory's frustration mounted as he and Noah walked to the end of the block looking for any signs of Smith. It was becoming extremely difficult to control his agitated wolf, who hungered to take down the man who'd wronged their mate, but for the last hour, every lead they'd followed had ended in a dead end, leaving him full of aggression with no one to take it out on.

At first, they'd gotten lucky and easily picked up Smith's trail in front of the bank. A number of business owners recalled seeing him and had been more than willing to help their search, enabling them to track his movements for several blocks.

Then, a couple of hours into their search, they'd lost the trail. Backtracking to the last person who'd seen him, they'd checked in every direction, talking to everyone they came across, but couldn't find anyone who recognized his picture.

It was like the man had vanished into thin air.

Jory came to a stop on the corner, then stood with his hands on his hips, looking back the way they'd come. "How could so many people have seen him go into that shop," Jory pointed to the store at the far end of the block, "yet nobody saw him leave?"

Noah shook his head. "I have no idea."

Jory frowned and considered the streets before him, then looked back the way they'd come. They could keep going on as they were, but he had a feeling it would just be a waste of time. "I'm not sure what's the best thing to do here. We can keep walking to see if we can pick up his trail somewhere further down. Or maybe it would be better to go back to the bank and see if he shows up there again."

Noah hummed. "Neither sounds like that great of an option."

"I know. But I'm out of ideas."

"Me too." Noah pulled out his phone. "Let me call Reid and see if Gilbert has found anything yet."

"Sure. And if he hasn't, I'd like to go back to the shop and check the alley again. Maybe we'll get lucky and there'll be someone new there who might have seen him."

"Sounds good." Noah pulled out his phone, then his eyes went wide at something he saw behind Jory.

Before Jory could turn to see what he was looking at, Noah was dragging him off the sidewalk. "What are you doing?"

"Shh. Don't attract his attention." Noah pulled him around the side of the building.

"Who's attention?" Jory whispered.

"Look around the corner, but be careful so he doesn't see you."

Jory peered around the edge of the building, then quickly pulled back. "Holy shit. That's Smith. Where did he come from?"

"I don't know, but here's our chance to follow him." Noah dragged Jory further down the building. They ducked behind a garbage can just as Smith walked past.

Waiting a few seconds, they snuck back to the end of the building. Jory poked his head around the corner and saw Smith was about half a block away, far enough he shouldn't notice them. "It's time to follow him."

"Okay," Noah said, leaning against his back. "You go first so I can stay behind you. We can't take a chance of him seeing me."

Jory nodded, then led them back to the sidewalk. He kept pace with Smith, his greater height allowing him to keep him in sight as they wove through the crowds on the street. Things got a bit trickier when Smith turned into a residential block and there were fewer people on the sidewalk to blend with. Jory slowed to put more distance between them, but relaxed after another block when it became apparent Smith had no idea he was being followed.

Or so he thought.

He wasn't sure if it was because they got too close or Smith finally sensed them, but Jory had only a split second to react when he saw Smith's shoulders tense and his back straighten.

By the time Smith turned around, Jory had Noah pressed up against a parked car and was kissing him. As his taste flowed over Jory's tongue, he quickly forgot where they were and what they were supposed to be doing, completely distracted by the small noises coming from his mate. Cradling Noah's jaw, he brushed his thumbs over his cheekbones, then slid his fingers in his hair. And stopped.

"Ugh." Jory pulled back, his nose wrinkling when he saw the sticky substance coating his fingers. He wiped his hands on his jeans, but whatever Noah used in his hair refused to come off. "What is this stuff?"

"Sorry," Noah whispered.

Jory glanced up at his tone, then mentally kicked himself when he saw he'd embarrassed his mate. That had been the last thing he'd wanted to do. Especially since

Noah had been brimming with self-confidence a moment earlier.

He took hold of Noah's hand. "Just ignore me. I'm being an asshole. There's absolutely nothing wrong with wanting to look your best." Jory kissed him gently in apology, then drew back, smoothing the few locks of hair he'd shifted out of place. "There. All fixed now."

"Thanks," Noah said, still not making eye contact with him.

He couldn't have that. Jory put a finger under his chin and tipped Noah's face up to him. "I really am sorry. I didn't mean to make you feel bad. I'm just not used to hair products. I mean, look at me." He gestured to his wild hair. "Does it look like I know anything about grooming?"

Noah chuckled, the shadows in his eyes falling away. "Not really."

"Exactly. So, don't pay any attention to me."

"I like the way you look." Noah reached up and sifted his fingers through Jory's hair. "And I love how soft your hair is. It feels like silk."

Jory pushed his chest out, feeling like strutting at his mate's words.

But Noah wasn't done. "Maybe one day I'll be brave enough to not care about the way I look either."

Jory sucked his chest back in and squinted at him. "Did you just insult me?"

Noah snickered. "Maybe a little."

Shaking his head, Jory laughed and gave him a quick peck on the lips. One kiss led to another, and before long, he was lost in his mate again. It took a car backfiring down the street to bring him to his senses.

Jory broke the kiss, then slid his lips along Noah's cheek, nuzzling his skin as he whispered in his ear. "Can you still see him?"

"W-who?" Noah stuttered, his eyes glazed.

Jory smirked. "Smith." Even though they had a job to do, he was disappointed when Noah's eyes cleared.

"Right." Noah shook his head, muttering, "You're so much younger than I am. How do you keep making me forget who I am?"

Jory snorted quietly into his hair. "I'm a wolf."

Noah peered up at him. "You're a wolf? That's your answer?"

"Yep." The eye roll was cute, but they had work to do. Playing with his mate would have to wait. Something he would need to work harder to remember. "Do you still see him?"

Noah looked over Jory's shoulder, then shook his head. "I think we lost him."

"Shit."

"No, wait. There his is. He's going into the yellow house on the next block."

"Let me know when he's inside," Jory said, tucking his face in Noah's neck and breathing deep, smiling to himself when he felt his mate tremble.

"Okay. He just went in the door," Noah said, his voice breathy.

Nipping the skin at the crook of his neck, then licking it to soothe the sting, Jory pulled back and grabbed Noah's hand. "How do you want to handle this? Should we bang on his door and demand answers? Wait for him to leave and then snoop around his house? Or we can—"

"We should follow him to see what he does next."

Jory blinked, not having expected that. "We should? Why?"

"Because either Smith's dead and whoever's pretending to be him has a disguise good enough to fool the bank's protection spell or this really is Smith, which means he's a thief and a killer and nothing like the man I know…or thought I knew."

"Which is why you want to see what he does next?"

"Yes."

Jory nodded. "Okay. Then we should look for a place to hide so we can keep an eye on him." He scanned their surroundings searching for possible spots they could use for surveillance.

After narrowing their options down to a couple of choices, Jory finally decided on a sheltered alcove across the street and a little down from the yellow house. Checking to make sure the street was clear, he took Noah's hand and jogged to the sidewalk on the opposite side before leading him to the hiding place he'd scoped out.

"This is where you want to watch from?" Noah asked in surprise. "Smith's house is right across the street. He'll be able to see us."

"Not unless he comes outside. We're hidden from the front window and we've got a better angle to watch for him if he goes out the back"

"What if he looks out the side window? We're right here. There's no way he can miss us."

"Then we have to make sure it doesn't look like we're watching him."

Noah eyed him suspiciously. "And how are we going to do that?"

Jory leaned in, pressing him up against the wall of the building. "Like this." Noah's eyelids fluttered, then closed when he kissed him. Jory pulled back until their lips were barely touching and whispered, "Uh, uh. You need to keep your eyes open."

"Right," Noah cleared his throat, then stared past Jory's head, blinking furiously.

Smirking, Jory licked the corners of his mouth, then slid his tongue between his lips, swallowing Noah's gasp. He dove deep into the kiss, a growl rumbling up his throat when Noah moaned and wrapped his arms around his back, pulling him closer. Jory fed on his mouth, knowing he'd never get enough of the wild energy of his mate's kisses, not even if he lived for a thousand years.

Sliding his lips along Noah's jawline to his ear, Jory hoarsely asked, "Are you still watching?"

"W-what?"

He chuckled and pulled back. "You need to watch Smith's house. Can you do that?" he asked, smoothing his thumb over Noah's cheek.

Noah licked his lips, then nodded, his breaths uneven as he blinked up at him.

"Good." Jory nosed along Noah's neck, breathing deep as he dragged his tongue over his skin. He really should stop, but the taste of his mate was hard to resist. Moving to his lips, Jory promised himself just one more kiss, then he'd concentrate on business.

"Don't forget to watch the house," he whispered, then covered Noah's mouth again."

Chapter Nine

Noah

Watch the house? How could he be expected to watch the house when all he could see was his mate. When all he could taste was the wildness of the wolf bursting over his tongue. When all he could smell was the cool darkness of a forest under a blazing sun. When all he could hear was the fierce pounding of his heart as it synced with his mate's.

Noah's skin burned, needing Jory's touch to cool him off. His body thrummed with a hunger only his mate could fill. His dragon wrestled for control, wanting to be free, to claim what was theirs, Noah holding him back by the barest of margins.

Then Jory's teeth scraped against the inside of his lip.

Between one breath and the next, he was looking through his dragon's eyes. His fangs dropped as he lost control, his dragon's fierce need roaring to the surface. He burned to show Jory what it meant to be mated to a dragon.

Clutching him closer, Noah attacked his mouth, fangs scraping tender flesh as he swallowed his mate's surprised cries. Sucking, then licking closed the small wounds, Noah growled, smoke wafting from his nostrils as his passion flared, igniting his blood. The air glimmered as magic swirled around them.

Tearing his mouth free, Noah sucked in a harsh breath. He opened his mouth, gasping as he filled his lungs so he could tell Jory they needed to find somewhere private, immediately, or he was going to mate with him right here in the street.

Before Noah got more than his name out, he was interrupted by a loud brrrrp. Colored, flashing lights lit up the night, then a bright beam shined directly on them, highlighting where they stood in the shadows.

Jory growled and spun around, pressing Noah against the wall as he placed himself protectively between him and…the police? What were they doing here? Noah tried to push his way around Jory, sure this was some mistake, but his mate growled and shoved him back behind him.

Noah huffed out a breath. Did Jory somehow forget he was a dragon and could look after himself? Resting his hands on Jory's waist, he leaned forward and whispered, "It's only the police."

Jory looked over his shoulder, his wolf showing in his eyes. "I don't trust cops."

"We haven't done anything wrong, so why don't we see what they want before assuming the worst?"

"I think we should run and not deal with them at all."

Noah snorted. "We're not going to run. Don't worry. Everything will be fine."

Later, he'd have to apologize for not trusting his mate.

Instead of listening to Jory, who obviously had better instincts for trouble than he did, Noah waited patiently, smiling like a naïve fool as the police got out of their car and walked over to them.

He started to suspect he may have made a mistake when the police officers stopped a short distance away with frowns on their faces and hands hovering over the weapons strapped to their hips.

But, continuing with his foolish belief that because they were innocent, everything would be fine, Noah nudged past Jory—shaking him loose when his mate tried to hold him back—and stepped forward to greet them.

"Good evening, Officers. Is there something we can help you with?"

"Yeah," the one on the right said. "You can start by explaining what you're doing there."

Noah blinked at his abrupt tone. "We're not doing anything."

"Well, see now, that's where you're wrong," the officer said, spitting on the sidewalk before swaggering towards them. "We got a call about a couple of peeping toms disturbing the neighborhood, which means I get to take you two freaks in for questioning."

"Freaks? Who the hell are you calling freaks?" Jory growled, shouldering Noah aside.

Not liking the look in the officer's eyes, Noah quickly jumped in front of Jory. The second officer had obviously noticed the same thing and tried to head his partner off.

"Sanders," whispered the second officer. "You know you're not supposed to call them freaks. Remember what happened last time?"

"Shut up, Jones." Sanders slid his baton from his utility belt, the look in his eye daring them to challenge him.

Noah barely refrained from rolling his eyes. As if they were that stupid.

Except...at the implied threat, the tenor of Jory's growl changed, growing louder and more menacing. If

Noah didn't diffuse the situation immediately, somebody was going to die. And it wouldn't be his mate.

Holding up his hands placatingly, Noah gave the police his best business smile. "Officer, I believe there's been some kind of mistake. I can assure you we weren't spying." Which was mostly true. He'd been too caught up in his mate's kiss to keep his eye on anyone.

"Then why are you hiding in the dark?" Sanders asked. "Care to explain that?"

"Well, uhm." He turned to look at Jory, who raised an eyebrow as if to say, this is your show. Scowling at his unhelpful mate, Noah turned back to Sanders. "To be honest, officer, we were having a, uhm, well, a personal moment."

Officer Sanders' nose scrunched as if he smelled something bad. "You freaks need to keep your depraved behavior off the streets. Decent folks don't need to see that shit."

Noah's back stiffened. What the hell was this guy's problem? Since when was kissing your mate depraved? "Listen to me, officer—"

Jory bumped him aside before he could finish, which was probably for the best since what Noah had been about to say would probably have gotten him arrested.

"You need to step back there, boy," Sanders said, pointing his baton at Jory's chest.

Jory crossed his arms. "And you need to stay away from my mate."

Noah wasn't surprised at Sanders' sneer when he looked between them. But he was a little when Sanders smacked the baton against his palm.

"Are you threatening me, freak?"

"No, he's not," Noah said, coming up beside Jory. "And since we've done nothing wrong, you have no cause to detain us. Rather than wasting any more of your valuable time when you could be looking for criminals or protecting the citizens of this city, the job for which you are paid to do, we'll just be on our way."

"Oh, no. You're not going anywhere except to jail." Sanders' smile was mean as he smacked his baton across his palm again. "Turn around and put your hands behind your backs."

Noah's mouth dropped open in shock. "Why? We haven't broken any laws."

"That's not the way I see it."

"Because you're an idiot," Jory growled, his top lip lifting, flashing a bit of fang.

"I'm feeling threatened," Sanders said, pointing his baton at Jory. "You feeling threatened, Jones?"

"Not really," the other officer muttered.

"Well, I do." Sanders raised the baton as if he was going to hit Jory.

Amber flashed in Jory's eyes as claws burst from his fingertips.

"Jory, stop. You're just going to make it worse." Noah grabbed his shoulder to pull him back. "This idiot isn't going to listen to anything we say," he whispered in his ear.

"I know."

"Then let's not provoke him more that we have. We still might be able to get out of this."

Jory gave him a look like Noah was still acting like a naïve fool, which to be fair he probably was, but he pulled his claws in and took a step back.

Noah had just let out a relieved breath, sure he could get everything to work out, when Jory glanced over his shoulder. Whatever he saw caused him to snarl and put himself between Sanders and Noah again.

And out came his claws.

Proving how much of an idiot he really was, Sanders bared his teeth at Jory, then poked him in the stomach with his baton. Jory's muscles bunched and the stream of growls coming from him rose in volume, but he stayed in control, not moving from where he stood protectively in front of Noah.

Noah's eyebrows shot up when Sanders poked him again. Didn't he realize how dangerous it was to challenge a wolf? Especially one protecting his mate. Noah would have rolled his eyes at the ridiculousness of it, except the situation was rapidly getting out of hand and needed to be stopped before it could escalate any further.

He jumped in front of Jory. "Officer, please. There's no need for this."

"There's every need. Now turn around." Poke. The baton jabbed Noah in the stomach. "You're under arrest for public indecency, disturbing the peace," another poke in the chest, "and resisting arrest."

"Resisting…what?" Noah exclaimed. "We're not doing any such thing."

"I don't see you cooperating." Another poke.

"Touch him again and you'll be eating your baton," Jory snarled, yanking Noah back.

"Threatening an officer of the law now?" Sanders said gleefully as he flipped his baton up, grabbing both ends to hold it horizontally before him. "That means I can use any means necessary to force you to cooperate."

He slammed the baton against Jory's chest. That is, he tried to slam it against Jory's chest, but Jory took a step to the side, his hand shooting up and grabbing hold of the baton. When Sanders tried to pull it free, Jory held firm, refusing to let it go. Yellow flashed in his eyes.

When Sanders realized he couldn't get it back, he let go, stepped out of Jory's reach, and pulled out his gun, aiming it at Jory's head.

"Sanders! Stop." Jones shoved his arm down. "You can't shoot them."

"I can if I'm in fear for my life." Hatred filled his eyes as Sanders glared at Jory and raised his weapon again. "And I'm feeling pretty damned threatened right now."

Okay. This had gotten totally out of hand. Noah held up his hands and stepped in front of Jory. "Nobody is going to shoot anybody. This is all just a big misunderstanding."

Jones pushed Sander's arm down again and turned to them. "It might be best if you both cooperate. We can sort this out at the station."

"But we haven't—"

"Forget it," Jory said. "They're not going to listen."

"They've got no grounds to arrest us."

"They don't need grounds. They're the cops."

Glaring at them, Sander lifted his gun again. "Both of you shut the hell up, turn around and put your hands behind your back." He cocked his weapon, his eyes gleaming as if hoping they'd resist.

"Let's just leave," Jory whispered. "It's not like he can stop us."

Movement across the street caught Noah's eye. A curtain parted as someone looked out the window toward them. Noah quickly spun around and put his hands behind his back.

"What are you doing?" Jory asked.

"Smith's watching. Turn around and cooperate before we cause more of a scene than we already have."

"Shit." Jory turned around with him. "Do you think he recognized you?"

"I hope not." Cold metal locked around his wrists. Noah sighed. So much for trying to prove he wasn't a screw up. Getting arrested sent completely the wrong message.

Jory grunted as he was slammed into the rough brick wall.

Glaring sideways at Sanders when he tightened the cuffs around Jory's wrists then grabbed him by the hair and smacked his face into the wall, Noah silently vowed to make him pay.

Nobody messed with a dragon's mate and got away with it. Not even the police.

———

"Well, well, well. What do we have here? Looks like a couple of jailbirds."

Noah closed his eyes and dropped his head. He'd recognize that taunting voice anywhere. Why, out of everyone who could have come, did it have to him?

Deciding to get it over with, Noah looked up from where he and Jory were being processed, shaking his head in disbelief as Carlos and Gideon walked through the police station toward them, grins on both their faces.

"How did you even know we were here?" Noah asked. "They haven't let us make our one call yet."

"One of Roman's enforcers saw you two being picked up," Carlos said with a smirk. "I told him we'd be happy to bail you out."

Noah rolled his eyes. "Of course, you did."

"Yep. Couldn't resist the opportunity to see another one of you dragons hauled in by New Orleans' finest." He grinned. "The police in this city sure have a thing about arresting you guys."

It took a moment for Noah to realize Carlos was referring to when Gideon had been arrested for suspected murder. He snorted. As if anyone in their right mind would think the dragon prince could murder someone. You'd have to be pretty stupid— He blinked. What were the odds Sanders was the same officer who'd arrested Gideon?

When he turned back and saw the way Sanders was glaring at Carlos and Gideon, he knew he wasn't going to take that bet.

He also didn't think Carlos and Gideon were going to be able to get him and Jory out of there. In fact, if he was reading Sanders correctly, they'd soon be joining him and Jory in a jail cell.

Noah looked toward the entrance of the police department. "I don't suppose Roman came with you? We might need his help to get out of this."

Gideon shook his head. "Sorry, Roman couldn't get away. You've just got us."

"That's right," Carlos snickered. "Mostly because I wanted to see how you handled being arrested. It's not something you dragons are used to."

"Unlike you," Jory shot back.

Carlos laughed. "You got that right. Especially when Officer Stupid is on patrol."

"Hey." Sanders slammed his hand down on the desk. "No talking to my prisoners. Go sit your asses down over there or I'll have you locked up."

Instead of listening, Carlos hitched his hip on Sanders' desk and flashed a big grin. "Still arresting innocent people, huh, Sanders?"

"Innocent, nothing. I caught them red-handed committing a crime."

"Is that right?" Carlos leaned in. "Or are you lying and faking evidence the same way you do when you try to arrest me?"

"I never lied about you, Rossi." Sanders said, his ears turning red.

"No? That's strange. I seem to recall being innocent every time."

Sanders shot up from his chair and pushed Carlos off his desk. "There's nothing innocent about you, asshole."

"Sanders," Jones cautioned.

"And yet, you could never prove I did anything, could you?" Carlos taunted.

"That doesn't mean you weren't guilty. It just means you were sneaky," Sanders snarled. "You and I both know you're nothing but a lowlife bloodsucking scumbag. "

"Tsk, tsk. Careful Sanders, your bigotry is showing. Keep it up and they'll take your badge again."

"One more word out of you, Rossi, and you'll be the one behind bars."

"Oh yeah. On what grounds?".

"Disrespecting an officer, for one."

"Too bad you're not a real—"

"Let it go, treasure," Gideon said, dropping his hand on Carlos' shoulder. "I'd rather Roman not have to come down here to free us again."

"Fine." Carlos turned to Sanders and smirked. "Later, Officer Stupid."

Sanders lunged at him. "Why you fu—"

"Sanders! Step away from him."

Noah tore his eyes away from Sanders, whose body was vibrating with so much anger he was afraid he might stroke out, and turned to the gray-haired man who'd stepped out of the corner office.

"Sir. You don't under—"

"Now, Sanders." Expecting his order to be obeyed, the man walked over and held out his hand to Carlos.

"Good to see you, Carlos. Keeping well?"

"Yes, Chief." Carlos shook his hand. "You remember my mate, Gideon."

"I do. Nice to see you again, Gideon."

After shaking his hand, the Chief stepped back. "What brings you boys here today?"

Carlos tipped his head at Jory and Noah. "Your officer arrested a couple of my friends. We're here to pick them up."

"Let's see if we can speed that up." He raised his eyebrow at Sanders. "What are the charges?"

"Public indecency, loitering, disturbing the peace, and resisting arrest." Sanders said, lifting his lip in a sneer. "And threatening an officer of the law."

"Hmm. That's quite a list."

"Yes, Chief. About what you'd expect from associates of Rossi's."

"I see." The Chief turned to Sanders' partner. "Jones, what were they doing?"

"But Chief," Sander said, "I just told you we caught them—"

The Chief held up his hand, cutting him off. "I wasn't asking you. Jones, why did you arrest these two men?"

Sanders scoffed. "They're not men."

Looking like he'd rather be anywhere else, Jones said, "They were kissing when we pulled up."

"Kissing?"

"Yes, Chief."

"Where?"

"The lips, sir."

Carlos snorted.

His lip twitching, the Chief tried again. "I meant, where were they when you found them kissing?"

"Oh. Magnolia Street, sir."

"Okay. What else were they doing?"

"That was it."

The Chief's eyebrow shot up. "So, there was no public indecency? No disturbing the peace?"

"No, Chief. Just the kissing."

"And the resisting arrest and threatening an officer?"

His eyes shifting toward Sanders, Jones shuffled his feet uncomfortably. "There may have been a small misunderstanding and some heated words."

The Chief's eyes narrowed. "Did these men resist arrest or not?"

"No, sir."

"And what about threatening an officer?"

"Uhm," Jones looked down, then shuffled a few inches away from Sanders. "Nothing was really said by the prisoners. Sanders might have—" He snapped his mouth shut when his partner took a step toward him. "Nothing happened, Chief."

The Chief's head slowly turned to Sanders. "Do you want to explain yourself or should we skip right to the part where I take your badge and you complete another round of sensitivity training?"

"Chief, we had no choice," Sanders spluttered. "Someone called in to report a couple of peeping toms. When we got there, we caught them red-handed being indecent in public."

"Because they were kissing?"

"Yes, Chief. They shouldn't be doing that in a public place where normal people can see them. It's disgusting."

"Are you fucking kidding me?" Carlos flashed his fangs. "Just because no one will kiss your ugly face doesn't mean it's disgusting for two grown men to kiss."

"They're not fucking men. They're a couple of paranormal freaks," Sanders shouted. "It's not right they can just go anywhere and do whatever they want."

"Hold up." The Chief raised his hand. "You arrested them because they're paranormals?"

Not seeming to realize the hole he was digging for himself. Sander nodded. "Yes, sir. They shouldn't be hanging around where decent folk live, lurking in the shadows. They need to keep that kind of lewd behavior off of our streets and stay in their own communities."

"Arresting them for no cause is a hate crime, Sanders."

"It can't be a hate crime because they're not human."

"Yes, it is. Paranormals have the same rights as everyone else," the Chief yelled. "You can't arrest them just because you don't like them."

"But, sir." The idiot actually seemed confused.

"Just stop. I've heard enough," the Chief said, rubbing his hand over his face before looking at the ceiling.

Noah was sure he cracked a tooth getting his anger under control. When the Chief spoke again, his voice was controlled. And quiet. Ominously so. Not that Sanders seemed to notice.

"Please wait for me in my office, Sanders, while I deal with these charges."

"Yes, Chief." He sneered at Noah and Jory before pausing next to Carlos. "I'll get you next time, Rossi." He clipped Carlos' shoulder when he shoved past him.

When the door to his office closed, the Chief signaled to Jones. "Release them."

Once they were freed from their handcuffs, Noah was surprised when the Chief shook their hands. "I'm sorry you were treated like that by one of my men. I truly thought Sanders had learned his lesson from the last time he did this, but I see now I was mistaken."

"It's not your fault, Chief," Carlos said, even though his tone said it was.

"Yes, it is. I should never have allowed him back on the street." He sighed. "Well, this was his last chance. I'll be taking his badge permanently after this, no matter how angry it'll make my wife."

"Your wife?"

The Chief nodded. "Her youngest sister's son. I've tried to give him every chance I can, but he has an inexplicable hatred for paranormals I've never been able to get to the bottom of." He closed his eyes and sighed again, before giving them a look filled with so much fatigue, Noah wanted to give him a hug. "But that's my problem. My apologies again that you were brought in for no good reason. Please let me know if you wish to press charges."

"That won't be necessary," Noah said, winding his fingers through Jory's, the last bit of stress leaving him when his mate's fingers squeezed his. "If there's nothing else, we'd like to leave."

"Of course." The Chief motioned to Jones. "Show them out." He turned to his office, then stopped and called over his shoulder. "Carlos, Sanders seems to have a personal hatred for you. Any idea why?"

"No, Chief. I've never done anything to him. Well, except being an ass."

"That's what I thought." He sighed again. "If you can, please try to avoid him. I'm certain he's going to blame you for losing his job and I'd prefer it if you didn't kill him."

"I'll do my best to stay out of his way, but I'm not going to run from him."

"Understood."

The Chief walked into his office and closed the door quietly behind himself. The yelling started before they made it to the exit.

Noah felt for the man, but he should never have put a loose cannon like Sanders on the street with a badge and a gun, nephew or not.

"So, they caught you kissing, huh?" Carlos teased as they walked down the steps in front of the police station. "What kind of kissing were you doing that you didn't notice the cops pulling up?"

"Well, uhm, it was…" Noah trailed off, his cheeks growing hot, not sure how to answer that. But Jory did.

"Obviously, it was the right kind. Why? Do you need any pointers?"

Carlos barked out a laugh. "Trust me, pup, I don't need any pointers from you."

"Are you sure? If your kisses can't make your mate forget where he is, then you're not doing it right."

"There's nothing wrong with my kisses." He looked at Gideon, "Right?"

"Of course not, treasure."

"See." Carlos shoved Jory. "You heard him."

"What I heard is you having to ask. I know exactly how I affect my mate." Jory pushed Carlos back. "I guess you're not as irresistible as I am."

"Oh, for the love of—" Noah whispered. What was even happening right now?

"I'm absolutely irresistible to my mate." Carlos thrust his chest out. "He's perfectly satisfied."

"Uh, huh. You keep telling yourself that," Jory scoffed. "I think we all know who the irresistible one is between the two of us."

"Why you little shit." Carlos jumped and put a headlock on Jory, who laughed and grabbed him around the waist before tripping him. They tumbled down the last few stairs and started wrestling on the sidewalk.

Noah stopped and stared at them, then turned to Gideon. "What are they doing?"

"Fighting for our honor."

"Are you sure? It sounded more like they're fighting for bragging rights."

Gideon snorted. "That too."

"Shouldn't we stop them?"

"Nope. I know Carlos loves me, but he doesn't show it in public very often. I'm enjoying watching him fight for me." Gideon glanced at Noah from the corner of his eye. "Besides, he's pretty hot when he's like this."

Noah's mouth dropped open. Since when did Gideon want PDAs? Especially ones where his mate rolled around on the ground fighting with another man in front of the police station, of all places. There was nothing at all dignified about what they were doing. And dignity had mattered a great deal to the Gideon he'd been in a relationship with. He'd have been appalled if Noah had done anything like this. When they were together, everything was respectable and controlled, with no messy emotions for either of them.

Turning to watch their mate's fighting, Noah wondered if that's why he and Gideon hadn't worked out. Because when he was with Jory, control and dignity never crossed his mind. His mate had his entire focus, and brought forth all kinds of heated and messy emotions from him. Maybe it was the same for Gideon with Carlos.

Echoing what he was thinking, Gideon nudged him. "This is why we never worked out. Not enough passion. Neither of us cared enough about each other to throw down."

No, they really hadn't. As he watched their mates roll on the ground, exchanging insults, and trying to wrestle each other into submission, he realized Gideon was right. Having his mate fight for him was hot. So very, very hot.

Noah winced when Jory took an elbow to his ribs. He should really stop this. He didn't want to disrespect his mate, but there was no way Jory could win against Carlos, who was an experienced brawler and completely invulnerable to injury because of his bond with Gideon. Then Jory drove his elbow into Carlos' sternum, actually causing the vampire to cry out. Maybe not then. But when Carlos retaliated and rubbed Jory's face into the hard packed dirt between the sidewalk and the street, Noah knew it was time to step in before Jory got hurt.

Which is why he was shocked to hear himself say, "A thousand dollars says my mate takes yours."

Gideon didn't even hesitate. "You're on."

Chapter Ten

Jory

Heading back to the scene of the crime…

Jory reached between the seats and pointed to the corner. "You can drop us off over there. We'll walk the rest of the way."

Carlos nodded and changed lanes, pulling the SUV to the curb. Twisting in his seat he looked at Jory. "What are you guys up to?"

His eyes held more respect than Jory had seen from him before, so even though he'd lost their impromptu battle, Jory had obviously proven something to the vampire. And impressed his mate, if he was correctly reading the heated glances Noah kept giving him.

Taking hold of Noah's hand, Jory answered Carlos. "It's just a small project Noah and I are working on."

Gideon looked at him in the rearview mirror. "Do you guys need any help?"

"Sure," Noah said. "That would—"

Jory cut him off. "Thanks, but no. We've got this." He pushed open the door and pulled Noah after him. "Appreciate the ride."

"Try not to get arrested again," Carlos called out.

"You too." Jory said, flipping him off. He could hear Carlos' laughter as he drove away.

"Why didn't you want Gideon to help?"

Jory turned to Noah, thinking that should have been obvious. "Because nobody needs to know someone is stealing from your hoard. Not even your prince."

Noah seemed surprised by his words. Then he smiled and squeezed Jory's hand. "Thanks. I know Gideon wouldn't think any less of me, but it would be hard to live it down if everyone else found out."

"Which is why we'll keep it to ourselves." Tugging on Noah's hand, Jory pulled him down the street, hiding his wince when the movement irritated his bruised ribs. Stupid Carlos and his lucky shot. Or perhaps he should say lucky shots, since the vampire had gotten in a few good hits in the same place.

Jory grinned, knowing he'd left marks on the vampire as well. Even if they'd healed by the time he and Carlos had finished their mock battle, he remembered where each of them had been.

When they neared Smith's house, Jory slowed and began looking around. "We need to do a better job of hiding this time. And maybe stay more focused on what we're supposed to be doing."

Noah snorted. "You think?"

"We should at least try. Especially me. I just kind of have trouble keeping my mind on business whenever I'm near you." Jory grinned, bumping shoulders with Noah. "My wolf keeps pushing at me to claim you."

"I know the feeling. My dragon is doing the same thing." Noah glanced up at him, guilt flashing in his eyes. "I'm sorry. This is all my fault for running from our mating."

Jory pulled him to a stop. "Don't be sorry. I'm sure you had a good reason." Which he hoped his mate would one day share with him.

Noah shook his head. "I'm starting to wonder if I did. The more I get to know you, the less my reasons make sense. We might both be suffering for nothing." He gave a strangled laugh. "And now we don't even have time to complete our bond because we have to find Smith."

"It's okay, Noah. What we're doing is important. We'll get to our mating soon enough."

Noah squeezed his hand. "I know. I'm just—" He shrugged. "I wish I'd made better choices when we first met."

"But then I wouldn't have gotten to chase you. Think of all the fun we'd have missed out on."

Noah snickered, then sobered and rested his hand on Jory's cheek. "As long as you're not hurt, because that's the last thing I wanted to do.

"I'm not." At least, not any more. Jory pulled Noah close, breathing him in. "Don't take on guilt for doing what you needed to do. Whatever your reasons, they were valid at the time."

"They were, but—"

"No buts. We'll be fine. Everything will work out the way it's supposed to."

"You really believe that?"

"I do."

"Okay," Noah sighed. "I'll try to let it go." He leaned his head on Jory's shoulder.

"Good." Jory pulled him close, giving them both a moment to just be, then kissed him gently on the cheek and moved back. Threading their fingers, he said, "How about we go find ourselves a good place to spy on your thief?"

"Sure." Noah squeezed his fingers, his eyes filled with emotion, saying everything Jory needed to hear.

Tugging gently on his hand, Jory led him down the sidewalk.

They eventually decided to watch from the recessed doorway of a building a few houses down from Smith's. Jory crouched in the small space, pulling Noah down beside him.

"Do you think you can put up some sort of shield so nobody can see us?"

"I can. But it'll only work if we're not moving." Noah gave Jory a wry look "We should probably have done that before. It would have saved us from being hassled by the police."

"And miss out on the wonderful experience of being arrested?"

Noah gave him a flat. "Trust me, I'd have been fine to miss out on that experience. It wasn't nearly as thrilling as Gideon made it out to be."

Jory couldn't resist poking at him. "Then maybe next time you'll listen when I tell you to run from the cops."

Noah rolled his eyes, then flicked his fingers. Magic sparkled in the air before settling around them.

As Jory watched the magic take hold, he could admit to being a little—okay, a lot—envious at how easy Noah made it look. Whenever he tried using his powers, it took a lot of effort and usually ended in disaster. But then again, Noah had had centuries to perfect his skills. Jory really hoped it didn't take him that long to get better. He glanced sideways at his mate. Maybe it didn't have to.

"Say, Noah."

"Hmmm," Noah murmured, keeping his attention focused on Smith's house.

"Do you want to teach me how to control my magic?"

Noah turned to him and frowned. "I thought Bryan and Lysander were teaching you."

Jory shrugged. "They are, but it's not going very well." Which was an understatement. "Bryan's all, *think about what you want and wrap the magic around your will.* Except when I try to do that, things explode." He shook his head. "And working with Lysander is even worse."

"Explosions are fairly common when you're first learning how to channel greater amounts of power."

"That's what Bryan says. I just think it might be easier to learn from you because I can see what you're doing."

Noah's eyes widened. "Are you saying you can see my magic?"

"Yeah. Every time you use it."

"Wow. That's uhm, incredible."

"Why?"

"Because you shouldn't be able to see it."

Jory shrugged. "It's probably just a mate thing."

Noah shook his head and gave him a strange look. "I's not. But something is definitely going on with you and my magic."

"As long as it helps you teach me, I'm not going to worry about it." He bumped Noah. "You are going to help me with my magic, right?"

"Sure. As soon as we have some time."

"Great. I can't wait." Jory also couldn't wait to tell Bryan he was off the hook. He'd be as relieved as Jory was. Probably more so. Just then, movement from the yellow house caught his attention. "Smith's leaving."

"I see him," Noah whispered, leaning against him.

They watched as Smith closed the front door then headed down the sidewalk. Once he turned the corner, Jory and Noah got up to follow him.

They'd only gone a short distance when Jory realized this wasn't going to work. He grabbed onto Noah's sleeve, pulling him to a stop. "There's not enough cover out here." He waved at the mostly deserted sidewalks. "He's going to notice us if we don't find a way to stay out of his sight."

After a small pause, Noah turned to him. "There's one way we can prevent him from seeing us."

"What's that?"

Noah grimaced. "You're not going to like it."

Jory tensed, knowing exactly where this was going. "You're talking about flying, aren't you?"

Noah nodded.

"You can't think of anything else

Noah shook his head. "Not if we want to follow him without being seen."

"Damn." Jory looked around as if another option would magically appear. "What I wouldn't give for a cloak of invisibility right about now."

Noah snorted. "I don't think that's actually a thing."

"Too bad. It'd sure be handy to have."

Noah moved in and wrapped his arms around Jory's waist. "I know this is hard for your wolf, but I promise, I won't let you fall."

"I know you won't. At least my head does. The rest of me isn't so sure."

"I'm sorry. Flying should get easier for you over time. Unfortunately—"

"Time is something we don't have right now," Jory said with a sigh.

"No, it's not."

He took in a deep breath and blew it out noisily. "Okay. Let's do this before I talk myself out of it."

Noah pressed their foreheads together and whispered, "Just remember, I won't let you fall." He let go and moved to the center of the street and shifted into his dragon.

Determined to be stronger than his fear, Jory ran into the street and was scaling Noah's back before he could think about what he was doing. Then it was too late to change his mind because they were in the air.

Feeling his mate's encouragement and remembering his promise helped keep Jory's fear of heights at bay. Or it could have been the bands of magic that wrapped around his legs, holding them firmly in place.

A couple of blocks after they started following him, Smith flagged down a taxi. Squeezing his eyes almost shut to protect them from the wind, Jory held tight onto Noah's scale ridge and leaned slightly forward so he could keep his eyes on the taxi.

It took Jory a bit to realize the random directions the taxi was going weren't so random after all. For some reason, the taxi kept backtracking down a lot of the same streets it had been on before, but never once stopped to let Smith out. When they went through the same intersection for a third time, Jory started to think Smith knew he was being followed and was trying to throw them off. Not that he could. There was no hiding from a dragon who had his prey in sight.

After a couple of hours of following its meandering route, the taxi eventually headed toward the Port, coming to a stop in front of a warehouse next to a small wharf.

Noah circled high above the warehouse.

Now that he wasn't distracted watching the taxi, Jory's stomach was making itself known. He swallowed hard as Noah made another pass, silently urging Smith to get a move on before he lost his lunch…not that he'd actually had any given they'd been at the police station at the time.

After what seemed like ages, but couldn't have been more than a few minutes, Smith finally walked into the building, allowing Noah to land. He dropped down behind a tall stack of shipping containers and adjusted his wings so Jory could slide down. After a couple of minutes, Noah's head twisted back to look at him.

Giving his mate a weak smile of apology, Jory forced his fingers to let go and slid down Noah's wing. Once on the ground, he tried to step back, but his legs refused to cooperate, so he ended up leaning against Noah's side and taking a moment to give his stomach time to settle and his legs to stop trembling. Once he felt like he could stand on his own without falling, Jory stepped back.

As soon as Noah finished shifting, he grabbed hold of him. "Are you okay?"

"Yeah," Jory croaked. At his mate's disbelieving look, he swallowed and tried again. "I'm good. Really. Let's see what's going on inside."

"You sure?"

"Yeah. Let's go."

Using the stacks of shipping containers for concealment, Jory and Noah made their way over to the warehouse, then snuck down the side of the building, looking for a way in. Around the back, they found an overhead door that hadn't been properly closed, leaving a small gap at the bottom. Lifting it high enough to slide under, they were inside and hidden behind a forklift parked along the back wall within seconds.

Waiting until they were sure their entry had gone unnoticed, they began slowly working through the warehouse toward the front, where they hoped to find Smith.

Reaching the end of a row of double-stacked crates, Jory peered around the corner, then gasped and quickly pulled back.

"What is it?" Noah whispered.

Jory whispered back, "There's a bunch of people locked in cages."

"There's what?"

"See for yourself." Jory motioned around the corner. Noah leaned past him, then sucked in a breath. Jory knew exactly what he was seeing; two large cages filled with young men and women lying on the ground. And none of them were moving.

He really hoped they were just unconscious and not dead.

Noah pulled back, the shock in his eyes a match for Jory's.

Jory leaned close. "What did we just walk into?"

"I don't know. But we can't leave them here."

"No, we can't." He looked around the corner again and did a quick headcount, stopping when he hit thirty. How were they supposed to get this many people out of here? Especially when they were unconscious. He turned back to see if Noah had any ideas and found him staring at the ground, deep in thought. After waiting a couple of minutes, Jory nudged him.

Noah blinked and looked up. "What?"

"What are you thinking about so hard?"

"I was trying to figure out if this has anything to do with the trafficking operation Reid ran into in Ireland?"

"What makes you think this has anything to do with a trafficking operation in Ireland?"

"It probably doesn't. But the one Reid stumbled on was linked to a trafficking ring in NOLA that Max and Bryan had shut down a few months previously."

"And you think someone is starting it up again?"

Noah shook his head. "More like Max and Bryan only cut off one head and there was another waiting to take its place."

Jory stared at him. If Noah was correct about the trafficking rings being connected, there was one possible choice. "Smith?"

"That would be my guess."

"Shit. Is there anything that guy isn't into?"

"I'm starting to think not." Noah shook his head. "I can't believe he fooled me and Reid so badly."

Jory took another look around the corner. "Well, we can't let Smith have them."

"I know. But it's going to be almost impossible to get them out of here when they're unconscious."

"Do you think your magic could wake them up?"

Noah's nose wrinkled. "I'm not sure. I've never done anything like that before." He paused. "But before I try, we should have a plan for how to get them out of here. Once they're awake, we're going to have to move fast."

Thinking of all the obstacles they'd have to overcome, Jory knew a plan wasn't going to be enough. He slumped against the crate. "There's no way we can do this on our own. We're going to have to call my brothers for help."

"Or Gideon."

"Let me try Lysander and Bryan first." Jory pulled out his phone. He'd just pulled his brother's number up when

Noah grabbed his arm. "What are—" Then he heard footsteps. His eyes flew to Noah. "What should we do?" he mouthed, flicking out his claws in case they had to fight their way out.

Noah shook his head and pressed down on his hand. "Not that." He pointed to the end of the row. "Let's hide."

Jory nodded and followed Noah down the side of the crates.

The footsteps came closer.

Shit. There was no way they'd be able to get to the end of the row in time. Not without running, which would give them away. Jory tugged on the back of Noah's jacket. When he looked over his shoulder Jory pointed up, then began climbing the stack of crates. Reaching the top, he crept to the edge and flattened out so he could peer over the side. A few seconds later, Noah crawled up beside him. They both froze when Smith, along with two armed men, passed in front of the row they'd just vacated and stopped in front of the cages.

"Have they given you any trouble?"

"No, sir. We drugged their water as ordered. They should sleep for another eight hours."

"Good. The last transfer will arrive this evening. When it gets here, I want all the cargo loaded onto the ship. It needs to be ready to leave at midnight."

"We'll have them ready to go, sir."

"See that you do." Smith turned to leave.

Jory tensed. Now that they knew what was planned for the prisoners and had Smith in their sights, it was time to take him down. He glanced at Noah and cocked an eyebrow. Noah nodded. Good. They were on the same page.

Jory slowly pushed himself up, his muscles coiled as he prepared to jump down.

But before they could make a move, one of the guards laughed and said something too low for Jory to hear.

But not too low for Smith.

Irritation crossed his face, then Smith, moving much too fast, spun back and grabbed both men by the front of their shirts. He lifted them in the air until their feet hung above the ground and shook them. "You dare to touch my stock?"

"It was a joke," the man on the left shouted. "I swear. We didn't go near them."

Smith slammed their bodies together, then tossed them up high as if they weighed nothing.

Jory gaped at the men suspended in the air, their legs kicking and fingers scrabbling frantically at their throats as if they were being choked by invisible hands.

Who the hell was this guy?

He glanced over at Noah and saw him frowning at Smith.

Jory turned back. The men's faces were now turning blue. Not that Smith seemed concerned. Jory shifted restlessly, trying to decide if he should try to save them or not, when Smith made a motion with his hand and stepped back.

The men dropped to the cement floor with loud splats, then rolled slowly to their sides, curling up as they gasped for air.

Smith strode over to them. "Keep your mouths shut, your hands off my stock, and do the job you're being paid for." He kicked the man nearest to him. "If anything happens to any of my inventory, you'll both take its place."

He flicked his hand sideways and sent the men tumbling toward a stack of crates. The sound of snapping wood—or possibly bones—was loud in the silence broken only by their pained cries.

"Are we clear?" Smith asked, his hands raised threateningly.

Jory couldn't see his expression, but whatever was on Smith's face terrified the guards more than being nearly choked to death. His nose wrinkled when the smell of fresh urine hit the air, along with the rank smell of terror.

"Y-yes, sir," the man who'd first spoken gasped out. "W-we won't l-let anything h-happen to them."

Tumbling them across the ground with another sweep of his hand, Smith said, "See that you don't." Then he headed toward the exit without looking back.

Jory tensed, ready to chase after him.

Noah grabbed hold of the back of his shirt and yanked him down.

"What are you doing? Smith's getting away."

"That's not Smith."

"What are you talking about? Of course it is."

Noah shook his head. "Smith doesn't have magic."

Not have magic. Jory looked at the guards lying on the floor next to the smashed crates. "Did you see what he just did?"

"That's what I'm saying. The Smith I know doesn't have magic. He's human. But whoever this fake Smith is, does."

Jory's eyebrows shot up "Oh, shit. That means the real Smith—"

"Is probably dead." Noah motioned towards the guards. "But there's something wrong with this Smith's magic."

"What?"

"It doesn't feel right, dark and twisted. Until we know more about it, I don't think you should go near him."

Jory leaned forward and craned his neck. He could just make out the top of Smith's head. But he was almost to the exit. "Then you need to go after him."

"I don't want to leave you on your own here."

Jory glanced back at him. "I'm sure I can handle a few guards. Now go, before we lose him again."

"No. It's not worth putting you at risk."

"At risk from what? Go. I'll be fine."

"I'm not leaving you alone."

Jory was going to argue some more but the stubborn set to Noah's jaw told him he'd be wasting his time. But he hated that Smith was getting away after everything he'd done.

He almost offered to go with Noah so they could stay together. But that would mean leaving the prisoners alone with the guards. He glanced over to the broken men, who were still groaning on the ground where Smith had left them. He didn't think the prisoners would be in any danger from them—being that they were too afraid of Smith to step out of line—but Jory didn't want to take any chances. But still, Smith, or non-Smith was getting away. "We have to do something. We can't just let him leave."

"We're going to have to. At least for right now."

"But—"

"Smith said he's coming back later. We'll get him then."

Jory startled, then nodded. "I kind of forgot about that."

Hearing a noise, he looked back to the guards as they staggered to their feet and slowly limped toward a small office in the corner of the building. He pointed at it. "We need to remember to have a look in there later."

"After we get everyone out of here."

"I better call my brother then, so we can get started on the rescue plan."

"Make sure you let him know they're bringing in more people tonight."

"I will." Jory pulled out his phone and dialed as he moved away from the edge of the crate. Before his brother could say anything, he whispered, "Lysander. I need your help."

A few minutes later Jory disconnected his call and returned to Noah. "We've got help coming, but because this looks like it might be a trafficking thing, Max wants to have his brother Ian look after it."

Noah tilted his head. "Do they think it's connected to the other trafficking operation?"

"They're not sure. But if it turns out this is part of it, Roman didn't want to send in his enforcers in case it messes up Ian's Special Op."

"Which it probably would," Noah said. "When's Ian supposed to get here?"

"Not for another few hours."

"Oh." He looked at the prisoners, then back at Jory. "What about them?"

"Since we're already here, Max asked us to stay to keep an eye on them until Ian arrives."

"Like we were going to leave them alone."

"Exactly what I said. But this works out for us. Ian's team should be here by the time the rest of the prisoners arrive."

"And Smith."

"Yes," Jory said, a hard smile on his face. "And Smith."

Noah pointed at him. "Just remember, he's mine to handle."

"I think you mean ours." He touched Noah's arm when he saw he was about to argue. "I won't go near him if I can avoid it, but I'm not going to let you deal with him on your own."

Obviously seeing the determination in his eyes, Noah huffed out a breath. "Fine."

Grinning, Jory bumped Noah's shoulder. "Don't fret, pretty dragon. I promise not to get in your way."

Noah rolled his eyes. "I'd rather you promise not to get yourself hurt."

"Don't worry. I won't get hurt." Jory stretched his muscles, then propped himself up on his elbows so he could keep an eye on the prisoners. "You might want to get comfortable. We're going to be here awhile."

Clothing rustled as Noah settled beside him.

Jory shifted closer until their shoulders touched, smiling to himself when Noah hooked an ankle over his.

They waited through the afternoon, watching over the prisoners and keeping track of the guards' movements, filling the quiet moments learning everything they could about each other and strengthening their bond.

But in the back of his mind was a worry about what Smith was getting up to now.

Chapter Eleven

Jory

Waiting at the Port…

A few minutes past sunset, something landed with a soft thunk on the crate behind him. Before Jory's brain had time to process the sound he'd already flipped around into a crouch, claws extended, with a warning growl vibrating in his chest. He hesitated when he saw the strange vampire, thinking it might be Ian, but when the vampire didn't say anything, Jory bared his fangs and tensed, ready to take him down.

Then the vampire winked, pulling him up short.

The fuck.

"Max said you were expecting me."

"Ian?"

"The one and only."

"Why the hell didn't you identify yourself?"

Ian shrugged. "I wanted to see how you'd react."

Jory's eyes narrowed. "Max didn't mention you were an asshole?"

"No? I'm surprised," Ian said with a grin as he crawled across the wooden crate toward Jory.

"Hi Ian." Noah whispered, holding out his hand. "I'm Noah. It's good to meet you."

"And you as well." Ian turned to Jory. "You too, pup." Ignoring Jory's growl, he moved to the edge of the crate and settled on his stomach. Peering over the edge, he said, "So what do we have here?"

"Some people we think might be part of the trafficking ring you're looking into," Noah said, lying down next to him.

Ian's head snapped to him. "Did Max tell you about that?"

Noah shook his head. "My brother, Reid, told me about running into you in Ireland."

"Reid, huh. I'd hoped he'd keep his mouth shut."

Noah shrugged. "He's my brother. We don't keep secrets from each other."

Ian gave him a long look, then grunted. "I get it. Max and I don't keep secrets either."

Jory cleared his throat. "Uhm, I hate to break it to you, but we all kind of know about your mission."

Ian huffed out a laugh. "I guess it was too much to ask that it would stay need-to-know. Especially with the way I keep tripping over you guys every time I turn around."

Jory snickered. "It really was. Someone's always in someone else's business. You have no idea how hard it is to keep secrets in that house."

"I'm starting to realize that. You guys are deeper in each other's pockets than any military squad I've ever seen." Ian said, shaking his head. He faced forward and motioned to the prisoners. "Do we know how long they've been out?"

Jory shook his head. "No. They were asleep when we got here. But we did overhear one of the guards say they drugged their water."

"Hmm. It'll be easier to get them out of here if they're awake, but we can make it work if they're not."

"According to the guards they should be waking up in another hour or so," Noah said.

"That gives us plenty of time to get this place locked down. How many guards have you seen?"

"So far we've counted eight of them," Jory said. "Two were injured by Smith, so they've been hanging around the office." He pointed toward the far wall. "The other six have been doing rounds, switching out in pairs every couple of hours."

Ian nodded. "And there's another four patrolling the outside of the building, so that's twelve we have to deal with."

"And Smith," Noah said. "We can't forget him. He said he'd be back when it was time to ship everyone out."

"We'll watch for him."

"Okay. What do you want us—"

Ian held up his hand, his body suddenly on alert. "I hear a train coming. That must be the transfer we're waiting for." He turned to Noah. "When it pulls up and the guards move in, I want you to freeze them. My guys will take their places and bring the prisoners in here and put them with the others, so we can protect them in one place. When your Mr. Smith shows up, we'll grab him and finish this."

"Be careful with Smith," Noah said. "There's something wrong with his magic."

"What do you mean?"

"I'm not sure, but it feels dark. Warn your guys to stay clear of him. Something tells me he's too dangerous for them to handle."

"Are you going to take care of him?" Ian asked.

"If I can."

Ian blinked, then nodded slowly. "Alright. I'll let my guys know."

"Good."

"Stay sharp. Things are about to get lively." With that, Ian sprang up and jumped to a stack of pallets far behind them, then jumped again before disappearing from sight.

———

Jory stayed back as more prisoners from the train were put with the others in the cages. He wished there was more he could do to help, but Ian's soldiers worked together so seamlessly, he'd probably only get in their way.

Noah nudged him. "You feeling a bit unnecessary?"

"Yep. How about you?"

"The same." Noah turned to him. "I feel like we'd get in their way if we tried to help."

Jory snorted. "I was thinking the exact same thing."

"Hey," Ian called out, walking up to them. "Can you two keep an eye out back and watch for the cargo ship?"

"Sure," Jory said.

Noah spoke at the same time. "We'd love to."

Ian seemed taken aback by their quick responses, but recovered quickly. Looking at Noah, he said, "As soon as it docks, I want you to freeze the crew, then come back. My men will look after the rest."

"Okay."

"If you run into any problems—"

"We'll be fine, Ian," Jory said. "Don't worry."

"I'll send one of my guys to you as soon as we get the train unloaded." His communicator crackled to life. *"Sir, we have a situation out front with one of the prisoners."* Ian hesitated, glancing toward the front then back to them.

"Go," Noah said. "Jory and I have this."

Nodding, Ian pressed the button on his communication device. "I'll be right there, Johnson." Looking back at them, he said, "Thanks." then sped off.

Jory looked at Noah and grinned. "Ready to go take out a cargo ship?"

"So ready."

They raced to the back overhead doors and waited in the entrance, watching the river. A short while later, an empty cargo ship floated toward their location.

"This must be the ship Smith's waiting for," Jory said to Noah.

A fact proven a few minutes later when it berthed itself next to the loading area.

Jory and Noah grabbed a couple of vests from hooks by the door and stepped outside, waving to the crew onboard. They hustled to the edge of the quay in time to catch the heaving lines the crew tossed to them. Working quickly, they pulled up the heavy thick ropes attached to them and hooked them over the posts lining the river.

Once the ship was secure, Jory wiped off his hands and gave a thumbs up to the crew, then groaned when he noticed a couple of them throwing him suspicious looks. Crap. What had he done wrong?

He edged backward, aiming for the doors, then stopped when the two crewmen pointed guns at him. Once the rest of the crew saw what was happening, they dropped whatever they were doing and pulled out their weapons as well, keeping them trained on Jory and Noah.

Jory cleared his throat. "Uhm, Noah. We've got a bit of a problem."

"Oh?" Noah looked up from where he'd been attaching one of the heavy cable ropes, "Ooh. I'm on it." He wiggled his fingers, freezing the crew in place.

Thanks," Jory said. "I wasn't planning on getting shot today."

"I'd prefer it if you didn't plan on getting shot any day."

"I'll keep that in mind." He frowned at the guns the frozen men were holding. "I know Ian said his team would look after the crew, but I don't like leaving the weapons out here where anybody can find them."

"I'm sure Ian's man will be along shortly."

Jory glanced back at the warehouse, crossing his arms as he waited. Five minutes later there was still no sign of the soldier who was supposed to join them. He turned to Noah. "How much longer should we wait? We really need to get back so we can watch for Smith."

Noah squinted at the empty doorway, then nodded. "You're right. We do." He turned back to the cargo ship and snapped his fingers. The guns disappeared from the sailors' hands and appeared in a heap in front of him. He passed his hand over them and flames sprang up, rolling across the pile of weapons. Noah motioned again and the fire turned from red to orange, then to yellow. He squeezed his fist, and the flames went even lighter until they turned blue-white.

Jory had to shade his eyes and look away. When Noah told him it was safe to look, the pile of weapons had been melted into a twisted heap of metal. He snorted. "I guess that's one way to make sure no one can use those guns again."

Noah chuckled and picked up the misshapen chunk of metal and carried it to the river. A cloud of steam erupted when he dropped it in, the hiss as the hot metal made contact with the cooler water fizzling out when it sank from sight.

"Holy crap. Doesn't that hurt?" Jory asked, running over to him.

Noah shook his head. "Dragon, remember. Fire doesn't hurt me."

"Still. That had to be hot enough to burn your hands off." Jory grabbed Noah's hand and ran his fingers over his palm. His skin was warm and slightly pink, but otherwise he was fine.

"Told you I was okay."

"I just had to be sure." Jory took his hand, threading their fingers together. "I wonder how your flame will work against Smith and his weird tainted magic?"

"Let's go find out," Noah said, tugging him toward the warehouse.

Jory grinned. If Noah's fire worked on Smith as well as it had on the guns, Smith would finally get what was coming to him.

———

Meanwhile, out in front…

Smith leaned forward in his seat to pull out his wallet and saw the train had arrived. As he paid the taxi driver, he kept an eye on his guards as they unloaded and moved his cargo into the warehouse. He stepped out of the vehicle and slammed the door, satisfaction filling him when he heard the screams. He breathed deep, taking in his prisoners' cries of desperation, their tears coating his tongue as their terror was absorbed by his skin. All of it feeding his ever-present hunger.

But it wasn't enough. Even the anger and turmoil of the dragons couldn't sate him for long, leaving an emptiness that burned. But Ruth's memories had provided a new avenue to pursue, one full of power he could devour until he was full. A Paranormal Council that would provide an endless source of pain to fill the void that had been empty for so very long.

When he learned their weaknesses, he would exploit them; when he discovered their most prized possessions, he would take them; when he uncovered what they held close to their hearts, he would destroy them. He would feed off their suffering until they were empty. Then he would eliminate them and rule over everything with none left to challenge him.

Swallowing the last bit of misery floating in the air, Smith flicked his tongue over his kips and walked toward the warehouse. The train pulled out as he neared it so he altered course and headed to the rear of the building to supervise the loading of the cargo ship. As he passed a row of containers, something moved. He stopped, then went back, pausing at the end of the row.

A vampire thrashed about on the ground. It stilled, as if sensing his presence. Its head turned, then it struggled to its feet and stumbled toward him.

As the vampire came closer, one of the entities he'd consumed whispered its identity. He changed from his Smith persona to another, one known to the intruder, then moved to intercept.

Red glowing eyes tracked his movements. "Ruth, is that you?"

"Leon. What are you doing here?"

Confusion settled over the vampire's face. "I-I don't know." He blinked, then looked past Ruth. "Where'd the other guy go?"

"I'm the only one here."

"No. There was someone else. A man." He pointed to the end of the row. "You must have seen him." He turned in a circle, stumbling and falling against one of the stacked crates. "Where is he?"

"Don't worry about him. Why are you here?"

"I, I…someone said to come." Leon rubbed his head, blinking a few times. "Was it you? Did you call me?"

"No." But someone obviously had. How intriguing. "How did you get here?"

Leon squinted, then shook his head. "I don't remember." Then he looked up, his expression clearing as lucidity came into his eyes. Pushing himself off the crate, Leon stood to his full height, his eyes hard. "You were supposed to give me my reward, Ruth. But you left me."

"I had things to do."

"Where did you go?"

"It's none of your business." Ruth moved closer.

"It is my business. You owe me."

"Do I?"

"You know you do. I did what you asked. I want what was promised."

Ruth shifted until she was standing in front of him. "I can give it to you now if you'd like."

"You'd better. I've waited long enough."

"Then I'll make sure you get everything you deserve." Ruth placed her hand on Leon's head. The vampire jerked, his eyes filling with terror, his mouth opened on a scream that was cut off after the first cry. Leon slashed his clawed fingers across her arms, scoring lines that immediately healed. A high-pitched wail was torn from his throat before cutting off abruptly as he stiffened and crumpled to the ground.

Ruth stared dispassionately at the body as it withered, sinking in on itself, before collapsing into a cloud of dust, the vampire's clothes settling to the ground, coving it.

Sucking in a deep breath, Ruth closed her eyes, then breathed out. Her image shifted, changing to Leon's before flashing through other shapes and forms until settling once more into Smith's angular features. Brushing particles of vampire remains off his suit, Smith exited the row of containers and continued toward the ship docked at the wharf.

As he neared the water, he heard voices. Ones that didn't belong. His steps slowed. He cocked his head and listened, anger growing when he recognized one of them. What was the dragon doing here?

Smith sped up, pulling on his magic as rushed toward the back of the building.

"I thought I heard a scream."

"Wait for me, Jory. I'll go with you."

"I'll be fine. I'm just going to have a quick look around."

"Not without me."

Rounding the corner, Smith saw shadows moving in the doorway, backlit by the lights of the building. He charged forward, then stumbled, staggering sideways and falling to his knees. Reaching out with his arms, he gave a strangled cry when he saw pulsing lines of red and black moving violently under his skin. Getting back to his feet, he took a few steps then was blinded by a scarlet fog that slid over his eyes. Stretching his hands in front of him, he took another step and slammed into a barrier, pitching forward, his short fall ending in a splash.

The waters of the Mississippi closed over his head. Unable to move as black and scarlet flames burned through him, he was helpless to do anything but breathe them in as he slowly sank.

———

Jory ran out of the back of the building, stopping at the water's edge. He glanced at the captured ship, then looked up and down the quay, then turned to Noah as he rushed up beside him.

"I can't see anything."

"Me either." Noah frowned out at the water. "I thought I heard a splash."

"Let's check out the ship. Maybe someone slipped on board."

They jumped on board and wove through the frozen bodies, then circled the ship, but didn't find anything.

"There's nothing here," Jory said. "Maybe we should check over there." He pointed toward metal containers stacked near the warehouse.

"Sure. Let's have a look."

They jumped off the boat. As they started walking toward the containers, Jory noticed Noah kept looking back behind them.

"Do you see something?"

Noah shook his head. "No. But there's something strange in the air near the water. I just can't figure out what it is."

"It's probably the funky smell from the river."

Before Noah could respond, one of the soldiers poked his head out of the warehouse. "Excuse me, Mr. Davenport. Ian asked me to come and get you."

"Right now?"

"Yes, sir."

"I wonder what he wants," Noah said, glancing at Jory.

"There's only one way to find out," Jory said. "You go and see and I'll keep looking around."

Noah looked indecisive.

"Just go. I'll be fine."

Noah raised his head. His eyes glowed. After a minute he nodded. "Alright. I can't sense anyone out there."

Jory rolled his eyes at his mate's overprotectiveness, but didn't say anything since he would have done the same in Noah's place.

Nudging him, Jory said, "Go see what Ian wants. I'll come find you in a few minutes."

"Be careful."

"I will."

When Noah headed inside with the soldier, Jory began searching around the containers in the staging area. Coming around the corner at the end of one of the rows, he stumbled to a halt when an acrid odor stung his nose. Covering his face, he cautiously moved toward a dark shadow on the ground, his eyebrows going up when he saw the pile of clothes.

Toeing at them, Jory coughed when he kicked up a cloud of dust, then gagged as the smell of decay filled his nose and coated his tongue. He turned to leave when something glinted in the moonlight, catching his attention.

Squatting, his heart kicked up a notch when he saw the red stone nestled in the folds of the dusty garments. He picked it up from the gritty ash, catching a whiff of ancient dryness through the stench of decay. Vampire.

Wiping his fingers on his jeans to clean off the remains of the vampire that stuck stubbornly to his skin, he pocketed the stone, then raced back to the warehouse to show Noah what he'd found.

The moment he stepped inside, Jory was put to work helping escort the groggy—Noah had just woken them up—scared, and confused ex-prisoners out the back and along the escape route the soldiers had set up that took them to SUVs parked further down the quay.

By the time he was done, he'd forgotten about the stone in his pocket.

———

Over the next few hours, all of the prisoners were smuggled out the back of the warehouse and were enroute to a safe location, Smith's guards and the cargo ship crew were locked in the cages, and the remaining weapons had been disposed of.

Ian, Jory, and Noah were doing a final sweep of the warehouse while they waited for the soldiers and SUVs to return.

All in all, the rescue mission had been a huge success, with one glaring exception.

There'd been no sign of Smith.

Jory stared out the front of the building with his hands on his hips. "I don't understand it. He should have been here by now."

"Something must have tipped him off."

"But what? Everything went perfectly."

Noah shook his head. "I don't know. But there's nothing we can do about it now."

"Shit."

"We might still be able to find him."

Jory turned to him. "How?"

"Knowing how arrogant this Smith is, I wouldn't be surprised if he tried hitting our accounts again."

Jory wasn't sure he agreed. "I don't know, Noah. If we have scared him off, wouldn't it make more sense for him to disappear and start up somewhere else?"

"If this were anybody else, sure. But from what we've learned about Smith, I don't think he'll give up that easily."

Jory thought about it, then nodded. He had a point "I suppose it couldn't hurt to check out his house. If we're lucky, we might even find him there." He shrugged. "And if we're not and he's long gone, we might find something important he left behind." He turned to Noah, feeling a lot more positive about their chances of finding Smith. "Let's go tell Ian what we're doing."

Jory walked through the office doorway and stopped, his eyes immediately going to the open safe, its door twisted and hanging half off, then to Ian who was bent over the desk. "Doing a little safecracking, are we?"

Ian glanced up and snorted. "Yes. And it's a good thing I did." He gestured to some folders spread over the desk. "Come see what I found."

Noah pushed past Jory and joined Ian. "What have you got?"

Ian flipped open a folder and spread out the pages. "Complete dossiers for everyone we've identified as being part of the trafficking operation, but these contain a lot more information than anything we've been able to get our hands on." He scooped up the papers and shoved them back in the folder. "But the biggest find is these." Ian held up two folders. "There eeere a couple players we were unaware of. High level government officials, and from the information contained in these, it looks like they're top tier of the tracking operation. And using the blood money they're getting to buy their positions." Ian dropped the folders to the table, his eyes going hard. "It's going to be a pleasure showing them the error of their ways."

"Which is no less than they deserve," Noah murmured as he flipped open one of the folders, his eyebrows going up when he saw what was inside. "Damn. I never would have expected Carlysle."

"Me either. I also found this." Ian held up a USB stick. "I'm sure whatever is on here will be everything I need to shut down the whole operation."

Jory, who was reading the dossier over Noah's shoulder, looked up at his words. "What makes you think that?"

"Because the only person who could possibly have had this much detailed information has to be whoever's in charge. The mysterious shadow leader we've never been able to identify." He clutched the USB in his fist.

"Smith," Jory and Noah said at the same time.

"Yep. And given what Noah said about his magic being wrong, it would explain how he's managed to elude us so far."

"Man, I'm really regretting him not showing up tonight," Jory said, shaking his head.

"Me too. If Smith is the mastermind behind this operation, then he has the knowledge and connections to easily start it up again. We need to find him and make sure he can't."

Jory took that to mean Ian was going to kill him, which he didn't have a problem with. He glanced at Noah. Or maybe he did since Smith was the only one who knew where his mate's money was. Pointing at Ian's fist, Jory said, "If you find any information on that flash drive about money transfers that aren't related to the trafficking operation, could you let us know?"

Ian frowned. "Why?"

"Uhm," Jory turned to Noah, not sure how to explain without giving away his secrets.

Noah cleared his throat. "Smith stole a significant amount of money from Reid and I and we haven't been able to track down where he's hidden it."

Ian's eyes narrowed as he studied Noah. "And I suppose if I find anything, you want to keep that information need-to-know?"

"If possible."

Ian nodded. "All right. If there's anything on here, I'll pass it along."

"Thanks."

"Yes, thanks Ian," Jory said, shoving his hands in his pocket. His fingers brushed against a hard round object. "Oh, shit. I meant to show this to you earlier, but I got so distracted, I forgot." He pulled out the red stone. "I found this when I was looking around outside."

He handed it to Noah, who shouted and flung it across the room. He shook out his hand. "What the hell did you just give me?"

"A stone. Why?" Jory grabbed Noah's hand, cursing when he saw the blisters on his fingers. "Holy shit. How did that happen?"

"I don't know," Noah said, pulling his hand back and looking at it.

Feeling like crap for harming his mate, pulled him into a hug, burying his face in Noah's neck. "I'm so sorry. I never would have given it to you if I thought you would get hurt."

"I know you wouldn't." Noah pushed him back, then stared at his hand, brushing his fingers over his red skin. "I don't know why it burned me. Not much can harm a dragon." He paused. "Well, other than a demon. Something I found out the hard way."

There was a story there Jory wanted to hear, but first. "You think it could be a demon stone?"

Noah shook his head. "Probably not." Then he looked at his fingers. "Then again, it might. There was a demon in our world not that long ago. Who knows what was left behind?"

Jory went cold. "If that's really a demon stone, I'd better find it."

"I'll help you," Ian said.

They looked around the floor, Ian taking one side of the room and him the other. When Jory didn't see it, he dropped to his knees and peered under the desk, then checked behind the filing cabinet. He finally spotted it under a table in the corner of the room. He was reaching for it when he realized he probably shouldn't be touching it with his bare hands.

He didn't even want to think about what it might have done to him while he'd been carrying it around in his pocket the last few hours.

Looking around the room for something he could use to pick it up, he spotted some paper towel next to a small sink. Ripping off a few pieces, he wadded it up and used that to pick up the stone. Then brought it over to Noah and unwrapped it, holding it out to him.

Noah gave him a surprised look and quickly stepped back.

"Sorry." Jory pulled it away from his mate. "I'll make sure it doesn't touch you, but can you look at it with your dragon's eyes and try to figure out what it is?"

"Uhm, sure." Noah tentatively stepped forward and focused on the stone. He closed his eyes. When he opened them again, they'd shifted from deep green to his dragon's sparkling gold, split down the center by a vertical pupil and filled with swirls of magic.

Jory was transfixed. Gazing into his mate's eyes, he got lost in the wonder of his sparkling orbs. The connection between them grew stronger, pulling at him. His wolf perked up, excitedly pushing at Jory to get closer to their mate. His gums tingled, then his fangs broke through. Jory inched forward, drawn by the lure of the dragon, urged on by the needs of his wolf, ensnared by Noah's soul calling to his. Swept up in the tide of overwhelming emotions, he shifted again, not realizing he was bringing the stone dangerously close to his mate.

A hand landed on his shoulder and yanked him back.

Jory blinked and shook his head, coming back to himself in a rush. Seeing how close the stone was to Noah, he jerked it away and quickly wrapped it in the paper towel. Then he shoved it behind his back for good measure.

Holy shit. That had been too close.

"You in control again? Is it safe to let go?"

Jory swallowed and turned to Ian, meeting his concerned gaze. "I'm good. Thanks for stopping me."

"No problem." Ian hesitated, then said, "I don't want to tell you your business, but you might want to think about completing your bond. The longer you put it off, the harder your animal spirit will push at you, until it forces you to claim your mate."

"I know. And we're going to. It's just, well, things have been pretty hectic." Jory huffed out a breath as he shook his head. "So much has happened, I can't believe it's only been a few days since we met. It feels like so much longer."

"Probably more so for your wolf. You don't want to be in the middle of something and have him take over because he needs to be with his mate."

"I know. You're right. This isn't the first time I've gotten distracted by my feelings—like almost getting arrested, he thought—but it was the most dangerous."

"So far," Ian said, a note of warning in his voice. "And it'll only get worse, so don't put it off too long."

"We won't." And they wouldn't. Because as soon as Jory had some privacy to talk to Noah, he'd find out what his hesitation was. And if he said it was because he needed to prove something or that he didn't deserve a mate, Jory would have things to say back. Because after seeing Noah in action for the last few days, he knew none of that was true. And he would take great pleasure in proving to Noah how strong and amazing he really was, until he had no choice but to believe it.

He turned back and saw the gold had faded from his mate's eyes. "Did you pick up anything from the stone?"

Noah nodded. "I could feel traces of demon magic. It's diluted and transformed in a way I don't understand, but still enough to cause damage." He held up his blistered fingers, as if Jory needed any proof.

"Then we have to get rid of it. But where?" He glanced around the office as if there was a demon-containing box just sitting on the shelves waiting for him.

"I have an idea," Noah said. "Make sure the paper towel is wrapped tightly around the stone, then hold it out to me."

Jory squinted. "How is that going to—"

"Just trust me."

Ookaay. Not sure what he was planning, Jory nevertheless did as he asked, then held out the paper-wrapped stone.

Noah fluttered his fingers over it. After his magic settled, Jory was left holding a small stone cube.

"Whoa." He turned it over in his hands. "Did you just turn the demon stone into regular stone?"

Noah snorted. "I wish. Unfortunately, my magic can't touch it, so instead I transformed the paper towel. I just hope it'll be enough to protect us from any taint until we find a way to get rid of it."

"Huh." Jory tapped his finger against the cube, then brought it to his nose and sniffed, but it looked and smelled like normal stone, except for a slight tingle that came from Noah's magic. "That's kind of impressive."

Noah flushed. "Thanks."

Jory flipped it up, then caught it. "We should take this to Lysander and Bryan and see what they think. They've got a lot more experience with demon magic than I do."

"That's a good idea."

"Except…we're supposed to be checking out Smith's house?"

"Wait a minute," Ian said, looking between them. "You guys know where he lives?"

Jory nodded. "At least, we know where he's been staying."

"Give me the address. I wouldn't mind having a look around myself." He handed Jory his phone. "In fact, I'll have one of my guys keep an eye on the place so you're free to take the stone to the Galways."

"Okay. Thanks." Jory input the info and handed the phone back to him.

Ian shoved it in his pocket. "Just try not to be too long. My team's got a lot of work to do now that we have all of this new information."

"Don't worry," Noah said. "It won't take us long to get to the mansion and back. Depending on how long the discussion takes, we should probably be done in a couple of hours or so."

Ian nodded. "That'll work. My guys should be back soon. By the time we get this place wiped, you should be able to send my man back."

Seeing another dragon ride in his future, Jory tried to think of another option. Then one came to him. He nudged Ian. "Any chance there's a vehicle left we could borrow?"

Ian shook his head. "Sorry. We used them all to transport the prisoners."

Jory sighed. He'd thought as much, but it had been worth a try. "I guess we'll have to fly."

Ian gave him a strange look, like how else would he get there? Which was reflected in his words. "Flying with your mate is a lot more efficient and quicker than going by vehicle."

"Right. What was I thinking?" But since they were on a tight timeline, Jory tried to push back his nervousness. He took hold of Noah's hand, squeezing only a little bit too tight. Or maybe not. He loosened his hold when Noah winced. "I, uh, guess we'll see you later then."

There was a pause as Ian studied him, then obviously catching on to what the problem was, snorted. "You bet. Have a nice flight."

"Asshole." Jory tugged on Noah's hand and started walking away.

"Yes, I am," Ian yelled after him. "Just ask Max."

Jory laughed and shook his head.

Noah bumped against him as they walked out of the warehouse. "You know I won't let anything happen to you."

"I do. It's just—"

"Your wolf."

"Yeah."

Noah's smile was kind. "Just try to keep in mind that we'll never let you fall."

Jory nodded. He couldn't wait for the day his stomach didn't twist at the thought of flying. Please Goddess, let it be soon. Because he was getting damned tired of looking weak in front of his mate.

Chapter Twelve

Noah

Meeting with the gang at the Galway mansion...

Noah tapped his fingers impatiently on his leg and checked the time, huffing when he saw only five minutes had passed since the last time he'd looked. His leg started bouncing as he glanced around the office, stopping on Roman, who was focused on his computer screen, then moving to Bryan and Max, who were having a whispered conversation off to the side, then finally landing on his mate, who was watching him with a smirk on his face. He narrowed his eyes, then looked away, holding back a smile when Jory snorted.

His mate made it hard to stay irritated at Lysander for being late.

Jory's hand covered his, stopping his restless motion. "Try to relax."

Noah turned to him and whispered, "We told Ian we wouldn't be too long."

"I know. I'm sure my brother will be here soon."

As if hearing his words, Lysander rushed into the office and sat in the chair beside Roman. "Sorry, everyone. I didn't mean to keep you waiting. There was a small emergency in the children's wing."

"Is everything okay?" Bryan asked.

"Yes. Just a game of hide and seek that went a little sideways." Lysander laughed. "One of the pups fell asleep in the back of the closet and no one could find her."

"Is she all right?"

"Yes. Everyone's fine. They were all in the kitchen having cookies and ice cream with Dychelle and Mrs. Davies when I left them."

Bryan snorted. "I'm surprised you didn't stay. I know how much you love cookies and ice cream." He stopped and squinted at Lysander. "Are those crumbs on your shirt?"

Lysander's eyes went wide. "No," he said slowly, then turned away and quickly brushed them off.

Noah snickered, something about knowing the Consort had been having cookies with the children melting the last of his irritation away. Lysander raised his head and winked at him before straightening in his chair, a look of complete innocence on his face...except for the slight twitch of his lips.

"I can't believe you didn't bring any with you. Especially after keeping us waiting," Bryan said, shaking his head.

"Sorry, there were none left."

"Uh, huh. And how many did you have?"

"A few," he answered cagily. "A couple of yours. And maybe some of Max's." He glanced sideways. "And possibly Roman's."

"Sandi!"

"What? They were chocolate chip. What did you expect me to do?"

"Not eat all of them, that's for damn sure. They were ours."

"Not anymore," Lysander said, wiping his thumb over a suspicious looking smudge in the corner of his mouth.

Noah burst out laughing and leaned against Jory. "I'm surprised he didn't eat yours as well."

Jory snickered. "He doesn't know where they are."

Noah sat back. "What?"

"Dychelle likes me more than Lysander, so she—"

"Hey. That's not true."

Jory's eyes sparkled with humor as he turned to Lysander. "As I was saying, because she likes me best, Dychelle hides my portion of cookies in a secret place where Lysander can't find them." He made a face at his brother. "No matter how hard he tries to."

"Don't get too cocky, little brother. I'll find your secret stash one day.'

"Uh, huh. Sure, you will." Jory turned to Noah, shaking his head and mouthing, *no, he won't.*

Noah snorted, then realized that after all of this talk about cookies, he wanted one. Luckily, he knew someone who had some. He leaned close and whispered in Jory's ear, "Any chance you'd be willing to share your cookies with me?"

Jory's eyes went hot. "I'll give you anything you want." His rumbly voice stroked Noah's nerve endings.

Noah swallowed, trying to clear his suddenly dry throat. "We're, uh, not talking about cookies anymore, are we?"

"No, my pretty dragon, we're not."

"Right." Noah shifted in his seat, starting to feel a bit warm. "So, uhm, that escalated pretty quickly."

Jory's quiet chuckle was drowned out by loud laughter from across the room.

Looking up, Noah realized everyone was watching them. His cheeks burned. "Sorry."

"There is no need to apologize. Unbonded mates have a tendency to become easily distracted," Roman said, his lips twitching with amusement.

"So, I've found out," Noah said dryly, giving Jory a quick jab with his elbow when he wouldn't stop snickering.

"Oh," Lysander said, leaning forward in his seat. "Did something happen?" He smirked. "Other than you two being arrested."

Jory barked out a laugh. "Nothing that's any of your business."

"So something did happen? Time to spill, Jory."

"Not a chance, big brother, no matter how much you beg." Winking at Noah, who could only shake his head at him taunting Lysander, Jory turned to Roman. "Did Ian catch everyone up on what happened at the Port?"

"He did," Roman said. "His men were on their way back while we were speaking with him. He wanted me to pass on a message that he anticipates they will be finished within the next two hours, at which point he will be recalling his man."

Noah nodded. "Okay. So we should probably get started then."

"Whenever you are ready."

Jory stood and dug around in his pocket. "We're hoping Lysander and Bryan might be able to help us with this." He pulled out the stone cube.

"What is it?" Bryan asked, staring at Jory's hand.

"It's a stone I found near the warehouse. It, uh, was in a pile of vampire ash."

Roman and Max stiffened. Max immediately stood and started toward the door.

"Max—" Roman started.

"I'll look into it immediately and let you know what I find out," Max said, nodding at him, before striding from the room.

"Do you think it could be one of ours?" Lysander asked Roman quietly, resting his fingers on his arm.

Roman shook his head. "I do not believe so. I would have felt if we lost anyone, however—" He lifted his hand.

"It's best to make sure," Lysander finished quietly.

"It is."

Jory cleared his throat, drawing everyone's attention. Before he could speak, the phone on Roman's desk began to ring.

Roman looked at the screen and frowned, then glanced up at Jory. "My apologies, Jory, but I should take this call."

"Of course." Jory's hand dropped to his side.

"Who is it?" Lysander asked.

"Eric."

"Isn't he at the Council building?"

"He is."

"Why would he be calling?"

"Why indeed?" Connecting the call, Roman said, "Eric. How can I help you?"

"I'm sorry to bother you, Prince, but can you and the Consort please come to the dungeons? Something's happened to Ruth."

———

As they turned the last corner, they ran into an acrid wall of wrongness.

"What is that?" Bryan choked, quickly covering his nose and mouth as he fell into a fit of coughing.

"Dear Goddess," Lysander cried, his eyes watering as he looked around. "It's like being surrounded by dark magic and death."

Holding his breath, Noah fluttered his fingers to clear the noxious fumes from the area.

"Thanks," Lysander said, rubbing his nose. "Any idea what that was?"

"Yes," Noah said, exchanging a glance with Jory, who nodded in agreement. "We smelled something like this in New York when we found our Finance Director's body, or what we thought was his body."

"You're not sure?"

"No. But if the same thing happened here—"

Lysander's eyes widened in realization. "Ruth!" Not waiting for the rest of them, he ran to the end of the corridor and around the corner. "Damn it!"

Noah and Jory joined the others gathered in front of Ruth's cell.

"Shit," Jory whispered. "She looks just like the body we found at Smith's."

Lysander turned to him. "Who's Smith?"

"The Finance Director I was talking about," Noah answered, as he squatted to get a better look. "The body Jory and I found at his place looked the same as this."

"She should have been safe here," Lysander said as he crouched next to Noah. "The cells are warded to protect the prisoners from all threats, internal or external. No one should have been able to get to her."

Noah tested the magics protecting the cell, confirming Lysander was correct. Mostly. The wards wouldn't stop a dragon, but they would be effective against anything else. Or should have been.

"Well, someone obviously got in," Bryan said. "The question is who."

"Or what," Lysander said slowly. "Something feels very wrong here."

"I agree," Noah said as he got back to his feet. "I wish I had answers for you, but we still haven't figured out how the person at Smith's house died."

Lysander frowned at Ruth's body, then looked over his shoulder at Roman. "Do you know of anything that could drain someone like this? Could it have been some crazy ass feral vampire?"

Roman shook his head. "No, beloved. This is not the work of a vampire. Unfortunately, I cannot bring to mind anything that would cause a death such as this."

"I need to get in there," Jory said, grabbing hold of the cell door and pulling on it. "Can someone please open this?"

Lysander frowned. "Why? There's nothing more we can do for her."

"I'm not worried about Ruth. I need to check for something."

"What?"

"I want to see if there's a stone near her body."

"A stone?" Lysander asked, standing and throwing him a puzzled look. "What kind of stone?"

Ignoring his questions, Noah turned to Jory. "You think a stone might be here?"

Jory nodded. "There was one next to the other body and another where I found the vampire's ashes. If the same thing killed Ruth, there should be one here."

"You might be right. I'll help you look." Noah waved his hand at the cell door, which immediately opened. He bit his lips to keep from smiling when Bryan started muttering about damned dragons and why bother using protection spells when they didn't work to keep them out?

"Thanks," Jory said absently, patting Noah on shoulder as he walked past him and began checking the ground around the body.

"What's this stone you guys are talking about?" Lysander asked again.

"Something I found next to Smith's body. And the vampire's."

"And you think there's one here?"

"Yes. It should be a small black gemstone." Jory paused. "Or possibly red."

Lysander nodded. "Okay. We'll all help you look."

"I'll start over here," Noah said, as he walked into the cell and began searching along the far wall.

Bryan and Lysander quickly followed, checking the other half of the space, while Roman went to arrange for someone to move the body.

After he'd finished searching his section, Noah turned to Jory. "I can't see it."

"Me either," Jory said, dropping the sleeve of Ruth's dusty robe. "There's nothing around the body, but I know it's got to be in here somewhere."

Lysander brushed off his knees. "Maybe the stones you found didn't have anything to do with whatever killed Ruth."

"Maybe not, but I think they do." Jory began crawling across the floor, brushing aside any loose dirt or small fragments of rock that were scattered on the ground.

Seeing he wasn't going to give up, Noah moved to the other side of the cell and began looking along the base of the wall, thoroughly examining every small gap where the wall didn't reach the stone tiles embedded in the ground. He was checking a wider opening under the wall when his fingers brushed something cool and smooth. He pushed his hand further under the edge, then growled in frustration when he knocked the object out of reach. Letting his claws out, Noah jammed them under the lip of the wall and pulled up sharply, breaking the rock and revealing a small black stone resting in a dip in the ground a few inches back.

"I found it," Noah said, retracting his claws then picking it up.

Jory rushed over and took it from him. "It's exactly the same as the one I found next to Smith."

"Can I see?" Lysander asked, coming over. He plucked the stone from Jory's fingers and held it up to the light, frowning as he stared at it. "You said you found more of these?"

"Yes. Another black one and a red one," Jory said. "What do you think it is?"

"I'm not sure. But something about it…" His voice trailed away as he handed it back to Jory. "I have a feeling these stones are more important than we know."

Bryan looked at him, then sighed. "Of course, you do."

As they were walking up the long path out of the dungeon, Lysander grabbed Noah's jacket sleeve, holding him back.

A couple of seconds later, Jory must have realized Noah wasn't with him and turned to look for him, frowning when he saw Lysander holding him. "What are you doing with my mate?"

"Nothing. I just want to talk to him."

Jory started walking back to them.

"Not you, Jory. Just Noah."

Jory stopped, his eyes glinting yellow.

"It's fine," Noah said. "Your brother probably just wants to know my intentions."

Jory's eyes slid over to Lysander. "Is that true?"

"No." Lysander shook his head, then shrugged. "Maybe a bit."

"You do realize you have no say in what happens between me and my mate."

"I know. I just have something I want to ask him."

"That you can't ask if I'm there?" Jory asked.

"Well, I could, but I don't want to."

Jory crossed his arms. "Then maybe I don't want you talking to my mate without me."

Noah couldn't help but laugh at the brothers. Annoyed eyes turned to him, making him laugh harder. "You don't need to protect me from Lysander. Go on without me while I see what he wants. I'll be right behind you."

Jory hesitated, his eyes flicking between Lysander, who rolled his eyes, and Noah, who smiled and nodded at him. "Fine." Giving his brother a warning look, Jory turned and continued up the path.

Once his mate was out of earshot, Noah turned to Lysander. "Is there something I can help you with, Consort?"

Lysander gave him a pained look. "Please don't start that Consort business. We're family now."

Noah startled, then chuckled. "I guess we are at that." He crossed his arms. "So, what did you want to ask that my mate couldn't hear?"

"I know this is none of my business—"

"I'm sure it's not."

"And I kind of promised not to interfere—"

"Then don't."

"I have to,' Lysander said. "Jory's my brother and I need to look out for him."

Noah hesitated, then nodded. "Okay. I can could respect that. What do you want to know?"

"Thanks," Lysander said sounding grateful, then a hardness came into his eyes. "I'd like to know when you're going to stop running and complete your bond with him?"

Noah couldn't say he was surprised by the question. Not after Reid told him how Lysander had pushed him and Fionn to get together. Still. "That's really none of your business."

"I know it's not and I should leave you both to figure it out—"

"You really should."

"But I can't. I'm worried."

Noah could see he was. And since his question came from a place of caring, he said, "I've stopped running."

Lysander's relief was instantaneous, telling Noah he'd been more worried than he'd let on.

"Is that all you wanted?"

Lysander shook his head. "There's one more thing. Please don't wait too long before bonding with Jory."

"Why? Because you have a feeling?"

Lysander surprised him when he laughed and shook his head. "Not this time." At the disbelieving look on Noah's face, he gave him a wry smile. "I know. I almost don't believe it myself, but it's true."

"Then why are you so worried?"

Lysander sighed. "Because Jory's my brother and I don't want him to get hurt. Everyone can see how much he cares for you."

His dragon rumbled happily hearing that.

"And you for him, for that matter. But mostly, I don't want anything bad to happen to either of you."

Noah's eyebrow shot up. "Why do you think it would?"

"Because every time one of us has delayed bonding with our fated-mate, something terrible has happened. I don't want that for you or my brother." He patted Noah on the shoulder. "I like the way you guys look together. You fit."

Noah stared after him, at a loss for words, when Lysander strode off to rejoin the others. They fit? Whatever he'd expected him to say, that hadn't been it. Then Noah smiled, because Lysander was right. He and Jory did fit.

———

They reconvened in Roman's office, this time joined by Gideon and Carlos. Additionally, because Ruth's death and the mystery of the stones had been deemed a matter for the Paranormal Council, Edgar and Jackson were also in attendance.

The only person who didn't seem to belong was Lysander's human friend, Tommy. When Lysander asked Tommy to join them as they were walking back to Roman's office, Noah had raised his eyebrow in question, but Lysander gave him a small head shake, so he let it go. He might not understand Lysander's insistence on Tommy being there, this didn't seem like the time to challenge his prophetic abilities.

"All right," Lysander said, once the office door was closed with two enforcers guarding the other side. "Now that we're all here, tell us everything you know about these stones."

"It's not much." Jory stood and pulled the two black stones he was carrying out of his pocket and laid them on the desk.

Noah noticed Tommy stiffen from the corner of his eye. A quick glance sideways showed that Lysander had also noticed his friend's reaction.

Jory tapped one of the stones. "The first one was next to the body we found at Smith's house in New York." He shook his head. "It was like walking into a nightmare. The way the house was destroyed, how it smelled, the taint of darkness in the air, and then finding what we thought was Smith's body, completely withered and drained…"

Noah interrupted. "And when Jory says it was drained, we're talking everything. There was nothing left behind. Not even the tiniest residual imprint of who he'd been."

"That's impossible," Bryan said. "Bones hold the memory of the soul long after life passes."

"Not this time."

Lysander frowned. "And Ruth? What about her? Did you sense anything? Because I couldn't."

Noah shook his head. "Her body was just as drained. Other than her physical remains, there was nothing left that could be sensed on a metaphysical level."

"What could do such a thing?"

"I don't know," Noah said. "But I'd sure like to find out. Because even though there's no way to verify it was Smith's body we found in his home, I'm convinced it was. Which is a bit of a concern since Jory and I've been following him around the city for the last couple of days."

"How can Smith be dead and still be running around?"

"That's the question, isn't it?" Noah said. "And I don't know if Ian told you, but he's convinced Smith is the shadow leader in charge of the trafficking operation."

"What the fuck is going on?" Carlos asked. "How is the trafficking operation tied to Ruth?"

"I don't know that it is. But…" Noah paused and glanced at Jory, who seemed to know what he was going to say and squeezed his hand in support. "Smith's also been embezzling money from Reid's and my business accounts."

"He's what?" Gideon looked stunned. "How is that possible? You and Reid have one of the best security systems in the world."

"I know." Noah swallowed hard, then told them the rest. "He also found a way to access our private accounts and managed to liquidate assets through our brokerage firm."

"Fuck me," Carlos whispered. "He got to your hoards?"

"Noah?" Gideon's eyebrows drew together. "Is this true? He's been stealing from your hoard?"

Noah nodded, shame washing over him.

"Gideon." The dragon prince turned to Jory. "You might want to check your finances as well. We think he found a way to breach all of the dragons' accounts."

"He better fucking not have touched my mate's hoard or I'll tear his fucking heart out."

"And I will help, treasure, as what's mine is yours and nobody steals from my mate."

"I don't understand," Bryan said, looking at them, his face a mask of confusion. "What's the connection between your hoard, a trafficking ring, and killing the remaining Elder?"

Noah shook his head. "We don't know. That's why we came to you."

"I recognize those stones," Tommy whispered, his eyes locked on the desk. "I've seen them before."

Noah's head snapped toward him. "You have?"

Tommy nodded. "In my dreams." He turned haunted eyes on Noah. "But there were more. And a red one. The center of everything. Where are they?"

Noah's gut clenched as he stared into Tommy's eyes. A demon infused stone could not be the center of anything good. How much danger was the human in?

"What is it, Noah?" Lysander asked, his eyes moving from him to Tommy and back.

"I-I—" He grabbed onto Jory's arm when his mate went to stand, suddenly afraid of what would happen once everyone saw the stone.

Jory looked at him. "We have to show them."

"Nothing good can come of it."

"Maybe, maybe not. But they still need to see it."

Not sure he agreed, Noah held him back for a few more seconds before letting go. He was hard pressed to hide his shiver when Jory pulled the cube from his pocket.

Jory held it out to him. "You need to take the protection off."

Still thinking this was a mistake, Noah flicked his fingers, dissolving the magic he'd put around the stone to keep his mate safe.

"Thanks." Jory carried the paper towel bundle over to the desk and opened it, letting the blood-red stone fall from its folds. It rolled across the desk and nestled up to the two black ones. "Tommy, is this the stone you saw?"

Tommy gasped and got shakily to his feet. He stumbled toward the desk, leaning heavily on it as he stared down at the three stones. "They're just like in my dreams. But…where are the rest of them?"

Jory shrugged. "That's all we have."

"No. That can't be. There's more. You need to find them."

Lysander got up and came around the desk. "Tommy, what are they for?"

"I don't know, Ell. But they're important." His hand hovered over them. Noah opened his mouth to warn him not to touch, but Tommy had already pulled his hand back. He stepped away from the desk, keeping his eyes locked on the stones. "We need to find them, Ell. All of them."

"We will, Tommy," Lysander said, the warning in his eyes as he looked at Noah and Jory telling them they'd better not make him break his promise to his friend.

"Good. That's good." Tommy gave Lysander a weak smile, then his eyes rolled back in his head and he collapsed to the ground.

"Tommy!"

———

Ian's team finishing up at the Port…

Hearing a splash, Johnson slowly worked his way around the back corner of the warehouse. He folded himself into the shadows and stilled, only his eyes moving as he scanned his surroundings. Though he couldn't see anything, he knew something was out there. Keeping his breaths steady, inhaling slow and deep, he waited for whatever was hiding to show itself.

Johnson's neck prickled. He pulled his knife free from its sheath with a whisper of steel against leather, then taking a deep breath, he flipped it to grip it by the blade, then spun and threw it at the man creeping up behind him.

His aim was true. The blade plunged deep into the man's eye. The man leaned over and clutched at his face. Before Johnson could close in, the man lifted his head and grinned—showing far too many teeth—then yanked the knife from his eye socket. Hefting it in his hand, he flung it at Johnson, piercing him through the shoulder.

Gritting his teeth against the pain, Johnson reached for his gun with his injured arm, but it flopped uselessly by his side. Before he had a chance to try with his other, the man was on him, grabbing hold of his head. Johnson punched him in the throat, but the man's hand dug into his skull, holding tighter. Johnson slammed his fist into the man's chin with an uppercut, then grabbed the back of his neck, pulling down as he drove his knee into the man's solar plexus. When that didn't force him to let go, he speared his thumb into the man's injured eye.

Then let out a strangled shout when a bolt of agonizing pain tore through his body.

Falling to his knees, Johnson could hear Ian calling to him. He gave a strangled gasp as pressure squeezed his head, and reached for his communication device to answer him, but his hand was knocked away before he could get to it.

Bearing down against the pain as blackness closed in on him, Johnson pulled the knife from his shoulder, determined to take the fucker out with him. Striking out blindly, the sharp blade made contact with something fleshy before it was torn from his grasp.

A presence forced its way into his mind, shredding his memories, and stealing his soul. Ian's voice shouting his name was the last thing Johnson heard before everything went dark.

The soldier's lifeless body toppled to the ground with a quiet thump.

"Johnson. Report."

The man pulled the weapons and communication equipment off the body, his face flickering like an out of tune picture, before settling into Johnson's hard features.

"Johnson. Answer me, damn it. Where the hell are you?"

He tapped the button on his mic. "Sorry, sir. I thought I heard a noise out back."

"Did you find anything?"

"Negative, sir. It must have been rats."

"Report up front. We're moving out."

"On my way."

As Johnson stepped over the soldier's body, a black stone fell from the cuff of his pants, bounced across the ground before landing with a soft splash in the slow-moving waters of the Mississippi river.

Chapter Thirteen

Noah

Noah's stomach churned as he paced Jory's room, trying to find the right words. What he needed to ask his mate was huge. He had no idea how he would react but hoped it wouldn't upset him too much. Especially since things were going so well between them. But he had no choice if he was going to protect Jory. This was the only way. But maybe he could...

"Noah!"

The sound of his name jerked him out of his thoughts. He stared blankly at Jory. "Did you say something?"

"I asked if you were ready to leave."

Leave? Oh, right. Smith. Noah shook his head. "We can't. Not yet. We have to talk first."

"Okay," Jory said slowly. "If you want. But I thought we were in a hurry to get to Smith's house before Ian's man has to leave."

"This is more important."

Jory's eyes widened in surprise. "Oh. What did you want to talk about?"

Where did he start? Did he just ask outright? Or maybe it would be better to explain the benefits, then tell Jory how—

"Just spit it out."

Noah stopped mid-thought. "What?"

"Whatever's got you all wound up, just spit it out."

"Okay." Noah licked his lips. "I'm trying to think of how to say it. I don't want to upset you."

"Is this going to upset me any worse than my mate running from me the first time we met?"

"It might."

Jory shook his head as if he couldn't believe such a thing, but Noah was being completely serious. "Just go ahead and say it."

"Okay. But try not to worry. What I have to do is, uh, it's necessary. You see…"

Jory sighed. "Noah, the only thing I'm worried about is you. I don't like you being this worked up, especially since I don't know how to help." Jory circled him and leaned against his back, his arms going around Noah's waist. "Whatever it is, we'll deal with it. Together." Soft lips nuzzled against Noah's neck. "Please tell me what's going on before you explode."

Noah swallowed. "I'm only asking this because of what's happening with Smith and those stones. I need to protect you. I need to be sure you're safe."

"And how do you plan on doing that?"

Noah paused for a moment before speaking fast, "I have to bathe you in the flames of my dragon." Then he held his breath.

Jory stilled.

Jory

Jory dropped his arms and stepped back. "You want to do what?"

Noah turned to face him. "I need to bathe you in the flames of my dragon."

That's what he'd thought he'd heard. Jory took another step back. "No."

"It's the only way."

"The only way for what?"

"To keep you safe?"

"By lighting me on fire?" That couldn't possibly have been what he meant. Right? When Noah shook his head, Jory blew out a relieved breath. "You scared me for a minute there. I thought you actually wanted to light me on fire."

"I do."

"What do you mean, you do?" Jory shouted. "Are you freaking crazy? I'm not going to let you do that."

"It's not real fire. Well, it is, but not like you're thinking," Noah said, grabbing his hands and pulling him closer. "It's a special flame used only between mates."

"Oh. Okay, then. Sure. What's a little fire between mates?"

"I'm so glad you understand." Noah's smile looked relieved.

"I don't understand anything. That was sarcasm, Noah. I'm not going to let you light me on fire." Jory pulled his hands free and stepped back from him.

"You have to."

"No, I don't."

"It's important. If you'll just give me a chance to explain."

"It had better be a damned good explanation."

Noah nodded. "It is."

Jory's eyes narrowed. He could see how important this was to his mate. That doesn't mean he was going to change his mind. Light him on fire? What the hell was he thinking? Crossing his arms, Jory growled, "Explain away."

Noah looked taken aback by his tone, but still reached out and touched Jory's arm. "I need you to have an open mind about this. Please. This is important."

Jory sighed, feeling like an ass. He let his arms drop. "I'm sorry. I'm listening."

"Thank you." Noah took hold of his hand and laced their fingers. "When I say I want to bathe you in the flames of my dragon, I'm not talking about my regular dragon fire but a special, once in a lifetime flame that can only be used between mates."

"What does it do?"

"It'll offer you protection from everything that could seriously harm you. Things like driving off a cliff or a building falling on you."

Jory thought about it. That didn't sound too bad. "Wait. You said seriously harm me. Does that mean other things still can?"

"Yes. The magic only protects from major injuries. Little things like cuts and bruises will still happen, but your wolf healing will handle those."

"Why not be protected from everything?"

Noah shrugged. "That's the way the magic works."

"Huh." Then a thought came to him. "Is this why Carlos can walk in the sun? Because Gideon's magic protects him?"

Noah nodded, looking uncomfortable for some reason.

Jory squinted at him. "What happened?"

"Would you believe me if I said, nothing?"

With the way his mate was avoiding looking at him? "Nope."

Noah seemed unable to meet Jory's eyes as he stammered, "I, uh, might have, just a little mind you, tried to kill him the first time I met him."

Jory blinked. "Why? I mean, I know Carlos can be an ass. I've wanted to kill him myself more than once. But why would you want to?"

"It's old news. Not important anymore." Noah cleared his throat. "So, let's get back to bathing you in my flames."

Jory shook his head. Cupping Noah's jaw, he tipped his face up. "Why did you try to destroy Carlos?"

"I'd rather not say."

"Why? Is it going to make me think less of you?"

"It might. But that's not the reason I don't want to tell you.

"Then what is?"

"I don't want you to be hurt."

Why would it hurt him? "Just tell me."

"Fine." Noah dropped his hand and moved a few steps away. Taking a deep breath, he blurted, "I might have been jealous."

"Of Carlos?"

Rolling his eyes like Jory was clueless, Noah muttered, "I thought I was in love with Gideon."

Jory froze. "And were you? Or perhaps I should be asking, are you?" When Noah hesitated, Jory rubbed at the sudden pain in his chest. The thought of his mate in love with Gideon hurt like nothing he'd experienced before.

"No, no, no," Noah said, grabbing onto his arms. "Whatever you're thinking, stop. I don't love Gideon. At least, not like that."

"But you still love him?"

"Yes. But I'm not in love with him."

"How is that any better?"

"Because one is how you feel for a lover, or a mate, and the other is how you feel about family." Noah rested his hand on Jory's chest, right over his aching heart. "I thought I was in love with Gideon. But when I look back, I think I was more in love with the idea of loving Gideon than actually being in love with him, if that makes any sense."

He squinted as he thought about it. "I guess."

"When we broke off our relationship, I let Reid convince me it could be rekindled." He smiled sadly at Jory. "But it couldn't. We didn't care about each other the right way. Unfortunately, by the time I figured that out, I'd already tried to kill Carlos, which ended any feelings Gideon had for me. That's when I realized I loved him as my friend, as my brother. But it was too late."

Jory thought about that. What Noah said made sense, except…he hadn't noticed Gideon's hatred in any of their interactions. But he had seen their brotherhood. "You seem to get along okay."

"Now, yes. We've had time to work it out." He shrugged. "It helped that I wasn't able to kill his mate. Luckily for me, Gideon made sure Carlos couldn't get away."

Jory frowned. "What do you mean?"

"When Gideon first met Carlos, he knew right from the start he was going to keep him. Not wanting to take any chances of him getting away, Gideon bit him and started the bonding process."

Jory's eyebrows flew up. "Without discussing it with Carlos first?"

Noah laughed. "Nope. He swooped in and staked his claim. From what I understand, Carlos fought him every step of the way, but Gideon knew what he wanted and took it. His bathing Carlos in his flames so soon after meeting him was the only reason I didn't kill him. Which, with Carlos being his True-mate, would have destroyed Gideon." Noah looked down and swallowed. "And probably me as well."

Jory felt for his mate, but he was still stuck on Gideon knowing what he wanted and claiming Carlos right away. Not running from him. And as much as he knew Noah had had his reasons, and was regretting his actions, he could admit to feeling hurt his mate hadn't fought for him as hard as he'd fought for Gideon.

"It's not what you're thinking," Noah whispered.

"What isn't?"

"You think I should be fighting harder for you. That I don't want to mate with you?"

"Because you don't. Or, you didn't." Jory wasn't sure which one it was, but knew one of them was true.

"That's not true. I do. I mean, at first, I didn't. Well, I did, it's just…" His voice trailed off.

"It's just what?"

Noah licked his lips, his eyes darting around the room.

"Tell me why you didn't want to mate with me," he said, hoping he was finally going to learn the reason Noah had run.

"Because, well…I'm kind of a screw up."

"And?" Jory asked, not seeing what that had to do with anything.

"And I need to prove myself, to show the Court I'm not useless, so they'll respect me. Or at the very least, ignore me." He gave a bitter laugh. "That was a big part of Gideon's draw. If I could have gotten the Prince of Dragonkind to love me, that would have shown everyone I was worthy."

"What are you talking about? You are worthy. Besides, who cares what they think?"

"I do."

"Why?"

Noah blinked. "Because they're dragons."

"So. You don't need to prove anything to them."

"I do. You don't understand."

"What don't I understand?"

"I need them to know I can protect my mate." He looked away when he whispered, "I need to prove I'm worthy of having one."

Jory stared at him, at a loss for words. He didn't get it. Noah was a dragon. The top of the paranormal food chain. If anyone should have to prove himself worthy of having a dragon mate, it was him. Not that he felt that way. But maybe him being a wolf was the problem.

"Is it because I'm a wolf?"

Noah's head whipped back to him. "Of course, not. Why would you think that?"

"I don't. I mean, at first, I thought my being a wolf was why you didn't want to mate with me. But that didn't feel right. And you say it's not—"

"Because that doesn't have anything to do with it."

"Yeah, I get that now." Jory gave a harsh laugh. "Turns out you have to prove yourself because you have a weaker mate." Saying those words burned.

Noah's eyes widened as he shook his head. "No. It's got nothing to do with you. It's because of me. I'm the one they don't respect. And because they don't take me seriously, I'm not sure if I can protect you from them." He drew himself up. "But I know I can do better. I promise, I will overcome the mistakes of my past to become who you need me to be."

Jory could only shake his head. Where was this coming from? Before he tackled that, he needed to make two things perfectly clear. "First off, I don't need you to become anything. You're perfect just the way you are."

"I'm really not—"

He held up his hand, stopping him. "And secondly, I don't need you to protect me from anyone."

"Yes, you do. You don't understand how vicious the dragons at Court can be."

"Like I care what they think of me. According to Carlos, they're nothing but a bunch of useless assholes anyway." Jory reached for him. "The only opinion that matters to me is yours. What do you think of me?"

"Oh." Noah's cheeks pinked up. "I, uh, I think you're pretty great."

Jory grinned, sliding his hands up Noah's arms to cup his jaw. "I think you're pretty great too."

"You do?"

"Yeah." He started to slide his fingers into his mate's hair, but stopped before whatever styling product Noah used got all over his fingers again. Then he frowned, a thought striking him. He tugged on the lock of hair that hung over Noah's forehead. "Is that what this is all about? Your hair, your clothes? Is this your way of impressing people?"

"Not impress them, no. More like, it's my shield. Something to hide behind, to give me confidence, so no one can get close to the real me." He gave Jory a sad smile.

"My armor, so I can pretend it doesn't hurt when they tell me how useless I am."

"You're not useless," Jory growled, angry at whoever had made his mate feel that way.

"I really am. That's why I need to prove myself first."

"You don't have to prove anything to anyone."

"Maybe I need to prove it to myself," Noah whispered.

Jory was going to tell him he didn't, then stopped. Maybe Noah did, at that, if only so he could believe in himself. And Jory suddenly realized how he could help.

"I don't think you're a screw up. In fact, you've proven to me you're anything but."

Noah looked at him in surprise. "You don't? I did?"

"What I see is a strong dragon who's been nothing but confident, especially when you were standing up to that arrogant asshole Boudreaux. I see my mate, who's not afraid to face danger and will do anything to protect the innocent." He smiled, resting his forehead against Noah's. "I see a mate I'm proud to belong to."

"Y-you really think all that?"

"I do."

Noah's eyes glistened. He blinked furiously. "I think it's you. You make me feel more confident, powerful." He swallowed. "Worthy."

"That's because you are all of those things, and I wish you would believe that." Except...would Noah believe what he said if Jory didn't show he trusted him...with everything? And even though he really didn't want to be lit on fire, he needed to prove to Noah he had complete faith and trust in him, so he could learn to have the same faith and trust in himself.

Swallowing his misgivings, Jory said, "Tell me more about this bathing in flames thing."

Noah's head snapped up. "What? You're going to let me bathe you in my flames?"

Jory nodded, knowing he would do anything to keep the joy in Noah's eyes. "But before you do it, I'd like to know what's going to happen."

"Sure. I just—" He stopped, frowning at Jory. "Why the about-face? A second ago you wanted nothing to do with this."

"Because you're my mate. And I trust you." Which was the right thing to say. Noah's smile lit up the room.

Then he got serious. "I have to be honest with you. Being bathed in my flames is going to hurt. A lot. But only for a bit," he said hurriedly when Jory started pulling away.

Jory swallowed. This was starting to sound like a really bad idea. He didn't want to disappoint his mate, but wasn't sure he'd be able to go through with it. Then again, Fionn had done it and he was only a little guy. How bad could it really be? So had Carlos. And Carlos, well, he was an asshole, but if he could stand it, so could Jory. He wasn't going to let the vampire show him up.

Jory took a deep breath and braced himself. "What do I have to do?"

"Just stand there," Noah said, pulling the collar of Jory's shirt to the side. "I'm going to bite you. It's not a true mating bite, but it will make our connection stronger. Then I'll release my flame."

Jory gulped. "Okay."

"Mating with a dragon isn't easy. It takes a strong heart, which I know you have."

"Sure."

Noah smiled and leaned in, the caressing slide of his lips on Jory's momentarily distracting him from what was coming.

Then Noah pulled away, his eyes filled with something Jory was too afraid to name, in case he was wrong. "Just remember, I have you. I won't ever let you fall. Not even in this." Noah allowed his dragon to rise.

Jory's wolf responded to the pull of his mate. Inflamed, he grabbed hold of Noah and attacked his mouth. Noah jolted, then yanked him closer. Jory groaned as the flavor of his mate spread over his tongue and magic danced along his skin. He pressed in deeper, sweeping his tongue along Noah's, knowing he'd never get enough of his wild, magic-filled taste.

Only when he had to breathe did Jory tear his mouth free. Panting, he pressed Noah's mouth against his neck and rasped, "Do it."

Noah licked his skin, then bit down.

Flames burst to life around them, engulfing Jory's body in a searing heat that burned down to his soul.

That's when he realized he might have been a bit hasty. But it was far too late.

"Fuck!" Fire stripped the flesh from him as the flames surged higher, burning brighter. His screams rose with the raging inferno until all he knew was pain.

"I'm here. I'm with you," Noah crooned.

"Hurts," Jory howled.

"I know. You're so strong, my mate."

"I'm not. Make it stop," Jory yelled. But it didn't. If anything, it burned hotter, a firestorm of scorching heat that poured over him, melting his bones.

"You have to see it through to the end."

"It's too much." Jory's knees buckled, only his mate's hold keeping him on his feet.

"You can do it. It's almost over."

"Can't."

"I know you can. Now hold on tight. This is where it gets worse."

Worse? How could it get any worse?

Then he found out. Jory's vision washed white when new agony tore through him, the flames tearing him down and remaking him new. His screams were lost in the roars of the fire and the cyclonic winds that swirled around them. He became one with the fire as the fire became his world, grounded only by his mate, who didn't let him fall.

It went on forever, until, flaring up one last time with a resounding boom that shook the room, the flames lowered and died. The winds slowed until only a gentle breeze brushed his skin. Then everything stopped.

Jory cracked open his eyelids. The first thing he saw was his mate, whose eyes blazed with pride. He gave him a weak grin, then darkness rolled across his vision as Jory fainted for the first time in his life.

———

Jory bolted upright, his mouth opened on a scream, then pulled it back when he realized he wasn't on fire. That he was in a bed with his mate reclining next to him.

"What happened?"

Noah smiled. "You fainted."

Jory scowled. "I did no such thing." Although he was pretty sure he had.

"Okay, passed out then," Noah said, his lips twitching. "Being bathed in a dragon's flames is not for the faint of heart. It can be a bit intense."

Remembering the feeling of his flesh being scoured from his bones, intense wasn't the first word that came to mind. Excruciating, yes. Feeling like he'd been thrown into a volcano and consumed by lava, also yes. But intense, no, that didn't even come close to describing what it had been like.

"You're not saying anything." Noah bit his lip. "Are you okay?"

Jory took stock of himself. If felt like everything was where it belonged, including the organs he could have sworn had melted. "I think so." He looked at Noah. "Am I all protected now?"

"Almost." Noah sat up and turned to him, crossing his legs. "There's one more thing I need to do."

Jory scooted up against the headboard, leaning away from him. "Uhm, is this going to be like the last thing? Should I be worried?"

Noah huffed out a laugh. "No. There's nothing for you to worry about. I just want to give you this." He held his hand out to Jory. A large, dark green stone, hanging from a silver chain, caught the light as it swung from his fist.

"That's beautiful," Jory said, reaching for it. "What is it?"

"It's a mating amulet, made with my own hands and forged in the fire of my dragon, as a gift for my mate." Noah took it from him and put the chain over Jory's head, the stone settling just above his collarbone. "While you wear this, you'll be protected against all magic. Even the magic of another dragon won't be able to harm you." He brushed his fingers over the stone, then sat back with a smile of satisfaction. "It looks good on you."

Jory could tell how pleased Noah was to see him wearing his gift. Almost as pleased as Jory would feel when his mate finally wore his mating bite. He went to take it off so he could have a better look at it, but Noah's hands stopped him.

"You can't take it off. It only protects you while you're wearing it."

"What if someone tries to take it from me?"

Noah shook his head. "They can't. Now that I've gifted it to you, the only one who can remove it is you. I want you to promise that you'll never take it off."

Seeing his intense expression, Jory nodded. "All right. I won't."

"Thank you."

Looking down, he ran his fingers over the cool stone, which was warming from contact with this skin, and along the filigreed edging. Jory suddenly realized he could feel his mate's pride and satisfaction coming through their bond. Weak though it still was, the connection between them was stronger than it had been before.

"Noah."

"Yes."

He looked up at him. "Since we've started our bond, did you want to finish it?" The link between them zinged with excitement, then it faded, regret taking its place.

"I do."

"But?" Jory could tell there was a but.

"I just—it might be better—" Noah's brow wrinkled, before he said, "I think we should wait."

"Why? Do you still feel like you need to prove something? Because you don't."

"I know that. Mostly. And I still want to prove something to myself, but after seeing how well you withstood my flame—"

"You mean by fainting?"

Noah laughed. "Before that. I realized you were right. You don't need me to protect you."

"No, I don't."

"I also understand we're stronger together."

"Which we are." Jory cocked his head, sure he was missing something. "You realized all of this because you bathed me in your flames?"

"Not totally." Noah flushed. "It has a lot to do with my dragon. While we waited for you to wake up, I got a lecture on how ridiculous I was being. How I was disrespecting you by not fully acknowledging your strength." He snorted. "And that he and your wolf are tired of waiting and we'd better get on with it."

"Those were his exact words?"

Noah snorted. "Pretty much. And he's right."

"He is," Jory said, reaching for his hand. "So, why are we waiting?"

"To be honest, I'd like for us to have some privacy when we complete our bond." He motioned with his hand above his head. "You may have noticed how the people in this house take an unhealthy interest in everyone else's mating."

Jory barked out a laugh. "You don't even know the half of it."

"I'm pretty sure I do. If it's all the same to you, I'd like to wait until we're somewhere private where we can keep it just between the two of us."

"We can do that."

Noah hesitated. "The only thing is, my brother, and yours for that matter, said we shouldn't put it off for too long."

Jory rolled his eyes. "I suppose Lysander had a feeling."

"He said he didn't."

"I find that unlikely. He always has a feeling."

"I know. But he did tell me that whenever anyone waited too long, something terrible happened."

Jory nodded. "He's not wrong about that." He ran his fingers over the skin where Noah had bitten him, but the bite mark had already healed. And would until Noah gave him his mating bite and permanently scarred him. "But don't let that pressure you."

"No?"

Jory shook his head. "I'm not going to rush our mating, no matter what anyone says. When the time and place are right, we'll know." Jory brushed his fingers across Noah's cheek. "Just promise me that if anyone tries to make you feel bad about yourself in the future, you'll let me know so my wolf can bite them.

Noah leaned into his hand, his dazzling smile stealing Jory's breath. "I promise."

Sheri Eleese

Chapter Fourteen

Noah

Surveilling Smith's house the following evening...

Noah crept as close as he dared, then ducked behind a shed and reached out with his senses. Once he was sure nobody was in the house, he motioned Jory back. They faded into the early evening shadows.

The sun was setting by the time they'd made their way down the street to the alley they'd chosen as their new place to watch Smith's house. Moving just past the entrance, they crouched next to a large trash bin that provided some concealment. Between that and the building's shadows, their presence would be mostly hidden from anyone passing across the mouth of the alley.

After they'd settled in, Jory whispered to Noah, "Was there anybody in the house?"

"No. The place is empty."

Jory frowned. "Then why didn't we go in and look around?"

"I'd like to wait for a bit in case he shows up."

"Couldn't we just wait for him in the house?"

Noah considered that, then shook his head. "I'm not sure how strong his senses are or if he'd be able to tell we were there. We've already scared him away once. I'd rather not risk doing it again."

Jory nodded. "Good point."

They monitored Smith's house through the evening, one of them watching while the other dozed, there not having been much opportunity for either of them to sleep over the last thirty-six hours.

After five hours had gone by with no sign of Smith, Noah came to the realization he probably wasn't returning to his house. He nudged Jory, waking him up.

Jory blinked, looking at him, then leaned to the side to check on Smith's house. "Did he finally show up?"

Noah shook his head. "I don't think he's coming."

"Did you try calling Ian again to see if his man saw anything?"

"There's still no answer."

"Damn." Jory looked around then back at Noah. "Well, what do you want to do? Keep waiting or should we just go in and have a look around?"

"We might as well go in. We're not accomplishing much sitting here."

"Okay." Jory stood and stretched, letting out a small groan.

Noah looked up and got stuck on his mate's lean frame, his eyes drifting to where Jory's sweatshirt lifted, revealing narrow hips above his low hanging jeans. His mouth started to water, wanting to lick the exposed skin, to nibble on the sharp jut of those bones. He swallowed as he imagined the taste of his mate's warm skin on his tongue.

A soft laugh sounded above him as the shirt was pulled down. "Not the time, pretty dragon."

Noah looked up and grinned wryly. "I suppose not." Then he sighed. "It never is, is it?"

Jory's fingers brushed across his cheekbone. "Don't worry. Our time will come."

It couldn't come soon enough for Noah. Now that he'd pulled his head out of his ass and realized how foolish he'd been by trying to avoid bonding with Jory, he wanted to get on with it.

They just needed everything to stop getting in their way so they could.

Noah pushed off the wall, then froze when the hair on the back of his neck rose. Holding up a hand for Jory to be quiet, he reached out with his senses, inhaling sharply when everything warned of danger closing in on them. Allowing his dragon to rise, Noah searched for the source of the threat, then jerked in surprise when he ran into someone he recognized. Someone whose presence could only mean trouble.

He quickly pulled Jory further down the alley where the shadows were deeper and offered better concealment.

"What's going on?" Jory murmured under his breath.

"Someone from my past is headed our way."

"Why are we hiding?"

"Because he's trouble and shouldn't be here. Confronting him will only create another commotion and draw unwanted attention to ourselves."

Jory nodded. "Which we don't need any more of."

"No, we really don't." Noah's voice dropped lower, until it was only air. "He's getting closer."

They both sank further into the shadows. Noah tracked the vampire who was steadily closing in on their position as if he knew right where they were. He threw up a distortion spell to hide their presence, hoping it would confuse him enough so he'd pass them by.

No such luck.

A shoe scuffed on the sidewalk as the vampire turned into the alley, his eyes unhesitatingly finding them in the shadows.

Noah rose and stepped forward, blocking Jory from his sight. "Leon. It's been a while."

"So it has, dragon." Leon leaned to the side, looking behind Noah. "Who's that with you?"

"No one who concerns you. Why are you following me?"

"What makes you think I'm following you?"

Did he think Noah was an idiot? Thinking back to their association, he probably did. "I know you are. Why?"

"You dragons," Leon sneered. "Everything's always about you. Why would I care what you're up to?"

"You shouldn't."

"Exactly." Leon took a step toward him. "But now I'm curious. Why are you lurking back here?"

"None of your business." Noah took a step back. "You still haven't told me why you're following me."

"Just coincidence."

Like Noah believed that.

Leon edged closer.

His dragon rumbled in warning. Noah held up his hands, fire sparking from the tips. "Don't come any closer, Leon."

"But I need your help."

"With what?" Noah shook his head. "You know what? I don't care. Just leave."

"Don't be like that. We were friends once, weren't we?"

"We were never friends."

Leon gave a harsh laugh. "I guess we weren't at that. I still need your help. Lukas is missing."

"Sorry. Can't help you."

"You owe me."

"I owe you nothing."

"After everything I did for you?" He inched closer. "I think you do, dragon."

Noah's eyes narrowed. The way Leon was acting wasn't ringing true. It was subtle, but something was definitely different from the last time he'd seen him.

"Get your gang of rebels to help you because I can't."

"They're all dead." Leon took another step forward. "Lukas was the only one left."

"I wonder if that's the vampire I found," Jory whispered.

"What was that?" Leon asked, coming closer.

"Stay the hell back, Leon," Noah said, throwing up a shield between them.

"So suspicious."

"Because I know what you're like. Now get out of here before I'm forced to make you."

"Not until I get what I came for." He took another step forward, stopping when he bumped into Noah's shield. Running his hands across the invisible surface, a sinister smile spread across his face sending chills down Noah's back.

A light breeze blew down the alley, kicking up dust. The air swirled around Noah, bringing with it an acrid scent that burned his nose. His eyes widened in recognition. Flames burst from his mouth, shooting toward Leon.

The vampire moved fast, dodging his fire and blowing past Noah's shield as if it wasn't even there. He stopped just in front of him, his eyes flashing crimson red.

"Shit." Noah jumped backward and threw up a thicker shield, hoping it would be enough to slow the demon. "Jory, run!"

"Too late." Leon broke through his shield and grabbed hold of him.

———

Noah's eyes opened. Or at least he thought they did, but he was still surrounded by darkness. A loud metallic crash echoed in the air, giving him an idea of what had woken him. He rolled to his side, then groaned, grabbing his head when the movement started a percussion of banging drums inside his skull.

Damn. How much had he had to drink?

Wait. There was something wrong with that thought. Noah squeezed his eyes shut as he tried to think through the fog in his brain. He couldn't remember drinking anything, but he and Jory must have gone out somewhere. No. That wasn't it. The last thing he could recall was watching Smith's house. Images crashed into his mind. Dark alley. Leon. Demon eyes.

Jory. Where was his mate?

Noah scrambled to his feet, then tripped over something in the dark. Something that moaned loudly…and gave him something soft to land on.

"Fuck. Why are you trying to crush me?" Jory shoved him away.

"Sorry. I didn't see you there. It's too dark."

"Then magic up a light orb."

"Good idea." Noah snapped his fingers, but nothing happened. He tried again. Still nothing.

"What's taking so long? It's just a simple light orb," Jory groused.

"Give me a minute. I'm working on it." Noah tried again. What the hell? His magic wasn't working. He reached for his dragon, but could barely feel him, his sense of him distant…muted. Uh, oh. That was bad. Really, really bad.

"What are you waiting for? It's black as night in here."

"My magic isn't working."

There was a beat of silence. "What do you mean it's not working? You're a dragon. Nothing can stop your magic."

"Almost nothing," Noah whispered, Leon's red eyes flashing in his mind. "Except for a demon."

"There's no demon. My brothers got rid of it."

"Uhm, yeah. I think we might have another one."

"Another one? Are you freaking kidding me?" Jory's voice went up.

"I wish I was. Before he attacked, Leon's eyes flashed red. But not regular vampire red. Demon red. And he broke through my shields. The only way he could have done that is if he was under the influence of a demon."

"Fuuuck," Jory groaned. "We're so screwed."

Noah nodded. They totally were.

Clothing rustled as Jory started moving around. Then there was a muted bang.

"Are you all right?" Noah asked.

"Yeah. I just hit my elbow."

A hand brushed Noah's hair before landing on his arm. "Do you have any idea where we are?" Jory asked.

"No. I just woke up."

"Help me search this place. We need to figure out how much trouble we're in."

"Okay." Noah climbed to his feet and held his hands out in front of him to keep himself from running into anything. Which proved to be no help at all when he tripped over Jory's foot.

As their eyes grew more accustomed to the pitch black that surrounded them, they were eventually able to make out enough detail of their shadowed surroundings to determine they were locked in a shipping container. If Noah had to guess, they were probably at the same wharf where they'd rescued the kidnapped victims the previous day. Or the day before that. There was no way to tell how much time had passed since they'd been captured.

But knowing where they were wasn't helping since they were trapped in a container they couldn't get out of. He and Jory had tried numerous times to force the metal door open, but whatever magic was sealing them in was something they couldn't break through.

"Son of a bitch," Jory yelled, when their last attempt failed.

"Jory? Is that you?" a faint voice called out.

Jory whipped around. "Ian?"

"Yes. Is Noah with you?"

Noah rushed to the wall to stand next to Jory. "I'm here. Are you all right?"

"Mostly. The five of us are a little banged up, but we'll live. I'm not sure what happened to the rest of my team." There was a pause. "I don't suppose you can help get us out of this tin can?"

"Sorry. We're locked in a container too."

"I was afraid of that."

"How did you get captured?"

"That thing pretended to be one of my men." There was loud bang, like something slammed into a metal wall.

"What thing?"

"Whatever locked us in here. It came back a few hours ago and grabbed Ben. We tried to stop it but it blocked us from getting near it, then drained Ben right in front of us. I've never seen anything like that before. Or smelled something so rank."

"It sounds like what happened to Ruth and Smith," Jory whispered.

"It does. Which means we're in more trouble than we thought."

Another loud bang came from the other container, startling them. "I told that fucker if it touched another one of my men, I'd kill it. It just laughed and said it would be back for me in four hours. Then it tossed Ben's body aside like it was garbage and left."

Noah stilled. Four hours. Why four hours? That was too specific not to mean something. But what?

Jory nudged him. "Noah?"

"Give me a second." Noah's mind raced, flashing through everything he could recall of dragon lore. Not finding what he was searching for, he unlocked a vault in his mind that contained all his knowledge of the ancient manuscripts. A whisper of a forgotten legend about an ancient being trickled into his mind. He pressed his hands against his forehead, trying to think where he'd seen it.

He must have made a sound because Jory's hand landed on his shoulder. Noah turned to him. Jory leaned close. "Are you okay?"

"I'm not sure. The four hours. It's important. I saw something, but I just can't think of where. Maybe a myth or perhaps —" Then it came to him. He'd been searching through the ancient texts for information on the demon dimension when he'd come across an obscure passage. Closing his eyes again, Noah brought up an image of the ancient manuscript, envisioning the curled and discolored page, smelling of dryness and age. He recalled the way he'd had to squint to make out the faded writing, some of the lettering lost to time. When he'd recalled everything he could, he locked the image in his mind and began working through the script, mentally translating it from its original language. A word in the last section jumped out at him. Oh shit. Their situation was far more dire than he'd thought.

Noah finished the rest of it, searching desperately for answers, a way to escape the danger, then swore under his breath when he reached the end and fully understood the hopelessness of their situation.

"Noah." Jory pulled him close. "What is it?"

He opened his eyes, his words a whisper as he said, "I know why it's coming back in four hours."

"Why?"

"Because that's how long it takes to process its victims." Noah swallowed, his heart racing at the threat they were facing. "Four hours to fully integrate whatever it consumes. If it hadn't killed Ian's man, Ben, before it found us, one of us would be dead."

"I don't understand. A vampire captured us."

If only that were true. "No. That was a soul wraith."

"What the fuck is a soul wraith?" Ian called out.

"A creature of nightmare. A being we can't defend against. One we can't stop."

"What are you talking about?" Jory asked.

Noah shook his head, pulling away to run his hands through his hair, not giving a damn about the condition he was leaving it in. "A soul wraith drains its victims and takes on their personalities and traits. That includes whatever powers and abilities they have."

"What?" Jory shouted. "Why didn't you mention this when we found Smith?"

"I didn't realize that's what we were dealing with. Soul wraiths are so lost in ancient times, nobody remembers they even existed. If I hadn't come across a reference to them recently…" His voice trailed off.

"How do we stop this thing?" Jory asked.

Noah shook his head. "We can't. Nothing can stop a soul wraith."

"There has to be a way."

"There isn't," Noah whispered, wishing on everything that wasn't true.

"Not even a dragon? I refuse to believe that."

"Not even a dragon, Jory. At least, not by itself. Soul wraiths are almost impossible to kill."

"Almost impossible isn't the same as impossible."

"In this case, it might as well be. It would take many dragons to handle it. A single dragon isn't enough. There's a slight chance I might be able to withstand its power and keep it from consuming me, but I still can't kill it on my own."

"You have me to help."

"You can't go anywhere near it. You have no way to defend against it. No matter how much power you have, no matter how strong you are, there's nothing you can do to prevent it from draining you."

"So, what? Are you saying we just give up? Let it eat us?"

Noah had no answer.

Jory growled. "No. I refuse to accept that. There has to be a way to defeat it. We just have to think of one." He stomped to the other side of the container, then swung around. "Wait. You said soul wraiths. Plural. There used to be more of them."

"Yes."

"So they can be killed."

"I suppose," Noah said, drawing it out.

"Tell me how they died."

He frowned, thinking again of the text, trying to unravel the meaning behind what he read. After a moment, he said, "According to the writings, they were violently territorial."

"You're saying they killed each other out?"

"I think so."

"But somehow this one survived.

"So it would appear."

"I wonder where it's been this whole time."

"I have no idea."

"So, if what you're saying is true, to get rid of this soul wraith, we need another soul wraith to kill it. That doesn't sound like much of a solution."

"Because it's not. There isn't one," Noah said bleakly.

"And you're sure there's no way we can fight it?"

"Us alone? No." Silence filled the container, until Jory made a sound he couldn't interpret. "What is it?"

"If a soul wraith is so powerful, so impossible to kill, why would it be interested in money? Why lead a trafficking ring? Why would it steal your hoard by pretending to be someone close to you? If it wanted money that badly, it could have just taken it since nobody could stop it? So, maybe this isn't a soul wraith. Maybe it's just something pretending to be one."

"It's not a pretender. It's a soul wraith."

"How can you be so sure?"

"A soul wraith inflicts pain in whatever way it can because it feeds off the suffering of others. Right now, it's toying with us, playing a game. A long drawn-out game of terror and torment it'll play until it gets bored and then it will destroy us."

"Stealing your hoard was to cause you pain?"

"Yes, because the best way to hurt a dragon is to threaten their hoard…unless a dragon's found their mate."

"Then I'm your greatest weakness," Jory said quietly.

"No. You're my greatest strength." But losing his mate was Noah's greatest fear. One that was going to come to pass because he knew he wasn't enough to stop the soul wraith. Not on his own. He was going to fail his mate and Jory would die because of it.

"Hey," Jory said, bumping him. "Whatever you're thinking, stop it. It's going to be okay. We'll figure this out. I just know it." He leaned against Noah's back, his arms coming around his waist to hold him tight. "Some stupid soul wraith isn't going to beat us."

But there was nothing to figure out. Jory didn't truly understand the danger of what they were facing. According to the passages he'd read, it had taken numerous dragons to eliminate just one of the foul creatures. And many of them had lost their lives doing so.

But what they faced now was so much worse. Because Noah had finally figured out why they couldn't escape their prison. What Jory hadn't realized, the thing that made this soul wraith so much more dangerous than any that had come before, was it had somehow absorbed the power of a demon. And demon magic was the one thing a dragon couldn't defend against.

Which meant he had no way to protect his mate from what was coming for them.

Chapter Fifteen

Jory

After another painful, yet failed attempt to break down the door, Jory stumbled over to his mate, and slumped against the wall next to him. "There has to be a way to get out of here.".

"I don't think there is," Noah said, the hopelessness in his voice tearing Jory apart.

Noah had been despondent and quiet since their discussion about the soul wraith. Jory was convinced if they worked together, they could find a way to defeat it, but Noah had already given up. Jory didn't know how to break him out of the pit of despair he'd fallen into, but he was determined to do so. If his mate had lost hope, Jory would have to have enough faith for the both of them. Because he was damned if he was going to let some stupid soul wraith have his mate. He would fight it with everything he had until he couldn't fight any longer.

He prayed to the Goddess it would be enough.

Taking Noah's hand, Jory pressed a kiss to his bruised knuckles. "What if we linked our magic the way my brother does. Maybe that would be enough to force the door open."

Noah shook his head. "I can't do that. I've never heard of anyone being able to do that, except for Lysander."

"We're mates. Can we somehow combine our magic? Weave it together?"

Noah gave him a doubtful look. "Maybe."

"You don't think it will work?"

"No."

"Well, let's give it a shot anyway. I'm not going to sit here just waiting to die."

"You're not going to die," Noah whispered. "I won't let the soul wraith touch you."

But there was no conviction in his voice. He might be saying the right things, but Jory could tell he didn't believe them, so his words were empty, without hope. Just like his eyes.

Which was pissing Jory off.

"Why won't you fight, Noah? This isn't like you to give up so easily."

"Because there's no way to fight against it. You don't…there's things…we can't win." The anguish leaking through their partial link was choking Jory.

Enough of this. He refused to let his mate give up or lose himself to despair.

Jory jumped to his feet. He was going to break down that fucking door and get them out of this tin can or die trying. He stormed to the back of the container, then crouching low like a sprinter waiting for the starting gun, took off, releasing an extended yell full of power as he ran full tilt at the door, slamming into it with his shoulder.

The resounding crash was loud in the enclosed space as he rebounded half the length of the container and slammed to the ground. Getting to his feet, Jory squared his shoulders and charged the door again.

Noah helped him up when he got knocked back for the second time. "Please stop. You're not going to be able to break through it."

Jory nudged him aside, then ran to the back of the container and rushed at the door again, putting every bit of strength he had into the blow. He bounced all the way to the back wall, landing against the ground with a loud crash. But as he slowly rolled over, he was smiling, convinced he'd felt a slight give in the door on his last attempt. With a bit more effort, he knew he could bust them out of here.

He got to his feet, swinging his arms to release the tension in his shoulders. Then he put his head down and barreled toward the door again.

Then tripped over his feet as he tried to stop so he didn't plow into Noah, who'd leaped in front of him at the last second. He grabbed onto Noah's shirt, his momentum taking them to the ground. With some quick maneuvering, he landed on his back with Noah on top of him.

Running his hands over his mate's face and down his arms to make sure he hadn't hurt him, Jory pulled him close. "What were you thinking? I could have hurt you."

"I was trying to stop you. If you keep going like this, you're only going to hurt yourself."

But he couldn't be hurt. Noah had told him that when he bathed him with his flames. He took stock of his body. Other than a slight ache in his shoulder, everything felt fine.

"I'm not hurt," he whispered, hope filling him for the first time since they'd been captured.

"What do you mean?"

"I mean, I'm not hurt." Jory gave Noah an exuberant kiss. "You said bathing me in your flames would keep me safe from injury. And look. It did."

Noah gasped and grabbed him by the arms. "Do you know what that means?"

"That I can't be hurt."

"Yes. And if we finish bonding, you'll be even stronger. Maybe even enough to keep you safe from the soul wraith."

Jory stilled. Was that possible? Could he be strong enough to keep them safe? Then he realized Noah was only talking about Jory, not himself. Then the meaning behind the rest of his words sunk in. For as much as he longed to complete their mating bond, knowing it was only a means to an end left a bitter taste in his mouth.

"Noah, I don't know—"

"I do," Noah said, pressing his forehead to Jory's. "I know this will work. We need to complete our bond. Right here. Right now."

"Because you want to protect me? Just me?"

Noah nodded, the smile on his face showing he hadn't heard the hesitancy in Jory's voice. "Yes. It's perfect." He pushed up and squinted around the dark container. "Well, not exactly perfect. I wish we were doing this somewhere more romantic, but as long as you're safe, that's good enough for me."

Jory gently eased Noah off of him, then stood, holding out a hand to help him up. "I don't know if it's enough for me."

Noah slowly climbed to his feet, finally realizing something was wrong. "What are you saying?"

"Completing our mate bond just to keep me safe isn't going to work for me."

"Why not?"

"Because we should be doing it for both of us, because we care about each other and want our souls united for eternity, not because it's expedient."

"I do care."

"For me, but what about yourself?"

"I-I don't understand."

"You're only talking about saving me. What about you?"

"You're what's important."

Jory shook his head, a growl escaping. "No. You are too, and I wish you'd realize that."

"But…I don't understand why you're upset. We can save you."

"What am I without you, Noah?" Jory shouted. "How am I expected to live without my mate? If you cared for me as much as I do for you, you'd understand why this isn't right."

"But I do care." Noah placed his hand over Jory's heart. "I have since the first time we met."

"When you ran."

Noah nodded. "I was overwhelmed. And scared."

"And the second time."

"Was because, well, because I was stupid. And still scared. Mostly about how much I was already drawn to you. And I was worried. I thought I needed to prove myself before I could have a mate."

"But now you know you don't need to prove anything. To anyone."

"I do. Because of you. You made me realize how ridiculous I was being when you didn't give up on me. When you kept chasing me, no matter how far or how fast I ran. You showed me I was worth it. That I was important. Then," his fingers tightened on Jory's sweatshirt, "the feelings I had for you grew into something more, something amazing, when I realized you accepted me just for me, the real me, not the person I show to the rest of the world. That's when I knew I would always be safe with you. That you'd never judge me."

"And I never will," Jory whispered, feeling raw from Noah showing his heart. "But none of this means anything if you don't care enough to want to live for me."

Noah froze. "Oh."

"Do you get it now?"

"I do. I only thought about saving you. I—"

"There is no me without you."

"No. I'm sorry for not realizing that sooner. It's just, it's…"

"Scary."

"Yes."

"But right."

Noah nodded. "It is. More than anything I've ever known."

"Then we do this together, Noah. For both of us, because we love each other, or not at all."

Noah's fingers slid up his chest and into Jory's hair. He pressed their foreheads together. "I do love you."

"Do you?"

"Yes. I wanted you from the first, even if I didn't think I could have you. But I knew for sure I loved you when I realized I could lose you."

"Yeah?"

Noah stroked his hand down Jory's face. "Yes. I'm sorry I made you doubt that. What I feel for you is so much bigger and brighter than anything I've ever felt before, for anyone. Even Gideon."

And though he hated thinking of his mate with another man, his words healed a hurt Jory hadn't realized he'd been carrying. "And I love you." And he did. So much so he couldn't imagine a life without his pretty dragon.

Noah's smile spread across his face. "Does this mean you'll mate with me? For the right reasons."

"Yes. It's all I've wanted since I met you." Then a horrible thought hit him. "Magic doesn't work in here. Will we even be able to complete our bond?"

"Oh. I never thought of that." Noah looked over Jory's shoulder, his forehead creased in thought. Then he looked up at him and smiled. "Mating magic is different than any other. I think all we can do is have faith and trust in the Goddess."

"Okay," Jory nodded slowly. "You do realize, if there isn't full acceptance on both sides, the bond won't take."

Noah pressed his check to Jory's. "I'm not worried. It'll take. "

"Yes, it will," Jory sighed. Nudging Noah backward to the container wall, Jory pressed up against him, then kissed him, sweeping his tongue inside when Noah's mouth opened on a sigh.

Groans soon filled the air as they feasted on each other, their kisses growing frantic and heated. Every noise he was able to coax from his mate sent Jory's passions higher until he was a throbbing mess of need.

He was taken by surprise when Noah spun them around, reversing their positions as he tried to take lead. Jory growled, nipping at his lips and spinning them back, crushing Noah against the wall and pinning him there.

Noah's excitement pulsed through their bond. He clutched Jory to him tighter, his willingness to cede control feeding Jory's hunger for his mate.

Scraping his fangs up the side of Noah's neck, Jory bit down on the fleshy part of his ear. "Your dragon likes submitting to my wolf, doesn't he?"

Noah's moan was a clear yes.

"That's good. I like being in charge." He licked down his mate's smooth skin until he reached his shoulder. Nosing the collar of his shirt aside, Jory bit down gently—not enough to break his skin—and whispered, "Last chance to change your mind."

"I'm not changing my mind. I want everything with you."

Groaning, he sucked the skin on Noah's neck where he was going to place his mating bite, then slid his fingers under the hem of his shirt, skimming his hands up his mate's body as he lifted it up and over his head, flinging it to the side. He reached over his shoulder to grab the back of his own shirt, a seam tearing in his haste to pull it off.

"Let me," Noah whispered, his hands sliding up Jory's ribs as he tugged it off.

Which seemed to be the signal for them both to get naked. Too impatient to care, Jory tore off the button on his jeans and yanked on his zipper so hard it got stuck, then came free when he pulled the tab again, tearing out some of the teeth. He toed off his shoes, slid his jeans down his legs, then kicked them aside, and turned to his mate, biting back a groan when he saw Noah taking his time, removing his clothes piece by piece, and folding them neatly before setting them to the side.

By the time Noah was finally done, Jory was growling with impatience, barely able to contain his wolf. Then the breath caught in his throat when he saw his mate's body for the first time, glowing in the shadowed darkness of the trailer.

"You're so beautiful," Jory whispered, tugging gently on Noah's hand and pulling him close.

"As are you, my strong and stubborn wolf."

Jory smiled and sank to the ground, pulling Noah down with him. Propping himself on his elbow, he stared down at him, unable to believe this was finally happening. He brushed a lock of hair off Noah's forehead, then trailed his fingers over his cheekbones, down his neck and rubbed his thumb over the spot his mating bite would go.

Noah sighed, his hand coming up and sliding around Jory's neck as he pulled him into a kiss. Lips touched softly, gentle with each other as they savored the moment it had taken so long to get to. Jory ran his hand along Noah's shoulder to the front of his throat, the pads of his fingers tingling from the magic that started sparking between them.

"Please touch me," Noah whispered against his lips.

"I am."

"More."

Smiling into their kiss, Jory took hold of Noah's hands and raised his arms above his head. Holding them in place, he whispered, "Keep them there." He drank down Noah's whimpers as he let go with one hand, trailing it down his arm and across to his chest, pausing to gently tweak his nipples, before moving on. He followed the sprinkle of hair bisecting his mate's abs to his navel, then slid to the side, tracing along his hip bone. Flickers of magic danced along Noah's skin as he slowly dragged his fingers across his lower abdomen.

"Yes," Noah cried into his mouth, thrusting up, leaving Jory in no doubt where he wanted to be touched next.

Teasing, he bypassed his center, skating his fingers down his inner thigh down as far as he could reach, then shifted to the other leg, Noah's skin pebbling as he dragged his fingers up with a light scrape of nails against his tender skin. Then stopped just short of his target.

Noah tore his mouth away and glared up at him. "Stop tormenting me and get on with it."

"Patience," Jory said, nipping at his lips. "I'll get there."

"Get there sooner."

Chuckling at his forcefulness, Jory rolled on top of him, hissing when their lengths brushed against each other. Keeping Noah's hands pinned, he leaned down, sliding his tongue between his parted lips and licked inside, letting the flavor of his mate fill him as he rubbed against him, keeping his pace slow to draw out their pleasure. And to torment Noah some more.

All too soon, his hunger for his mate flared. His hips began moving faster, pressing down harder and his fangs broke through his gums. Not wanting to reach the end too quickly, Jory slowed his movements and gentled their kiss, until only their lips touched, keeping them connected, as he sucked in deep breaths to get himself in control.

His eyes snapped open when Noah yanked his hands free and grabbed him by the hips, thrusting up hard, clearly out of patience. Quickly changing gears, Jory ground down against him. Noah moaned loudly, his long fingers flexing, digging into Jory's skin as his eyes rolled back in his head. Jory covered his mouth as he reached between their bodies and took them both in hand.

Swallowing his mate's cries, he finally let his wolf free.

Chapter Sixteen

Noah

Noah clutched at Jory's shoulders as his mate set a punishing pace, the thrust of his hips sending him spiraling higher and higher, Noah's tight hold on him all that was keeping him from flying away.

That and the glowing amber eyes of the wolf staring down at him.

His lids slid shut when the overpowering sensations became too much to handle.

A guttural voice growled. "Look at me."

Noah's eyes snapped open. Magic began to swirl around them.

Jory slowed and fell forward, propping himself on his forearms. He brushed the damp hair back from Noah's forehead and placed the other over his heart.

"It's time, pretty dragon. Are you ready?"

Looking up, Noah's breath caught when he saw his future in those fierce golden orbs. He nodded, all of his reservations and doubts gone as if they'd never existed, swept away by the love and trust he had in his mate. Needing to share what was in his own heart, he lowered all of his walls, letting his true feelings free, and sent them through their tenuous link.

Jory froze above him, his eyes locked on Noah's, the force of his stare stripping him bare, unlocking every secret in his mind.

Slowly smiling when he saw his feelings reflected in the eyes of his wolf, Noah whispered, "I'm ready, Jory. I've never been more ready for anything in my life."

A smile of satisfaction spread across his mate's face. "Me either."

Noah slid his fingers into his hair and pulled him close. "I love you."

"I love you too, pretty dragon," Jory husked, his eyes burning brighter. He softly brushed their lips together, his movements slow and gentle, where moments before they'd been hungry and fierce.

As his mate's mouth moved along his jawline, Noah tilted his head, baring his neck, shivering when Jory's fangs pressed against his shoulder.

His mate's deep voice, heavy with emotion, filled with love, spoke the words of the ancient mating ritual.

"Do you freely agree to become my True-fated mate, uniting our souls into one, as fated by the Goddess, bonded together through eternity?"

"Yes," Noah said, setting his own teeth to Jory's neck. They bit down together, sharp teeth breaking skin, then drank deep when blood started to flow.

Noah groaned when the wild, untamed flavor of his mate burst over his tongue, lighting up his senses. He drank down another mouthful, then released his hold on Jory's shoulder, licking up the spilled blood and closing the wound, as his mate did the same.

Above him, Jory slammed home one last time, then shuddered, filling Noah with warmth. He fell forward, resting his weight on him, and murmuring nonsense in his ear.

Noah pressed smiling kisses to his face, holding him close as he rejoiced in knowing they'd never be parted. Then his back bowed, the movement forcing his mate from his body and knocking Jory off of him. Noah cried out as bolts of lightning arced through him, lighting up all his nerve endings.

Beside him, Jory shouted and began thrashing around.

Fighting against the fire raging through him, Noah levered himself up and threw himself down on his mate, pinning him to the floor. Holding tight, he ignored the claws digging into his back and the teeth that clamped deep in his shoulder as Jory writhed beneath him.

Then they began to rise.

Noah locked his arms and legs around his mate when the magic, which had been swirling gently around them only moments before, grew turbulent. It pulled on his dragon magic, yanking it from him, and snagged on Jory's, doing the same. Noah squeezed his eyes shut against the brightness when their magics surged, uncontrolled streams of power that flowed around them, circling faster, spinning higher, ever increasing until the container was filled to bursting. The cyclonic forces of the wild magic rolled through Noah into Jory and back, again and again, until they were wrapped tightly. Then the magic slowed, sinking into their skin and weaving them together, binding their souls into one.

They floated in the air, magic pulsing softly, a warm blanket caressing them. It was a moment of calm, of peace, where they breathed and lived in the same space, and happiness filled their souls.

Then the magic exploded outward.

Noah clung tightly to his mate as they were tumbled around the container, banging off walls and bouncing off the ceiling as the combined forces of the mating magic built, the pressure rising higher until it reached its peak and shattered with an explosion strong enough to tear the fabric of the universe.

The echo of a thousand dragons' voices, roaring in exultation, filled the void left behind.

They floated down, landing on the bottom of the container with a soft bump, wrapped tightly around each other.

Jory was the first to find his voice.

"What just happened, Noah?" Jory asked, his voice shredded. "The magic…it burned right through me like fire."

"I'm not sure," Noah whispered, his words as shaky as his mate's. "I had no idea it would be like that." He pushed himself up onto one arm and ran his hand over his mate. "Are you all right?"

"Yeah. What about you," Jory asked, running his hands up Noah's back. "Are you okay?"

"Pretty sure I've never felt better," Noah said, pressing a soft kiss to his lips. He gave a startled laugh when Jory rolled them over until he was lying on top of him.

Jory grinned as he looked down at him, though his eyes looked a bit wild. "I guess with all the explosions and fireworks, that was a True-mating?"

Noah grinned back, then sent his thoughts into Jory's mind. *"Yes, my precious wolf, our mating is True."* He snickered when Jory's mouth dropped open.

"Did you…are you speaking in my mind?"

"I am. Just like you can speak into mine." Noah closed his eyes and took a moment to revel in their connection

before opening them again. *"I can see all of you, Jory. And all of you is beautiful."*

His wolf mate, looking uncharacteristically shy, responded through their new link. *"And I can see all of you, pretty dragon. And I love everything I see."*

As Jory's arms wrapped around him, Noah sighed, then tucked his face in his True-bonded's neck and breathed, fully at peace and not wanting to be anywhere else.

The throat clearing next to them was a surprise. Noah looked up, his eyes widening when he saw Ian standing over them, his eyes filled with laughter.

"Sorry to break up your special moment, but I thought you guys might want to get dressed."

"What?"

"You know," Ian waved his hand over them. "Put some clothes on, before you give us any more of a show."

Noah blinked, still not understanding how Ian got into their container. But when the vampire's eyes drifted down Jory's body, all of his possessive instincts came forth.

"Stop looking at my mate's ass," he growled, snapping his fingers. Magic swirled, instantly clothing both him and Jory.

Ian laughed and held his hands in front of him. "Sorry, I couldn't help myself. It was just there."

"Try harder next time."

"Why? Are you planning on giving us another show?"

"No," Noah said, scowling at him.

"That's too bad."

Noah growled.

Jory snickered and stood, then pulled Noah to his feet. "Try not to kill the vampire."

"No promises." Then Ian's words registered. What did he mean by us? That's when Noah noticed the men standing behind Ian. When they saw him looking at them, they began whistling and cheering.

"Don't mind the guys," Ian said with a cheeky grin. "It's not every day they get a ringside seat for a True-mating."

Noah flushed when he realized everyone had been listening in on their private moment.

Jory leaned in and whispered in his ear. "And to think we didn't want to complete our mating at the mansion in case anyone overheard us."

Noah snorted, then turned and buried his head in his mate's chest, his shoulders shaking with laughter. Dear Goddess, they should have just bonded when he'd given Jory his mating amulet. It couldn't possibly have been more intrusive than this.

Ian's next words made him thankful they'd waited.

"Who knew a True-mating carried enough explosive power to break us out of a soul wraith's trap?"

Noah lifted his head off Jory's chest, then he looked around, his eyes widening when he saw the containers toppled and tossed around all over the staging area as if a child had gotten bored and kicked his toys everywhere.

Next to them, a metal container creaked, then slowly tipped over, falling to the ground with a loud crash. A moment later, another crate further down the dock fell over

"You two sure made one hell of a mess," Ian said, his hands on his hips as he looked from left to right then back at them, cocking his eyebrow. "I'm just glad you waited until the sun went down, so I didn't burst into flames when our container busted open."

Noah exchanged a look with Jory, their eyes wide as they both realized they could have killed Max's brother.

But fortune, and the Goddess, must have been smiling down on them because they were all alive, True-mated, but most of all, free.

Jory

A few minutes later, Ian cleared his throat. His team immediately fell silent and came to attention. He smiled at Noah and Jory. "Congratulations on your mating. I'm happy for both of you."

"Thanks."

"I hate to cut this short, but we need to find the rest of our team."

"Of course." Jory said, curling his arm around Noah's waist. "We'll help. Where do you want us to start?"

Ian's eyes moved from the toppled containers surrounding them, to the warehouse where one of the overhead doors had been pushed in, revealing broken pallets and crates, then back to them. He motioned to the metal containers. "We'll start our search out here. If we were put into these tin cans, the rest of my men probably were as well. Between the three of us, we shouldn't have any problem figuring out where they've been stashed."

Using Jory and Noah's noses and Ian's heightened hearing, they quickly identified the containers holding the missing soldiers and got to work on rescuing them. Ian and his few soldiers working on one end of the pier, Jory and Noah on the other.

Jory and Noah, working together, lifted the end of a shipping container that was jammed up against one with

Ian's men trapped inside. Straining under its weight, they slowly shuffled sideways until they'd moved it enough to clear the entrance, then set it down. Rushing back to the other container, they worked on getting the door open, shoving and pulling on the twisted and bent metal. Finally tearing it free, they quickly scrambled inside and began tending to the wounded soldiers with the supplies Ian's medic had provided.

Jory sidestepped the soldier Noah was working on and carried the injured man he was tending to from the container and laid him on the cement. He was checking the wrapping around his chest to make sure his wound hadn't bled through when another of Ian's men limped over to him.

"Hey. Do you think you could give me a hand?"

Jory looked up, automatically scanning him for injuries and noted he was favoring his leg. "Do you need me to wrap or splint that for you?"

"Nah." The man shook his head. "It's fine. Just a twisted ankle. I can walk it off."

"You sure?"

"Yes. But I could use your help." He pointed his thumb over his shoulder. "A couple of our guys are trapped under a stack of pallets in the warehouse."

"Give me a minute to finish up here." Jory wrapped another strip of fabric around the soldier he was working on, then looked up. "Did you let Ian know?"

"Yeah, but he's got his hands full over there." He pointed to where Ian and some other soldiers were digging around a large pile of containers that were tumbled together like dominos. "He told me to get one of you guys to help."

"All right." Jory tucked the end of the makeshift bandage under, then patted the wounded man's shoulder. "Try not to move so you don't break open your wound."

"Okay." He looked past Jory, then gasped. Clutching at his hand, he stuttered, "T-that's n-not—" Then his eyes rolled back in his head, his hand dropping limply to the cement.

"Shit. Are you all right?" Jory pressed his fingers to his neck, blowing out a relieved breath when he felt a strong pulse.

"What's wrong with him?" the man waiting for help asked.

"I think he just fainted." Jory checked the wound on his chest, then listened to his breathing, but he didn't seem to be in any distress.

"Should I get someone else to help me?"

"No. I think he'll be okay, but I'll ask my mate to watch over him just to be safe." Jory stood and wiped his bloody hands on his pants, then jogged over to the open end of the shipping container. "Hey Noah, I'm going to go with—" He glanced over his shoulder. "What's your name?"

"Johnson."

He turned back to his mate. "I'm going to give Johnson a hand with a couple of soldiers trapped in the warehouse."

Noah sat back and wiped off his hands. "Do you need my help?"

Jory turned to Johnson. "Do we need any more help?"

Johnson shook his head. "Two of us should be enough."

"We're good, Noah. But while I'm gone, can you keep an eye on the man I just brought out? He was fine and talking one minute and passed out the next."

"Sure. I'll have a look at him right away."

"Great. Thanks." Jory turned toward Johnson and motioned with his hand toward the warehouse. "All right. Let's go rescue your men."

"Thanks, man. I appreciate your help."

"No problem." Jory rushed toward the warehouse. He was halfway there before he realized Johnson wasn't with him. Looking over his shoulder, he saw him following at a fast limp. He stopped to wait.

Johnson waved him forward. "Go. I'll catch up to you."

Nodding, Jory took off.

Behind him, Johnson's face flickered, switching to Smith's, then Leon's, before settling back into the angular, rough-hewn features of Johnson.

Entering the building, Jory slowed, taking in the toppled pallets, smashed shipping crates, and bent racking. Shit. It looked like a cyclone had gone off in the warehouse. Freeing anyone from this mess was going to take a while. Looking over his shoulder at Johnson, who was almost to the entrance, he yelled, "Where are they?"

"Near the back."

Jory raced toward the back of the warehouse, all too aware of the passing time, knowing a second's delay could mean the difference between life and death. His thoughts stuttered to a halt.

Ian, with his vampire speed, could have gotten here quicker than him. He was also stronger and would be able to tear through the obstruction trapping his men a lot faster than Jory could.

So, why would Ian have sent Johnson to them for help?

His unease increased when he reached the back of the warehouse and didn't smell blood. Just to be sure he wasn't missing anything, he lifted his head and breathed deep, his hackles rising when he confirmed there wasn't anyone in the warehouse but him and Johnson. And a bitter odor he'd smelled before.

He turned to face Johnson, who had stopped twenty feet behind him, and was watching him with an expectant look on his face. Jory let his wolf rise. His fangs dropped and claws burst from the ends of his fingers. "There's no one back here."

"No," Johnson said, swaggering toward him, his menacing smile showing more teeth than should bet in a human's mouth. "There's nobody here but us."

Quickly glancing around, Jory spotted an opening in the destruction behind him. He spun and darted away. Before he'd taken more than a few steps, Johnson appeared in front of him, blocking his way.

"Gotcha," Johnson said, his eyes flashing red as he reached for him. Jory ducked, but not fast enough to avoid the hand that clamped down on his head.

His wolf howled.

Slashing at Johnson's face, Jory threw himself backward, but couldn't dislodge his hand. He grabbed hold of Johnson's arm, his claws shredding the flesh down to the bone, and kicked out with his feet. But his efforts had no effect on Johnson, who kept a firm hold on his head.

His eyes bored into Jory's.

Jory's desperation to free himself ratcheted up when he felt an alien presence pushing into his mind, stopped only by the protection his mating-bond had given him.

When the itching on his brain increased, Jory quickly put up a personal shield—the first thing Bryan had taught him—gasping in relief when it slid into place. The pressure against his mind faded.

Anger filled Johnson's eyes. The fingers holding onto his head dug into his skin, but his shielding held firm. Time stood still as he and the Johnson soul wraith remained locked in a silent battle of wills. The longer it went on, the more confident Jory grew that he'd managed to stop it. He just needed to hold on until Noah came looking for him. Then together they could deal with the soul wraith and end it once and for all.

A few seconds later, his shield shattered.

Chapter Seventeen

Noah

Noah carried the last injured man out of the crumpled metal container and laid him on the ground with the rest of the wounded, then glanced toward the warehouse. Still no Jory. It had taken him longer than he'd expected to clear the container, so he'd hoped his mate would have been back by now. The fact he wasn't meant the situation in the warehouse must be more dire than Johnson had thought. They'd probably appreciate an extra set of hands. Which worked for Noah since he was missing his mate, even if he'd only been gone a short time. He grinned and amended that to his True-bonded mate, who'd be his forever.

Noah closed his eyes, happiness washing over him as he relived the moment their souls had become one. Yeah. He had it bad for his wolf. It was time to go find him.

With that decided, Noah looked around to see who could watch over the wounded and smiled when he spotted Ian. Catching the vampire's eye, he waved him over.

Ian appeared in front of him. "What's up?"

"I'm going to go give Jory a hand. Can you have someone take over here?"

"Sure. Where'd he go?" Ian asked, glancing around.

"He went with Johnson to dig out some of your men."

Ian blanched. "Johnson?"

Unease stirred in Noah's gut. "Yes. Why? Is that a problem?"

"It's a big fucking problem." Ian fisted Noah's shirt. "Where'd they go?"

"The warehouse."

"Fuck. We need to find him."

"Why?"

"Because that's not Johnson."

Ian took off before Noah could process what he'd said. Not Johnson. Then it hit him. Dear Goddess, the soul wraith. The soul wraith had his mate.

Noah started running after Ian, then stumbled, falling to the ground when Jory's panic and fear slammed into him through their bond.

Ian was back in an instant, hauling him to his feet. "Hurry."

"The soul wraith—"

"I know. Let's go."

This time Noah took the lead, fear for his mate making him run faster than Ian. They were almost to the warehouse when he cried out and grabbed his head, feeling like an iron spike was being driven into his brain. He cried again when he felt his skull being ripped open, the edges peeled back as an alien presence forced its way inside. Noah didn't notice when he fell to the ground, his senses overloaded by an agony that incinerated him from the inside.

He was lost in the fire burning in his mind when Ian picked him up and tossed him over his shoulder.

Noah landed on the ground, hitting his head, which helped jar him loose from where he'd been trapped in his mind through his link with Jory. Ian shaking him and yelling in his face brought him the rest of the way back.

Struggling to his knees, Noah's heart seized when he got his first look at Jory. His beautiful mate, his heart, the other half of his soul, was suspended in the air, in the grip of the soul wraith. Noah froze, unable to move as he stared at his worst nightmare come to life.

Fortunately, Ian wasn't similarly affected. Noah was shocked out of his paralysis when Ian shook him again. Once he saw Noah was back with him, Ian let him go and sped toward the soul wraith with his claws extended. "Get the fuck away from him, you bastard."

Johnson's eyes flashed red.

Ian slammed into an invisible shield and rebounded, flying through the air and crashing into a jumbled stack of wooden crates a few yards behind them.

Noah staggered to his feet and rushed to his mate, bouncing off the same shield. He got up and ran at it again, this time sending his magic before him. As before, he slammed into it, stumbling backward when his dragon's nulling magic had no effect on it.

The third time he tried, Noah was more cautious and slowed his approach. When he made contact with the shield, he called up his dragon, then set his hands on the barrier and pushed against it, but whatever demonic power was fueling it resisted his efforts. Unwilling to give up, Noah didn't stop until his arms finally collapsed and he fell forward, his body pressed up against the shield keeping him from his mate.

Tears rolled down Noah's face when Jory's anguished eyes slid toward him, the terror and pain in them shredding his heart. Then their mate-link vibrated as though struck a jarring blow, ringing out a sour note that reverberated through him, hurting him down to his bones. The strands of their link pulled taut, then began snapping one by one by one.

"No!" Clutching his chest, unable to breathe, Noah watched helplessly as Jory's eyes rolled back in his head, his screams cutting off as his body writhed, his life force being forcibly pulled from him.

The soul wraith flung his head back, his triumphant cry rising above Noah's screams to let his mate go. "Yessss. More power. Give it to me. Give it all to me."

Noah slid down the shield, falling to his knees, watching in horror as Jory's body withered, the soul wraith draining him right before Noah's eyes. He was distantly aware of Ian next to him, slamming his fists against the shield, leaving bloody smears on its surface as he tried to break through, but most of his attention was locked on his mate, on Jory, his precious wolf, his entire world, whose body was turning gray as the soul wraith sucked him dry.

And there was nothing Noah could do to save him.

He closed his eyes, unable to keep watching, not wanting to see when the last breath of life was stolen from his mate. He'd know when the end came, when the last link snapped in the bond connecting their souls. He'd know…and he'd follow him.

Another strand snapped. It was almost done. Just a few more, then his precious mate would be free from the agonizing torture he was suffering. And a moment after that, Noah would join him and they could be together once again in the arms of the Goddess.

He bowed his head and waited for the end.

Then the soul wraith's cries of pleasure turned to screams of pain.

Noah's eyes snapped open.

"Stop! Too much. No more!"

Noah climbed slowly to his feet, unable to tear his eyes from the tableau in front of him, mesmerized as beams of light shot from the soul wraith's eyes and mouth. It swung its arm wildly, trying to shake Jory off, but Jory's hands were locked tight around its wrist, his claws digging deep as he refused to let go.

"Noah!" Ian pointed at Jory. "Look at his arms."

Noah gasped when he saw the light shining from his mate, his skin almost translucent.

Then Jory's shirt burst into flame, revealing his chest covered in stars. But not only stars, entire constellations were contained in his skin. Galaxies of planets and moons raced across his torso, chased by comets with streaming tails of flame, surrounded by flashes of exploding stars.

And all of that power of the galaxies living under his skin—all the immeasurable energy of the universe—was flowing through Jory and pouring into the soul wraith.

The soul wraith's cries grew higher and louder and more piercing, until Noah could no longer hear them, only feeling the vibrations of them in his bones.

And still Jory channeled power, until the soul wraith's skin began to split, unable to contain the vast amount of energy being forced into it. More power, and then more, until finally, the energy stopped flowing.

Everything went still as the universe held its breath.

The energy pulsed.

Then the soul wraith exploded.

Noah and Ian ducked as black stones shot from the epicenter of the blast. Then a wave of power slammed into them with the force of a sun going supernova and sent them flying through the air. When he was slammed into the ground, Noah distantly heard the tinkle of hundreds of stones bouncing all around him.

His vision dimmed, everything going dark, the power of the universe proving too much for even a dragon to bear.

"Noah. Noah. Wake up. Noah!"

He groaned, déjà vu taking hold as the percussion band living in his head started playing for the second time that day.

"Try not to move. I'll go get help."

Noah's hand shot out, grabbing hold of Jory before he could run off. "Stay," he croaked. "I just need a minute."

Hands stroked down his chest and arms before gentle fingers wove through his hair. Noah moaned as his headache receded. He lay still with his eyes closed, enjoying the soothing strokes for a moment, then memory returned. His eyes flew open. He stared up at his beautiful mate, whose face was lined with worry, but who was alive. So wonderfully, inexplicably alive.

"You're all right." Then he gasped as their mate-bond, frayed and almost broken, snapped back into place as strong as before. Or even stronger. Noah closed his eyes and tested it. Definitely stronger.

"Whoa. What just happened?" Jory asked.

"Our mate-bond. It's back."

"What?"

Noah pushed himself up, then almost fell over, only Jory's hold on him keeping him from face planting into the ground.

"Slow down," Jory said. "Take a minute before you try to move. You look like you were caught in the middle of an explosion."

Noah let out a strangled laugh. "I was."

Moving slowly, Noah sat back on his heels, looking fully on his mate, Jory's confused expression making him smile. Then everything hit him all at once. His mate was before him, whole and well. The soul wraith was dead, the Goddess and her gift to Jory the only reason he was alive. Noah lunged at him, knocking him to the ground. Jory grunted, then wrapped his arms around him, holding him as tightly as Noah held him.

After a moment, Jory rolled them to their sides and brushed the bangs off of Noah's face. "What brought that on?"

Noah took a moment before answering, smoothing his hands over Jory's wild hair—straightening the mess as best as he could—before sliding his palms down his neck, where he could feel his mate's steadily beating heart. He lingered over his pulse, taking comfort in the proof Jory was still with him. "I'm so happy you're alive. That I'm alive. That we're both alive."

Jory stilled. "Was that in doubt?"

Noah slowly nodded. "It was."

"What?" Jory pushed himself up. "Why? What happened?"

How could he not know? Noah sat up and leaned against him. "What do you remember?"

Jory closed his eyes and rubbed his forehead. "We were helping Ian rescue his men when one of them asked for help." Jory froze, his eyes flying to Noah. "Johnson. Only it wasn't Johnson. It was the—"

"Soul wraith. I know. What happened next?"

"We came to the warehouse. I got there first because Johnson's leg was hurt so he was lagging behind." His eyes narrowed. "That fucker. It was just a trick to get me to go ahead of him. So he could trap me."

"More than likely. Then what?"

"I realized something was wrong when I got to the back of the warehouse and I couldn't sense anyone. I tried to run but it stopped me." Jory's breath stuttered. "T-then it tried to drain me."

Noah swallowed and nodded. "Ian and I tried to get to you but the soul wraith blocked us."

"Then how come…why aren't I dead?"

"Because of you, Jory. You saved us all."

"What?"

"You channeled so much power into the soul wraith, it exploded."

"I did? What power? I don't have…how?"

"I'm pretty sure it's because of this." Noah tapped the skin over his heart.

Jory glanced down at his naked chest, his hand flying to the symbol inked into his skin over his heart. "What the? Where did this come from? It's…it looks like a galaxy."

Noah nodded. "I think that's exactly what it is."

Jory's eyes flew to him. "Why a galaxy?"

Noah frowned. Something about that wasn't quite right. But what? It took a moment, then the knowledge burst into his mind. It was so obvious it should have been the first thing he'd thought of. He was blaming being captured, blown up, and almost losing his mate for why it had taken him so long to put together.

"Noah? What is it?"

Noah rested his fingers against the mark on Jory's chest. "It's not a galaxy. I think your symbol actually represents the universe. Or rather, the heart of the universe."

"The heart of the universe?" Jory looked at his chest then squinted at Noah. "Why do you say that?"

"Because of the prophecy."

"What prophecy?"

"What prophecy? What do you mean, what prophecy? Oh." Realization dawned. "You weren't there when we talked about it."

Which meant Noah had to be the one to tell his mate he was an integral part of stopping what they suspected was a demon invasion. That he'd been chosen by the Goddess to stand with his brothers to lead the fight? That he would be the first line of defense protecting the earthly dimension and one of those most at risk. That he probably wouldn't survive. That his death would end Noah.

How was Jory going to react when he'd learned all of that?

"Noah?"

Of course, Jory had proven more than once he wasn't afraid of a challenge. But still. These were demons they were facing. Noah didn't want his mate at risk. But weren't they all at risk if it was demons? Maybe Lysander should explain it to Jory. He knew more about what they were facing than Noah did. Actually, that was a great idea. Lysander could explain it to both of them, because Noah needed to learn everything he could if he was going to keep his mate safe.

"Noah." Hands gently shook him. "Hey. It's okay. Just tell me whatever it is."

Blinking back to awareness, Noah could see the worry in his eye. "Sorry. I got stuck in my head."

"I noticed. What's going on? What's this about a prophecy?"

"It was a message that was burned into Fionn's neck."

Jory's eyes opened wide. He mouthed, *burned into his neck*, then asked, "Are you serious?"

"Yes."

"Who would do such a thing?"

Noah raised his eyes, looking skyward.

"You're saying—" Jory pointed his finger up.

Noah tilted his head and arched his eyebrows.

"Damn. That's not good."

Which was an understatement. "The message was written in an ancient dragon script. I'm one of the few who can translate the language. That's why I was at the mansion."

"What did it say?"

The words came easily to him, the memory and feel of them imprinted on his mind the moment from he'd read them.

When shadows of the abyss break the veil,
Beloved sons gather, secrets reveal.
Let light seek the soulless horde,
Tame the beast, loose it to gorge,
Rise forth, Liberator, embrace thy destiny,
Nexus to seal the gate and set all free,
The heart of the universe shall bolster all,
Lest chaos unleashed cause worlds to fall.

"What does it mean?"

"Everyone thinks it might be demons."

"Demons? Again?" Jory's face went pale. "And more than one?"

"Yes."

"And you think I'm part of it? The *heart of the universe* part?"

"I do. But I don't know what the whole thing means, which is why we need to talk to your brothers. I, uh, kind of missed whatever was discussed after I translated it." He found it difficult to hold his mate's gaze.

Jory gave him a puzzled look, then smirked. "Because you ran, right?"

Noah flushed. "Maybe."

"I think you mean, yes, that's exactly why."

"Fine. Yes, that's why I don't know more and why we need to talk to everyone."

"So, let's go." He looked around. "Unless there's something more we need to do here."

Noah stood, the bumps under his feet reminding there actually was something else they needed to do. "Just one little thing."

"And what's that?"

He gestured to the ground covered in black stones. "We need to gather up a few hundred stones."

Jory let out a loud groan when he looked around. "Where did they all come from?"

"The soul wraith. When it exploded."

"Shit."

Noah nodded. Shit indeed. But Tommy said they were important, so they didn't have much choice but to bring them to him.

Before they could start gathering up the stones, he heard feet scuffing on the cement floor behind him. Spinning around, he moved protectively in front of Jory, then relaxed when Ian limped into view.

Jory's hands landed on his shoulders as he whispered in Noah's ear. "We should probably check on Ian's soldiers again, shouldn't we?"

"Why?"

"Well, we did blow them up again. Or at least, I did."

"True."

Jory nuzzled Noah's neck as Ian came closer, looking bedraggled and a little shell shocked. "We should probably hurry because the sun's starting to come up. I don't think Ian would appreciate being turned into a pile of ash on top of everything else we've put him through tonight."

Noah snorted and covered his mouth to hide his smile, not wanting to offend the vampire as he slowly made his way over to them. It wasn't funny. Really. It wasn't. Except it was, in a thank the Goddess we're still alive kind of way. Jory must have been thinking the same because he was chuckling against the back of Noah's neck.

"Shit," Jory gasped. "This has been the most fucked up night."

Noah barked out a laugh, wincing when Ian glared at him. It really had been.

———

With the help of his magic, it took only minutes for Noah to collect all of the stones and put them in a bag he created to hold them. Then he and Jory helped Ian locate all of his soldiers, including the body they found behind the warehouse that Ian confirmed had been Johnson.

"I'm sorry about Johnson and Ben," Noah said to Ian.

"Me too." The vampire's lips were pressed together so tightly they were white. "If your boy hadn't exploded that thing, I would have torn it apart for killing my men."

Noah bit back on telling Ian he wouldn't have been able to do anything to stop it. All he would have done was killed himself trying.

"If you have no further need of us, Jory and I have to get back to the mansion."

"Go. We've got this."

"All right. Thanks." Noah motioned to Jory, who was talking to one of the soldiers whose chest had been bandaged. He nodded at Noah, fist bumped the man, then raced over.

"What's up?"

"We're leaving."

"Okay." Then he grimaced. "Flying, right?"

Noah snorted and nodded, trying not to smile. Jory's fear of flying, such an ordinary thing compared to being almost eaten by a soul wraith—which he'd easily taken in stride—was kind of amusing. Not that he'd say that to his mate.

"Maybe there's a vehicle we can borrow." Jory looked hopefully at Ian.

"Sorry. We still don't have one to spare."

"Damn."

Ian snickered, some of the darkness in his eyes fading. "You better get used to flying, pup. I see lots of it in your future."

Jory shoved Ian. "I'm not a pup."

"To me you are."

Rolling his eyes, Jory flipped him off. Then he looked at Noah and sighed. "Let's get this over with."

"I'm sorry flying makes you so uncomfortable," Noah said, pulling him to an open area.

"It's okay. I'm sure I'll get used to it one day."

That was Noah's greatest hope. He couldn't wait to show his mate the beauty of flying above the clouds at dawn to watch the sun come up. But seeing the slight tremble in Jory's jaw and the panic starting to creep into his eyes, Noah knew that day wouldn't be coming soon. He sighed inwardly. It was a good thing they had forever.

Pressing a quick kiss to Jory's mouth, Noah stepped back a few feet and shifted.

"Holy shit," Jory gasped, running over to him.

Noah's head swung around as he looked for a new threat, then became confused when Jory stroked a hand down his side.

"What did you do?"

Do?

"Nice armor, dragon," Ian said, walking over to them. He rapped his knuckles against the scales on Noah's chest. Metallic clangs filled the air. "When did this happen?"

Noah looked down, a small burst of flame escaping, barely missing Ian, when he got a look at himself. What the hell?

"You look like you're covered in metal," Jory whispered, awe in his voice as he ran his hands over Noah's blue-tinted silver scales. "Amazing."

"It probably has something to do with your mating bond," Ian said.

Noah's head went up.

Jory turned to Ian. "You think?"

"It makes as much sense as anything else." Ian walked around Noah, studying his chest closely. "Huh. Come look at this."

"What'd you find?"

"This," Ian said, pointing to the left side of Noah's chest. "See that scale there? The one that's darker."

Jory came over and peered at Noah's scales. "What about it?"

"What does that look like to you?"

Jory's face got close to his chest. Noah bent his neck forward to see what they were talking about, but their heads were blocking his view.

"It kind of looks like a shield." Jory looked up at Noah. "What do you think?"

He moved out of the way so Noah could look. Another puff of smoke escaped when he saw the scale they were talking about. It did look like a shield.

Waving the smoke from in front of his face, Jory leaned in and took another look. "What do you think it means?"

Ian shook his head. "I'm not sure, but I'd be willing to bet these scales are a hell of a lot stronger than they were before." Ian rapped his knuckles against Noah's chest again. "Impressive, dragon. Very impressive."

"Tell him thanks," Noah said.

Jory snorted. "He says thanks."

Ian grinned. "Let me know when you figure out what they can do."

Noah nodded.

Patting his chest again, Jory looked up at Noah. "I guess we should go now, huh?"

"Yes. I'd like to see what Gideon thinks about my scales," Noah said, preening a little. Okay, a lot. And why not? No other dragon had shiny metallic scales like his.

"We should see what my brothers have to say, too," Jory said, climbing up and settling in place.

"Are you ready?"

"Sure."

But Noah could hear in his voice he wasn't, so he would make sure this flight was as smooth as possible. He flexed his knees then sprang into the air. Once aloft, he circled the warehouse, roared out a goodbye to Ian, who waved back, then he set off for the Galway mansion.

Sheri Eleese

Chapter Eighteen

Jory

Jory's stomach lurched when Noah jumped in the air. He quietly moaned and squeezed his eyes shut, his legs gripping tightly to his mate's sides as his fingers locked onto Noah's scale ridge. Even though Noah had wrapped bands of magic around him to prevent him from falling, today, they didn't feel like enough. He could tell Noah was flying as smoothly as possible, but every tiny motion made his head spin and his stomach churn worse than they normally did.

It was probably a lingering effect from being almost sucked dry by a soul wraith.

When Noah's wing dipped as he turned, Jory fought back the nausea that tried to rise, his chin sinking to his chest as he held on even tighter.

Panting as he tried to keep the contents of his stomach down, he mind-spoke to his mate. *"Please get us there as quickly as you can."*

"Are you sure?"

"Yes," Jory wailed out loud. He needed this flight to be over before he got sick all over his mate. *"As fast as you can, Noah. I mean it."*

"Okay. Hang on."

Oh, he was hanging on. Hanging on for dear life.

He had his eyes squeezed shut, holding onto his mate's scale ridge with a death grip, silently urging him to go faster, when there was a loud pop, like the sound a bubble made when it burst.

"Dear Goddess."

Now what? Jory opened his eyes, then cried out and slammed them shut. He must be seeing things. He couldn't possibly have seen what he thought he did. Right? He cracked an eye, then squeezed it closed again. Nope. They really were flying in a sea of black.

"Jory? Are you all right?"

"I'm not sure. I think I'm going crazy."

"You're not. I see it too." There was a moment's silence, then Noah gasped in his mind. *"Amazing."*

"What?"

"Are your eyes open?"

"No."

"You might want to see this."

Jory didn't think he did, but the wonder in Noah's voice had him straining to open his eyes. Once he did, he let out another cry when streaks of light zoomed past him, the flashing strobe of the colorful streams disorienting him and making it hard to hold on. Shutting his eyes again, he tucked his head into his chest, swearing he would never fly again. Not even if his life depended on it.

A strange voice, filled with the depth of ages, crooned to him. *"Do not be afraid. We are with you. We will keep you safe."*

Yeah. That didn't make him feel any better. At all. Especially when the lights grew brighter and more numerous, flashing by him faster and faster, their brilliance lighting up his vision even though his eyelids were closed.

All he could do was hold on, try not to get sick on Noah's back, and trust in his mate to bring them safely home.

———

They burst out of the sea of black into the sky above the mansion. The moment Noah touched down, Jory let go and fell sideways, tumbling down the wing his mate helpfully angled to the ground and landed in the lush grass in a sprawling tangle of limbs. Groaning when his stomach lurched again—knowing this time he couldn't hold it back—he shakily got to his hands and knees, weaving in place as his stomach tried to turn itself inside out onto the lawn.

"Are you okay?" Noah's hand rubbed up and down his back.

"No," he croaked. "No, I'm not."

Noah rubbed his back. "I'm sorry. I had no control over what happened."

Jory disagreed, but his heaving body choked off what he wanted to say. Once it passed, he wiped his mouth and stared at his mate through teary eyes. "Why?" he wailed.

"Why what?"

"Why did you do that?"

Noah looked surprised. "It wasn't me."

"It had to be. That…that…what was that anyway?"

"I think we must—" He broke off with a laugh. "I can't even believe I'm saying this, but I think we teleported."

"Teleported? Fuuuck." Jory heaved again, then moaned and collapsed on his side.

"I know. Can you believe that? It was amazing."

Jory groaned when his stomach gurgled again. Amazing wasn't the first word that came to mind.

Noah rubbed his shoulder. "It wasn't that bad, was it?"

Jory opened one eye. "It was."

"But look how quickly we got here."

"Don't care. Now go away and let me die."

Noah snorted, but didn't say anything else, just kept rubbing his shoulder and back. After a few minutes, he asked, "Think you're going to live?"

Jory flipped him off. When Noah snickered, Jory rolled to his back and scowled. "I'm glad you find this so entertaining."

Noah's eyes sparkled. "I'm sorry you feel so bad, but do you have any idea what you did?"

"I didn't do anything except almost throw up on your back."

Noah made a face. "Yeah. Thanks for not doing that."

"No problem." Since it seemed like the spinning in his head had finally stopped, Jory tried to sit up. Noah's arm quickly slid behind him to help. He sighed and leaned against his mate.

"Are you ready to go in?" Noah asked.

"Not just yet." Jory rubbed his face on Noah's shoulder, a pitiful moan escaping at the thought of moving. "Please don't teleport ever again."

"Uhm, so, I hate to tell you, but that didn't have anything to do with me."

"Yes, it did," Jory groused. "Why didn't you tell me dragons could teleport?"

"Because we can't."

"Sure seemed like it to me."

"We really can't. That was all you."

Jory lifted his head and glared. If Noah didn't start talking sense soon, he was going to tackle him to the ground and grind his face in the grass, mate or not.

Once he got his strength back.

Correctly reading his expression—most likely because he could tell what he was thinking through their mind-link—Noah laughed. "I'm serious. We teleported because of you. I think it was because you were in such a hurry to get here."

"I think it was because of those fancy new scales of yours." Jory closed his eyes again. "Worst. Flight. Ever. Please don't ever teleport again."

Jory opened his eyes when Noah put his finger under his chin and tipped his head back. "You're not listening. That wasn't me. You did that."

Jory shook his head. "No way. That couldn't have had anything to do with me."

"It did. I could feel your power pushing at me. Hard. One minute we were over the Port, the next we popped out here." He tapped his finger on Jory's chest. "You funneled your power into me. That's what made me teleport."

"Fuck." Jory groaned, remembering his urgency to get home. And how off balance he'd been. Some of which probably had to do with the extra power he only now realized filled him. "Don't let me do that again."

"I don't think I can stop you."

"Why not?" Jory whined.

"Because it's your power. You control it." He rubbed his hand down Jory's back. "Don't worry. I'll help you so you only use your power when you need to."

"Or we can just make it so I can't ever use it again."

"That would be a bad idea," Noah said, resting his hand over Jory's Goddess mark. "I have a feeling your new power is going to be essential in defeating the demons when they come."

"A feeling?" Jory groaned. "Not you too."

"Sorry."

The laughter in his voice said he wasn't. "How is making you teleport supposed to help us win?"

"Because you can do more than that. If I'm right about this, you have the ability to increase anyone's power." Noah smiled down at him. "And that's what's going to help us win."

"You're saying I'm a power-up."

"Pretty much."

Jory blinked. "Fuck." He fell back onto the grass.

Noah laughed and pulled him to his feet.

———

In Roman's office…

Jory pressed his lips together to hold back his smirk. Somehow, seeing everyone's expressions—which ranged from shock, disbelief, thoughtful, or in Lysander's case, knowing—as Noah summarized everything that had happened since they'd left yesterday—that had been a surprise to find out they'd only been gone a day—made him feel a whole lot better. The old saying was true. Misery really did love company.

Bryan, as he'd come to expect from his pseudo-brother, was the first to speak.

"I can't believe you managed to get captured by a soul wraith—whatever the hell that is—broke out of a prison powered by a demon, saved yourself by bonding with your True-mate, and then killed a supposedly unkillable soul wraith by channeling the power of the cosmos through it.

And then, to top everything off, you juiced up your dragon with so much power he was able to teleport and get you home in time for breakfast. Does that about cover everything?"

Jory snorted. "Pretty much."

"Fuck."

"That's what I said."

Bryan shook his head. "I don't even know what to say about all that."

"Join the club."

"How did this soul wraith thing, that isn't even supposed to exist, wander around the world without anybody knowing it was there?"

"Or was it just hiding?" Lysander asked. "If, as Noah says, they were creatures lost to legend, it could have been in some kind of dormant state."

Bryan nodded. "You might be right. What do you think woke it up?"

"I have an idea," Tommy said. Everybody turned to him. "What if the fight with the demon woke it up?"

Lysander blinked, then turned to Bryan, who shrugged. He looked next to Gideon.

"It is a possibility. There was a great deal of power being thrown around that day."

"Well, whatever it was, you're going to have to live with not ever knowing," Jory said. "The soul wraith is never coming back from what we did to it."

"You mean what you did to it. With this new cosmic power of yours," Bryan said, raising a brow. "One that enabled your mate to teleport."

Jory shrugged, still uncomfortable about the whole thing. "I guess."

"I'm curious what power Noah got," Lysander said, studying him. "I can't sense anything different about you from before."

Jory felt Noah's amusement through their link. And his smugness. His dragon was sure proud of his shiny new metallic scales.

"Not much is different," Noah said casually. "You know, other than the fact my scales are now a dark blue-tinted silver."

"Ooh," Tommy said. "Maybe he's a steel dragon. No. Wait. Even better. Maybe his scales are adamantine."

Lysander rolled his eyes. "There's no such thing as adamantine."

"Are you sure? Because I've read about it."

"Yeah. In comic books."

"And online."

"Right," Lysander said, rolling his eyes. "Because everything you read on the internet is real."

"I hope it is in this case. How cool would it be if Noah really had adamantine scales?"

Jory couldn't disagree. Especially if it would help protect his mate from demons. Hmm. Maybe his new power could make the scales even stronger. But what was stronger than adamantine? He'd have to experiment and see.

Noah turned to him. "No."

"No, what?"

"You're not touching my scales."

"How did you know what I was thinking?"

Noah raised his eyebrow and looked at him until he got it. Stupid mind link.

"Why won't you let me play with them?"

"Because they're fine just the way they are."

"Maybe I could just experiment with the ones on your tail. The small ones."

"No."

"But—"

"No."

Jory rolled his eyes. "Fine."

Noah gave him a look that said he didn't believe he was going to give up that easily—which was smart because he wasn't—and stood.

"Before we get too far off track discussing my steel or adamantine scales, we have something else we need to discuss." He looked around the room then grabbed a large serving tray from the wet bar and placed it on Roman's desk.

Jory picked up the bag of stones he'd put next to his chair and handed it to him.

"Thanks." Noah poured the hundreds of stones he'd collected from around the docks onto the tray. Shaking the last one from the cloth bag, he folded it up neatly, then set it on the desk before reclaiming his seat next to Jory.

Lysander reached into the tray and scooped up a handful of the black stones. "Where did you find so many?"

"When the soul wraith exploded, so did the stones. I don't know if they were actually a part of it or if they're remnants from the beings it consumed."

"Amazing," Lysander said. "They're vibrating with energy, but I don't feel anything dark about them."

"Me either," said Noah. "The only time I felt anything negative was from the red stone, which I'm convinced contains traces of demon magic, however muted it might be."

Lysander pawed through the stones in the tray, then raised his eyes to Noah. "There are only black ones here. You didn't find any other red stones?"

Noah shook his head. "No. But since I used my magic to gather them up, it wouldn't have worked on a stone tainted by demon magic."

"True."

Noah frowned. "Speaking of the red stone, where is it?"

"I've got it." Tommy got up from his chair and approached the desk, his eyes locked on the tray overflowing with ebony gemstones. He stood over them for a long moment before grabbing a handful and laying them out on Roman's desk.

Lysander watched for a moment, then frowned. "What are you doing, Tommy?"

Totally focused on his task, Tommy ignored him and scooped up another handful. After a few minutes, everyone gathered around him, watching as an intricate pattern began to take shape.

"Tommy—" Lysander started, only to be shushed by Jory.

"Let him finish."

Giving Jory a look that promised he'd regret it if anything happened to his best friend, Lysander closed his mouth and kept watching

After a few more minutes, Tommy leaned back, frowning at the design he'd created on Roman's desk, then adjusted a couple of stones.

"Is that it?" Lysander asked.

"Not quite." Tommy reached into his pocket and pulled out the paper towel wrapped red stone. When he went to add it to the others, Lysander stopped him and gestured to the pattern of stones.

"Where did this come from, Tommy?"

He looked up, a dazed expression on his face as he whispered, "I've seen it in my dreams." Looking down, Tommy brushed Lysander's hand aside and set the red stone into an empty spot in the center of the pattern.

A loud chime sounded the moment the stone settled into place. The air above the pattern wavered, then the stones shifted and fused together with a loud click. The pattern of stones trembled, then began to rotate, the entire piece spinning faster and faster until the bell chimed again.

Then it began to rise.

"Shit," Bryan shouted. "Everyone. Get back."

When the stone pattern floated in his direction, Tommy cried out and jumped back, but in his haste, tripped over his feet and fell to the ground. Jory and Lysander dived at Tommy to pull him away.

But the stones were faster.

Before they could get their hands on him, the intricate pattern of black stones flashed through the air and wrapped around Tommy's left forearm. They sank into his skin forming a jeweled brace that covered him from elbow to wrist.

Tommy yelled and shook his arm. "Get it off of me. Get it off." When shaking his arm didn't dislodge it, he scraped his nails down it, but the stones only glowed, lines marking the path his nails took, then faded out.

Noah flicked his fingers and sent his magic toward the stones at the same time as Lysander, Bryan, and Gideon. There was a resounding crack when the streams of magic collided, striking the brace, then the magic fizzled out as though it had never been.

"Do it again," Jory said, taking hold of Noah's hand and trying to push power into him. Noah looked at him, then at his hand, raising an eyebrow when he saw it was glowing, then flicked his fingers at Tommy.

His magic spread around Tommy in a sparkling wave before converging on his arm. The decorative stone brace pulsed, then absorbed his magic.

Another chime rang out, then the stones sank further into Tommy's arm until they blended seamlessly with his skin, a shiny black brace, embellished by a red gem—centered in the middle of his forearm—that glowed with an inner light. Tommy's nails raked over his arm again, but as before, trails of lights sparked where his nails scraped, before fading, leaving unmarked skin behind.

Eyes spinning wildly, Tommy yelled out. "Someone give me a knife." When nobody moved, he glared at Carlos. "Now!"

Carlos looked around the room, then pulled a dagger from his boot and handed it to him.

Tommy stabbed the point into his arm. The dagger rebounded, flying from his grip. Holding up his arm, which didn't have a mark on it, Tommy turned to Lysander. "This is bad, Ell, isn't it?"

"I-I…" Lysander's eyes darted around the room as if looking for answers, then he squatted next to Tommy and ran his fingers over the pattern covering his arm, a thoughtful look crossing his face.

"How bad is it?" Tommy asked.

"I'm not sure if it is."

"I know it's bad, Ell. You don't have to lie to me."

"That's just it, Tommy. I don't know what this is, but it doesn't feel evil."

"What does it feel like?"

Lysander's eyes flared, a light sparking in them before he shook his head and sat back, covering his mouth.

"What is it?"

Lysander's eyes glistened, brimming with emotion, when he looked at Tommy.

"Ell. Seriously. What does it feel like?"

Resting his hand on Tommy's arm, Lysander gave him a warm smile. "I don't know how to explain it. But…it feels like hope."

Tommy's eyes rounded. "Hope?"

"Yes."

Tommy raised his arm up and shook it. "Does this look like hope to you?"

"No, but—

"Then why would you say that?"

"Because that's what it feels like." Lysander grasped Tommy's hand and held it between them. "It feels like hope. You feel like hope, Tommy."

"Me?"

Lysander nodded.

Tommy's breath stuttered. "T-that means I'm next. Aren't I?"

"I think so."

Tommy just stared at him, then closed his eyes briefly. "Shit."

"Everything's going to be okay."

Tommy shook his head. "You don't know that." He took a deep breath, then held out his hand. "Help me up. I have something I need to show you."

After Lysander pulled him up, Tommy stared at the floor with his jaw clenched. It was obvious he was waging a fierce inner struggle. He eventually looked up, his eyes were shiny. He tried to smile, but his lips were trembling too much to pull it off. "Remember how I told you I'd let you know when I was ready to talk about what happened to me?"

Lysander nodded. "I do."

"I'm sorry it's taken me so long." He touched his fingers to his ribs and flinched. Shooting Lysander a look, he said, "I'm sorry for making you wait. I know you wanted to help, but it just never felt like the right time."

"Whenever you're ready, Tommy," Lysander said softly. "I'm here for you. Always."

"Always," Tommy whispered back before closing his eyes and tugging up the hem of his shirt.

Nobody said a word as they stared in horror at the mutilated skin on his side. Blackened and red, scarred and puckered where someone had carved intricate runes into the tender flesh over his ribs with a sharp blade, then burned them into his skin, permanently marking him with the taint of dark magic.

"I need someone to tell me what these marks mean. Ell, I need you to tell me how much trouble I'm in."

"Tommy," Lysander said wetly. "How—"

Cutting him off, Tommy whispered, "I need you to tell me why it feels like a piece of me is missing."

Epilogue

Aldrich sank back against his cage when the demon queen released him. She'd taken more of his energy this time than she usually did, leaving barely enough to keep him alive. As he was fading in and out, he heard the queen order her demon servants to activate the stone. He was a witness to her telling her most trusted advisors to prepare for the invasion of the earthly dimension and the subjugation of all its inhabitants.

His heart quaked, knowing they were out of time, not sure if they were ready, or if the sacrifices each of them had made and the plans he'd put into motion, would be enough.

But they would have to be.

Because it had finally come. The war against chaos, prophesied so many eons ago, was about to begin.

He had to trust that the sons of his heart were prepared.

He had to have faith that the heart of his soul would bring him home.

Or all would be lost.

Fin

To be concluded in A Dragon's Faith…

If you enjoyed this book, it would be awesome if you could take a minute and leave a review on Goodreads and/or your place of purchase. Reviews really help authors attract new readers.

Thank you for your support.

Sheri

About the Author

Sheri is an MM Romance writer who believes that love should have no boundaries, in happily-ever-afters, that dragons are real…oh, and bacon; there's always room for bacon.

Her stories are romance with low angst, high action, fade to black or minimal sex, and characters who know how to kick butt.

She lives in Alberta, Canada with her husband, two sons, four cats, and one crazy, energetic dog.

You can visit her website @ https://www.sherieleese.com

Friend her on Facebook: sherieleesewrites

Or you can email her directly at sheri@sherieleese.com

276

Other Books by This Author

Please visit your favorite eBook retailer to discover other books by Sheri Eleese:

Reforming the Paranormal Council:

Forbidden Bonds - Book One
Feral Bonds - Book Two
A Paranormal Family Christmas - Book 2.5
Treasured Bonds - Book Three
Hidden Bonds - Book Four
Fearless Bonds - Book 4.5

Paranormal Council – Legacy

A Dragon's Healing – Book One
A Dragon's Promise – Book Two
A Dragon's Faith – Book Three

9 781777 893347